Praise for **Fl**

"A complicated tale told with deceptively simple ease. Clever in plot, exciting in execution, and tinged with mystery. What more could you want from a thriller?"

> —**Steve Berry**, *New York Times* and #1 international bestselling author of the Cotton Malone thrillers

"Loved it! *Flamingo Coast* is a clever, fast-paced thriller that features ex-IRS Special Agent Jennifer Morton as she digs into the sordid world of white-collar crimes, only to discover that her pursuit is much more personal, and dangerous, than she could ever have imagined. Highly recommended."

> —**D. P. Lyle**, *USA Today* bestselling and award-winning author of the Jake Longly thrillers

"*Flamingo Coast* is a bold, bracing, and blisteringly original tale that bristles with energy. Equal parts revenge and redemption, Martin Jay Weiss effortlessly blends the best of Nelson DeMille and Lisa Gardner."

> —**Jon Land**, *USA Today* bestselling author of twenty-five novels and the new Murder, She Wrote book series

"I loved *Flamingo Coast*. A fun, fast-paced ride through the dark, mysterious world of off-shore banking that will draw readers in from the very first page."

> —**Cristina Alger**, author of the bestselling international thriller *The Banker's Wife*

"Weiss has written a captivating financial thriller that packs a punch, starring a heroine—Jennifer Morton—who delivers a mean uppercut."

> —**Steve P. Vincent**, *USA Today* bestselling author of *The Omega Strain*

"A buzzsaw of a thriller! Weiss grabs you from the very first sentence and doesn't let you breathe again till he throws you into the thunderous climax. If you like novels with gusto, pizzazz, riveting characters, and fine writing, you'll love *Flamingo Coast*!"

—**Shane Gericke**, bestselling author of *The Fury*

"Weiss's fearless female protagonist, Jennifer Morton, exposes global corruption in a breathless, cinematic page-turner I couldn't put down!"

—**Carrie Smith**, award-winning author
of the Claire Codella mysteries

Praise for **The Second Son**

"*The Second Son* is that rare novel that hooks with the first line and never let's go. One of the best thrillers of the year!"

—**John Gilstrap**, *New York Times* bestselling author
of the Jonathan Grave thrillers

"[*The*] *Second Son*'s cutting-edge thrill ride through Silicon Valley spawns from a spiderweb of dark family secrets. Weiss's story is strikingly original, artfully mixing classic mystery themes with modern technology. A must-read for thriller fans."

—**K. J. Howe**, internationally bestselling author of
The Freedom Broker and *Skyjack*

"A riveting, cleverly plotted thriller for the modern age, *The Second Son* combines action, intrigue, and romance against the vivid backdrop of colorful California culture. Readers will keep turning the pages late into the night."

—**A. J. Banner**, *USA Today* bestselling author of *After Nightfall*,
The Twilight Wife, and *The Good Neighbor*

FLAMINGO
COAST

A Vireo Book | Rare Bird Books
Los Angeles, Calif.

MARTIN JAY WEISS

All my best,

Marty Weiss

FLAMINGO COAST

A Vireo Book | Rare Bird Books
453 South Spring Street, Suite 302
Los Angeles, CA 90013
rarebirdbooks.com

Set in Dante
Printed in the United States

10 9 8 7 6 5 4 3 2 1

Publisher's Cataloging-in-Publication data
Names: Weiss, Martin Jay, author.
Title: Flamingo coast / Martin Jay Weiss.
Description: First Trade Paperback Original Edition | A Genuine Vireo Book
| Los Angeles, CA: Rare Bird Books, 2019.
Identifiers: ISBN 9781947856585
Subjects: LCSH Fathers and daughters—Fiction. | United States. Internal
Revenue Service—Fiction. | Criminals—Fiction. | White collar crimes—
United States—Fiction. | Suspense fiction. | BISAC FICTION /
General | FICTION / Thrillers / Suspense
Classification: LCC PS3623.E45553 F43 2018 | DDC 813.6—dc23

For my father

Pleased to meet you
Hope you guess my name
But what's puzzling you
Is the nature of my game

—"Sympathy For The Devil,"
The Rolling Stones

CHAPTER 1

JENNIFER MORTON COULDN'T GET the last image of her father out of her mind. The look on his face—their shared countenance—weighed heavily. He was once her *raison d'être*, her anchor, now he was the reason she was on a runaway power cruiser seeking retribution.

The yacht hit a set of pounding whitecap swells and the unmanned wheel shuttered. Jennifer braced herself and watched the island lights fade away as they charged out to sea. There was no turning back, even if she wanted to. Two men were hunkered down somewhere in the bulwarks, planning their attack. It was time to make her move.

She slipped through a teak hatch, found her way into the engine room, and went to work. As she rigged a detonator to the fuse box, her mind drifted back to the earliest memory of her dear old dad, when she was barely five years old and he had taken her for a joyride on his most prized possession—a vintage mahogany Chris-Craft Capri—befittingly christened *The Great Escape*. She remembered how the classic Italian speedboat shimmered from endless pampering as it cut through the rippled surface of the sea like a skimming stone, the warm summer breeze flowing through her long auburn curls, and how safe she had felt as her father preached life lessons: *"When it comes to money, people will do unthinkable things…"*

She was too young back then to know that *The Great Escape* was more of a decision than a desire, or to understand the scope of her father's betrayals. Three decades later, it was payback time. She would soon feel safe again, or so she hoped.

She set the time delay. She had two minutes, which felt like an eternity, so she tucked behind two bolted-down ice chests and prayed for the first time in years. She asked to be forgiven for the sin she was about to commit. It was a big one, she silently confessed.

The hatch door sprung loose and she saw one of the men approaching through the relentless rain, then the other, and they were both about to fire their sanctioned Glock 23 pistols when the cruiser crushed a crestless six-foot swell, lifting them off their feet. They both landed face down. The yacht shimmied through a series of whitecap rolls, sending them back to the quarterdeck.

Jennifer checked the timer.

Twenty seconds left.

Her father's deep, throaty voice continued to echo in her head as she pulled herself back through the porthole: *"Whatever you desire—love, money, revenge—doesn't matter…"*

One of the men spotted her and fired.

Jennifer dived behind the downriggers.

The yacht struck another enormous wave and knocked the shooter back down.

Jennifer climbed up to the ledge.

Ten seconds left.

The islet lights were barely visible now. The cruiser had drifted too far out for anyone to see them. Jennifer shut her eyes and her father's final words resounded: *"The more you have, the more you want. And the more you get, the harder it is to protect yourself. Unless, you take it all and disappear…"*

Everything that had been murky was now perfectly clear.

Jennifer leapt, jackknifed into the raging sea, and descended into the ink-black void.

"…And there is only one way to truly disappear."

A thunderous explosion bellowed above.

CHAPTER 2

Four Months Earlier

JENNIFER MORTON WAS TRAPPED inside a six-by-six-foot windowless room on the forty-seventh floor at One Worldwide Plaza. The office—or closet—they had placed her in had been set at an uncomfortably cold temperature, but she had grown used to it. She had been auditing Global Currency Arbitrage since early November, spending every waking hour behind piles of financial documents, determined to find some hidden, undeclared gems. The hedge fund darling had been red flagged for years, not only because all four of their funds had been churning out extraordinary returns for far too long, but also because so many of their investments and acquisitions were in foreign countries that were hard to track, where tax evasion was common.

And this wasn't GCA's first barbeque. They had been audited three times in the past seven years, always passing with flying colors.

The IRS smelled smoke and wanted Jennifer to find fire, but after scouring through five years of corporate returns, company ledgers, backup records, statements, and receipts, she found nothing suspicious, inappropriate, or out of order. Their books were spotless. In fact, it seemed as if GCA overpaid their federal taxes and were entitled a substantial refund.

They were going to have a very merry Christmas.

As Jennifer was about to head back out into the coldest, wettest winter New York had had in years, her gut told her that she was missing something. There was something going on at GCA, maybe something nefarious, but she had nothing to go on…

And then there was a knock on her door.

The GCA comptroller, who had cooperated fully and provided her with every document request, came by to bid her farewell. He was a few years older than her, maybe late thirties, and he was handsome, smart, and charming to boot.

"Never thought I'd say this to an IRS agent," he said, "but I'm sorry to see you leave."

She laughed. "I appreciate you being so helpful."

He had been almost too helpful, she thought, *but that's not a crime.*

He checked the hallway to make sure no one was in earshot, and then shut the door.

Is he going to tell me where the bodies were buried? Is he looking for immunity?

He sat on the edge of her desk and leaned in close. His aftershave smelled good. And he looked good in his $5,000 custom Italian suit. "I just wanted to say…I was thinking…" He struggled to find the words, and then he came out with it: "Maybe we can go out sometime."

She was used to getting hit on whenever she planted herself in companies for too long. Despite her conscious efforts to wear the least-revealing navy Liz Claiborne business suits, layered sweaters, and no makeup, guys would inevitably look for excuses to pass by, make idle conversation, and offer unnecessary help. It may have been another reason her boss knew she was the right agent to send out to high-profile audits; her looks were disarming, and office crushes caused many men to make foolish mistakes.

"I'm flattered," she told the comptroller, "but we have a policy—"

"No one would find out," he assured her, lowering his voice, "I have a place in the city." He set his cell phone on her desk and touched her hair. "How 'bout tonight?"

Truth be told, the GCA comptroller would have been her type. He was attractive, well educated, age appropriate, and good at his job.

Unfortunately, he was also a creep.

She asked him, "Do your wife and kids know about your place in the city?"

He blushed, held up his left hand, and stuck out his ring finger, as if he were showing her a bank statement to support a capital loss. "What wife—?"

"I can see the indent," she said with a snigger. "Bet you a hundred bucks there's a wedding ring in one of your front pockets."

He turned a deeper shade of red. "It's kind of complicated, my situation."

"I'm sure it is."

"As long as we're discreet—"

"Not going to happen," she cut him off. If he was hiding things like a wife and three kids on Long Island, she could only imagine what he was hiding on the hard drive in his office. She was now absolutely certain he had been cooking the books.

He got up to leave, without a hint of shame, and then turned back at the door. "I had my phone with me—"

"You knocked it off my desk." She reached down and came back up with it.

He grabbed it back and headed out. "See you around," he said dismissively, like she just blew the deal of a lifetime. "Good luck."

"Good luck to you, too," she said. And he was going to need it, because while he was hitting on her, she had migrated all the data from his iPhone onto a highspeed backup device, where she would later extract all his passwords and company access passes.

The audit was over. But she was just getting started.

—

As night fell upon the midtown skyscraper, Max Culpepper entered the Global Currency Arbitrage boardroom and took a seat at the head, a formidable patriarch with a coiffed head of white hair and thick-rimmed Oliver Peoples that helped hide his shifty baby blues. "Congratulations," he began, "we made it through another review without a glitch!"

His band of four portfolio managers applauded.

He held up his hand. "But I still want to play defense for a while, just as a precaution."

The bleary-eyed PMs stared back, their smiles fading.

Culpepper knew they'd be expecting a celebration, some kind of bonus, and they would be disappointed. He also didn't give a shit. GCA was under a scope and he didn't want to draw any more attention. "I want to show losses on each of your yearend statements," he told them. "And not just a two- or three-point slide. Something substantial."

One of them whined, "We've suppressed profits for the last two quarters."

"The market's up," another added. "More investors will cash out."

"Come on, fellas," Culpepper countered. "We've pulled a boatload of cash from these deals. We get sloppy, we get *Madoffed*."

"When I joined the firm," the whiny PM said, "you assured me that we'd have a say in these matters. Can we at least discuss this?"

Culpepper looked around the room at their sorrowful expressions. *These thankless Ivy League pencil pushers should be kissing my ring,* he thought. *I had the brilliance to set up the systems, the balls to initiate the funds, and the generosity to hire them. The rate of returns sold themselves. They only had to keep a secret, which they were all only too happy to do, especially when they bragged about their Hampton homes, diamond dripping society spouses, African safaris, and debutant balls...*

Unfortunately, he also needed them to look legitimate. So he begrudgingly complied, "Of course we can discuss this. That's why we're here." He glanced at his $750,000.00 Patek Philippe (not what he paid, of course) and feigned what seemed to be a genuine smile. "Who would like to begin?"

He listened to their objections and then spent the next hour convincing them why they needed to comply, reminding them of the old adage: It doesn't matter how you make your money, it's how you keep it. They also discussed new ways to improve their systems and falsify statements to lure new investors. Culpepper thought it was a productive meeting. Of course, he was unaware that on the impasto portrait of Adam Smith hung behind him was a tiny recording device feeding their conversation through a fiber-optic portal, and that the IRS agent that had just wrapped up their audit was wearing wireless earphones in the office next door, listening to every word.

—

DISGUISED IN THICK-RIMMED GLASSES and a custodial uniform, Jennifer pored through every file on the comptroller's computer until she found the real company ledgers, which were completely different than the books and records she had been shown. Her heart raced when she realized what they were hiding. Global Currency Arbitrage had not only been evading taxes, but they were in violation of fraud. Big-time fraud. It was a now a criminal case. She just had to get the evidence out of the building.

She filled up a 5TB portable drive and then put in another. There was a lot of data and downloading seemed to take forever: 73 percent...75 percent...76 percent...

She heard footsteps approaching. *Damn!*

She peeked out into the hallway. A security guard was heading her way. She knew that the comptroller always left at six and cleanup on this floor usually began after midnight. The guard was making his rounds too early. Maybe it was because of the meeting next door. Or maybe he noticed the computer screen aglow in the comptroller's office. Either way, her window was closing, she had to move fast.

The guard called out, "Mr. Martinez?"

Jennifer glanced the drive: 82 percent...85 percent...86 percent... "Martinez has the flu," she said. "I'm covering."

"This is a secured floor," the guard said as his bulky form filled the doorway. "I should have been informed."

"It was last minute."

The guard moved inside and looked around.

Jennifer put a fresh plastic liner inside the trash to look like she was doing her job.

"Make sure they call me next time," the guard said as he headed back into the hallway.

"I sure will," she assured him.

She needed to be gone by the time he looped back. She put her hand on the drive, waiting...98 percent...99 percent...100 percent. *Got it!* She stuffed the drives in her jumpsuit pocket and peeked out again. When the guard turned the corner, she took off.

To avoid the security cameras, she took the stairwell sixty floors, just as she did when she arrived. And since she had disengaged the alarm when she was in the building earlier that day, she left through the boiler room emergency exit, unheard and unseen.

In the alley behind Forty-Ninth Street, she pulled a large plastic bag from a dumpster. Inside was the overcoat and briefcase she had planted earlier. She placed the stolen drives inside the briefcase, put on the overcoat, and headed toward Madison Avenue.

Gusts of snow whipped angrily at bundled New Yorkers moving down the slushy sidewalks en masse, all vying to get out of the bitter cold. Jennifer emerged and merged with the herd. The instant anonymity made her feel safe—and ironically giddy—lamenting like a homicide cop that just realized how easy it is to get away with murder.

Breaking and entering, robbery, larceny, and so many of Jennifer's escapades were indisputable violations of the law—the consequences unthinkable if exposed—but public sentiment had been on her side since she started at the service a dozen years ago, when the country wanted the government to do anything and everything to counter terrorism, even if it meant invading their privacy. The Patriot Act gave federal agents the authority to share information, monitor phone calls, surf web archives, search DNA databases, medical, and financial records. Jennifer took full advantage.

And Simon Brisco took full advantage of Jennifer.

Simon was the head of the New York City bureau, and Jennifer's boss. When she had applied for the job, she said that her dream was to become James Bond of financial crimes. Simon hired her faster than he had ever filled a position. He became her formidable mentor; she became his secret weapon with a self-imposed license to intrude. He often encouraged her—privately—to get results by any means necessary. He did, however, always add the disclaimer: "As long as you don't get caught." Jennifer paid little attention to that stipulation, convinced she was too careful, too clever, and her motives were too righteous. If the fat-cat scumbags she pursued were lying, cheating, and stealing, she wholeheartedly believed that it didn't matter how she exposed them. The end justified the means.

The Global Currency Arbitrage takedown would prove that it was all worth it. It was by far the biggest scandal she had ever uncovered, her *coup d'état*, and she couldn't wait to share the details with Simon over their next martini lunch.

When Jennifer got up to Sixty-First Street, she stopped in front of a Barney's window display, set down the briefcase, and pretended to peruse the dresses on sale. A few minutes later, a man in dark shades and a long trench coat nonchalantly lifted the briefcase and carried it away. They didn't exchange a word. Not even a glance. Wasn't necessary. The man in the trench coat was her contact at the US Attorney's Office, and she had just delivered everything they needed to prosecute.

CHAPTER 3

FBI AGENTS ESCORTED MAX Culpepper out of his Trump Tower condo in handcuffs. It was 4:00 a.m. None of his neighbors were awake to witness the arrest. No one from the press was waiting on Park Avenue. Culpepper was taken without warning, completely by surprise.

Sort of.

His lawyer had warned him that Global Currency Arbitrage had made the IRS blacklist—a little known subgroup of their dreaded Watch List that targeted extremely wealthy and high-profile individuals and companies they suspected were hedging the system. Culpepper took all the necessary precautions, of course, but he always knew that no one was immune from human error, an inside leak, or a cagey attack.

Staring out the tinted window of the government-issued black Escalade, he was well aware that it would be a long time before he would see these city streets again, if ever. The gig was up, and he was surprisingly resolved, even grateful, like an alcoholic finally thrown out of his favorite bar; he would soon wake up in a different bed, without hangover or headache, and he was ready to get off the roller coaster.

He had rarely seen the city at this hour, so tranquil. It was like watching a yellow-bellied sea snake sleep and his drive downtown was like a trek down memory lane, from his opulent Upper East Side home to his first one-bedroom apartment above a pornographic movie theater in Times Square, his humble beginnings paying his way through city college, making peanuts selling junk bonds, and his insatiable ambition to join the filthy rich.

They caught a run of green lights down to the Village, traversed SOHO down to Broad Street, then across the heart of the Financial District, the playground he had navigated over the past four decades. His rise to prosperity was nothing short of spectacular and he smiled as they passed by Bobby Van's Steakhouse, where he made so many deals over $90 bone-in specials and $900 bottles of wine, and Setai, a private club with a Michelin star-rated SHO Shaun Hergatt, where he celebrated every double-digit annual profit with his entire staff.

His thoughts turned to his PMs, also likely on their way downtown, awakened before dawn, heavy hands pounding on doors trumpeting their soon-to-be-plummeting social status. No more *pieds-à-terre* in the city; no more beach homes; no more excess of any kind. Their wives' sorrowful tears would be heartbreaking. Culpepper almost felt sorry for them. They too were money addicts, but unlike him they couldn't admit it. It never seemed to occur to them that he had chosen each of them to run his investment funds because they were malleable, unscrupulous, and as slippery as he needed them to be. Their naïveté and insufferable arrogance prevented them from acknowledging that the bottom could fall out at any time, and they were all ill-equipped to deal with the consequences. They would do time in prison. When they got out, they would be unemployable. Their families would blame them—if they were still there—forever disgraced.

That would not be Culpepper's fate. He would never let that happen because he knew what he was. He didn't need rehab or redemption, only an exit strategy, an escape hatch ready and waiting should things go off the rails. If his underlings didn't understand the risks and plan accordingly, it was their loss. He gave them fair warning, and that was all he could do, all he should do.

As the Escalade pulled up to One Police Plaza, he thought about his own wife. He couldn't remember if she was in Côte d'Azur or Montepulciano, or when she was supposed to return to New York. She had probably told him before she left, but he rarely paid attention to such details. She wouldn't be happy when she heard the news, but she wouldn't be shocked either. He had painted this possible scenario for her many times. She knew how to react when federal agents questioned her, seized their assets, confiscated their properties, and when their socialite friends deserted her. She knew the deal. And she wouldn't starve. She could survive on the ten or eleven million he had stashed away for her. She was taken care of.

Now he needed to make sure that he was taken care of, too.

When the police informed him of his right to one phone call, he pulled Barry Lynch's business card from his wallet. Barry Lynch was the lawyer who had warned him about making the blacklist and his home number was scribbled on the back of his card. Culpepper always knew that if he ever got caught, Barry Lynch would be his first call because the blacklist wasn't the only thing the Barry Lynch had told him about.

—

Barry Lynch sat up in bed, put on his reading glasses, and grunted, "What are the charges?"

"Seven counts of fraud," Culpepper told him.

Lynch knew that meant billions of contested dollars. "I'll start preparing your defense first thing in the morning—"

Culpepper cut him off, "I also want you to make that call for me. You know the one."

"You do know that I am a stellar attorney," Lynch said. "There's a good chance I'll get you off—"

"I sure hope so. But just in case, make that call."

Years ago, Lynch didn't care if his clients made the blacklist; he even reveled in it. White-collar criminals were hard to prosecute back then, and those on the blacklist were practically untouchable when they hired high-powered law firms like Lynch, Arnold, Heller, and Gold, who were staffed with brilliant tax lawyers that could easily outsmart, outwit, and outplay government counsel. It was the real reason why fewer than two percent of the wealthiest one-percenters' tax returns went into review, and why the IRS avoided litigation whenever possible. But that was before Main Street blamed Wall Street, and before financial inequality and the loss of the middle class became a focal point of two presidential elections. Law firms like Lynch, Arnold, Heller, and Gold could no longer guarantee outcome, only the best defense money could buy.

Their most vulnerable clients—like Culpepper—needed more assurance. They were told about a place that could perform miracles. It was expensive and risky, but sometimes necessary, like when there was a good chance that federal prosecutors had seized indisputable evidence proving their clients were guilty as sin.

Lynch called it Plan B. And Culpepper was opting in.

"So, you'll set it up?" Culpepper pressed.

"I will," Lynch assured him. "I'll make the call."

CHAPTER 4

J ENNIFER MORTON WAS CALLED to the stand.

As she headed up, she thought of her boss's, Simon Brisco, advice to explain the evidence in layman's terms and be as swift and concise as possible. He had always contended that an IRS agent should be felt and feared, never seen or heard. If she had to be a key witness in a media-crazed case, the goal was to present the facts and get out quickly.

After she was sworn in, the prosecutor from the US Attorney's Office began his introductory Q & A, presented Exhibit A—the basis for their discovery—and then set her up: "If you would, Ms. Morton, please walk us through what these documents are and what they represent."

Jennifer scanned the packed courtroom and saw the GCA gang staring back hatefully. She imagined their $5,000-custom Italian suits turning into $5 orange jumpsuits, and began, "Global Currency Arbitrage sold nearly five billion dollars of shares to investors...through funds that claimed to invest in high-end, low-cost computer equipment, electronics, and various high-tech devices...mostly from companies in Russia, China, and emerging markets—"

"Places that are hard to track."

"Correct."

The GCA comptroller and four PM's looked shell-shocked. She was about put it all out there for the world to see. The evidence was so incontestable, even their infamous attorney, Barry Lynch, looked tongue-tied. But she couldn't figure out why Max Culpepper—the big cheese CIO with the most at stake—looked oddly at ease. He was actually smiling.

"Please continue," the prosecutor said.

She did: "Global Currency Arbitrage never invested one dime in the production of anything whatsoever. They showed false profits—"

Barry Lynch sprung to his feet. "Objection! Before she makes such absurd and slanderous accusations, we need to establish how this evidence was acquired—"

"The IRS acquired the evidence through a thorough and legal audit," the prosecutor said, turning back at the judge, "they're trying to spin—"

"Yes. Overruled," the judge agreed, already growing impatient. "Go on, Ms. Morton."

"Thank you, Your Honor." Jennifer continued, "They showed false profits, so that more investors would pour in, and then they routed the money through personal bank accounts."

"But they never actually purchased anything, did they?" the prosecutor prompted.

"No. Nothing."

"And the money that went into personal bank accounts was never reported, was it?"

"No."

"And all the assets they had claimed to have purchased overseas…?"

"Were used as collateral to borrow more money to finance other acquisitions—"

"Objection!" Lynch pounded his fist on the table.

"On what grounds?" the judge asked, clearly annoyed.

"She could not possibly know those things from her audit—"

The judge peered over his bifocals. "What are you suggesting?"

Lynch didn't have an answer because the only way for him to prove that the evidence could not have been acquired during her audit would be to admit that GCA provided false or doctored documents.

Jennifer had him. She felt unstoppable.

The judge said, "Counsel, approach the bench."

Jennifer turned away, so it didn't look like she was listening to the conversation. But Lynch was irate and loud. "My clients have been targeted unfairly," he told the judge. "This is their third... fourth audit. The IRS is going after conservatives that applied for tax-exempt status again, clearly a case of political profiling—"

"You don't think your client's dealings with Russian oligarchs shows probable cause?" the prosecutor asked mockingly.

Lynch hissed, "If the evidence was gathered without going to a judge, it's a violation of FISA, at the very least..."

"Not if the purpose was intelligence," the prosecutor shot back. "We do not need to show probable cause if they were doing suspicious business abroad. Trailing terrorists is admissible."

Lynch's face turned beet red and he sprayed saliva, "Our clients are not terrorists! They are goddamned upstanding American businessmen for Christ's sakes—"

"Who apparently just got their dirty little hands caught in a heinous Ponzi scam," the judge concluded as he looked out to the horrified, thwarted GCA mob. "I'm allowing the evidence. And watch your goddamn language, counselor."

Jennifer watched Lynch storm back to his seat seething.

Culpepper, still oddly calm, leaned over and whispered in Lynch's ear, "What are you doing?"

Lynch reached for his Tums Ultra Strength Antacid bottle. "Trying to get a mistrial."

"Don't give yourself an ulcer," Culpepper told him. "Just get this over with so I can get on with my life."

Jennifer could read lips and she laughed to herself. Culpepper was delusional if he thought he was getting on with anything but a hefty prison sentence.

But she didn't know about Plan B.

—

BARRY LYNCH WAS STANDING on the federal courthouse steps fielding questions from a News 12 reporter when he noticed Jennifer leaving the building. He had been following her career closely, knowing that she was frequently assigned to the most maligned tax manipulators, the kind he often represented. He found this ironic since he knew her father long ago, a brilliant tax attorney renown for some of the most aggressive tax avoidance strategies ever.

And this wasn't the first time Jennifer had testified against one of Lynch's clients. A few years ago, he had defended a media heiress accused of embezzlement, and that trial hadn't gone well for him either. After that debacle, he had sought revenge through his client's newspapers, claiming the investigation was part of a government witch hunt, and compared Jennifer Morton to Joseph McCarthy. He thought the attack would send a message and reign her in, but she responded on a *Wall Street Journal* Webcrawler video with the most audacious statement Lynch had ever heard: "My beat is Broadway to South Street and I'm going to defeat every cheat." The clip was shared on Facebook pages throughout the Street, but people wrote it off as an overambitious federal agent, and it didn't get her fired.

Lynch was now feeling more vengeful, and knowing that an IRS field agent's anonymity was as vital as her calculator, he decided to give exposure another try.

He stalked toward Jennifer, the News12 camera crew in tow, and went on a rant, hoping to provoke her: "Why don't you ask that young lady how she acquired the evidence, if she obtained a FISA warrant, why she violated search and seizure protocol, why the IRS is invading our privacy…?"

All eyes, and cameras, were on Jennifer. Instead of avoiding the press like she was expected to do, she responded, "We can no longer allow people like Max Culpepper to cheat America and force honest tax payers to pick up the tab."

A reporter countered, "But the defense claims Fourth Amendment rights are being ignored, weakening the protection of civil liberties, eliminating government accountability."

Jennifer looked square into the camera lens, as if she were running for office, and said: "The IRS doesn't make policy, we just enforce it."

Lynch revealed his first smile of the day. Her words came off her lips like a Nuremberg defense. The press pounced with more questions and she proudly answered them all.

She was digging her own grave and he had handed her the shovel. He walked away, the pangs in his belly finally relenting.

He lost the case, but he would get the last laugh.

CHAPTER 5

JENNIFER BURST INSIDE THE drab New York City field office of the Internal Revenue Service, a politically charged justice seeker returning from battle with enemy heads on a plate.

Government hackers in ill-fitting suits that draped their out-of-shape bodies delivered a hero's welcome as she powered through the maze of cubicles, despite their envy. They were used to her exceptional performance, frequent promotions, and preferential treatment, but the comments she made to the news outlets on the courtroom steps were unprecedented, so none were surprised when their boss, shouted across room, "My office, right now, Morton!"

Simon Brisco—large and in charge—never had to scream to be heard, and the ovation subsided the moment his star agent was sequestered.

At first, Jennifer thought this dramatic greeting was just for show. She was prepared for the obligatory lecture on adhering to protocol, possibly even being sentenced to that week of media training, followed by an under-the-table bonus, three martini lunch, and promise of a future endorsement. She quickly gathered something else was going on when Simon slammed the door so hard he knocked a stack of old tax journals off their rickety shelf that nearly fell on little man sitting in the corner.

"This is Mr. Sanders from DC." Simon said before he sucked a desperate hit from his inhaler.

Jennifer reached to shake hands. "Nice to meet you, Mr. Sanders."

But Mr. Sanders didn't get up, didn't shake her hand, and didn't smile.

Simon barked, "Take a seat."

She did.

"I don't know why you can't get it through your skull, Morton," Simon began, "trumpeting to the press like we're above the law pisses people off."

"So do tax schemes and corporate scandals," Jennifer said, despite her mentor's unyielding glare and Mr. Sanders' lack of warmth. "Everyone knows that greed is the enemy. And we can do something about it. We just *did* something about it. Congratulations to all of us. It's a proud day. Are you just in the city for the day, Mr. Sanders? If you're staying overnight, maybe we can show you some of the newer hot spots in the city?"

Both men stared back, stone cold, and Jennifer realized she had grossly misread the situation. Her boss wasn't just delivering a perfunctory reprimand to cover his bases before he rewarded her in private; he was genuinely upset. And then he told her why: "Unfortunately, greed just got away," Simon said as he rubbed his aching temples. "Max Culpepper disappeared sometime in the middle of the night."

It took some time to register.

"Did you hear what I just said?" Simon asked.

Her voice cracked, "That's impossible. He's on electronic monitoring, ten-million-dollar bail. The court has the deed on his condo—"

Mr. Sanders finally spoke. His voice was high-pitched, adeptly affected, and blatantly sarcastic. "Yeah, well, the court just became the proud owner of a Trump Tower penthouse. I hear it's fabulous, furnished with a lovely ankle bracelet."

Jennifer couldn't imagine a man like Culpepper walking away from the fortune he spent his life thieving. "They seized all the GCA assets."

"Assets they could verify, yes, less than two hundred million dollars," Sanders said.

Jennifer knew what Sanders was insinuating. "The judge would have revoked bail if he had more—"

Simon cut her off, "Do you think a guy who had been running a con job for so many years, given the scope of it, wouldn't have hidden much more than that?"

Mr. Sanders pulled out a small pad of paper with numbers scribbled on the front. "I'm guessing it's more than a billion."

"You're guessing?" Jennifer said, as if there was no way to know such a thing. But she knew they were right. It would be easy to walk away from $200 million if Culpepper had transferred a billion or more offshore. And with a guarantee to flee before his sentencing, it would explain why he had been so calm at the trial. But Jennifer felt defensive and didn't feel that she should be taking all the blame. She had done her job. She found the Ponzi scheme that none of the prior auditors could find. She testified simply, as she was required.

Then Mr. Sanders explained, "The court will take some of the blame, but we'll get the brunt of it because you came off on FOX News making us sound like the deep state, which the president has been on a Twitter rant about, and our commissioner wants to deflect—."

"I'll fix this." Jennifer sprang to her feet. "I'll find him!"

"No, you won't," Simon said. "He's probably halfway around the world by now." Simon looked like he was taking it harder than she was, and he stared out the window as he delivered the kill shot: "Been nice working with you, kid."

When Jennifer turned around, two security guards were waiting in the doorway.

She had come to work that day expecting to celebrate a victory, to share in the revelry, to make her mentor proud. Someone like Mr. Sanders should have been there to offer her an appointment in DC, an analyst position, maybe even something better. But Mr. Sanders was only there to make sure her termination was done swiftly and legally, so there would be no chance of further embarrassment.

Simon wouldn't look at her as they escorted her out. His secret weapon was no longer a secret, and she was no longer his.

—

SIMON BRISCO LEFT THE office a disheveled mess. He bummed a cigarette from a stranger in the elevator on the way out, despite quitting the habit three years ago, and pushed through the rush-hour swarm down to the subway station he had sojourned for the past twenty-five years. It seemed unusually crowded. He looked around at the other beaten down faces and it made him feel exceptionally depressed. What had his life been about? He thought about his pending retirement. He had once looked forward to a quiet place near a lake where he could fish and breathe fresh air, but since his wife left him six years ago, all his prospects looked dim. He was sure he would end up all alone and he had just terminated the one agent he had hoped to carry on his thankless legacy.

The ride home on the train was even more bleak. He thought about the martini lunches he had had with Jennifer, their shared contempt for rich pricks who thought they were above the law, as well as the tax laws and loopholes they manipulated. He recalled the closed-door meetings where he and Jennifer speculated on rumors of insider trading, high-frequency trading, market manipulation, and front running. The Culpepper verdict should have been the culmination of everything he had groomed her for.

Simon was devastated. He got off at his stop on the southern part of Bayside, Queens, picked up a bottle of Jack Daniels at a corner market, and walked six chilly blocks to his home in Oakland Gardens, a musty turn-of-the-century row house his ex-wife gladly let him keep when she moved in with the butcher four blocks away.

He made his way inside his unkempt, dilapidated home, ignored the pile of dishes in the sink, filled a glass of Jack Daniels over ice, and proceeded to the den where he spent most nights watching bad TV until he passed out. He plopped down on the couch, found the remote control, and powered on the TV. The light from the TV revealed a form waiting in the corner. His body stiffened.

And then the form spoke: "We have to talk."

It took him a moment to register that it was Jennifer. "Jesus, Jen... How the hell did you get in here?"

"Seriously? You had me trained by professional thieves to break into buildings with state-of-the art security, and you leave a key under your front mat."

"I didn't have you trained—"

"Fair enough. You only made suggestions."

Simon took a swig and sank further into his well-warn sofa, hoping that she wasn't there to blackmail him. "I shouldn't be surprised," he said with a goaded stammer, as if the Jack Daniels had already taken effect. "We all take a personality test when we join the service. You showed excessive tenacity and an excessive sense of justice."

Jennifer forced a smile. "Which means I'm valuable—"

"Which means that you *were* valuable. When you started working for me, people cared more about their safety than their privacy. But the pendulum is swinging back, like it always does. People want change. And change always needs a scapegoat."

His explanation fell on deaf ears. "You've threatened to fire me before," she said, "for show, to make a point, to save face. I'll play this any way you want."

"I didn't threaten to fire you today," he reminded her, "I actually fired you. I'm sorry. My hands were tied."

"If I find Culpepper, we could reverse this," Jennifer said. "I'll go on my own dime, I'll drag him back—"

"What? Like a bounty hunter—?"

"Whatever it takes. I'll find a way."

Simon sighed. "See?"

"What?"

"Excessive sense of justice."

Jennifer looked like he had just smacked her in the face, which was his intent. "You're a smart girl," he said. "You're young enough to start over. Do something else. You deserve better. Look at the shit-hole I live in. You want to end up like me?"

"I don't care about money."

"You will," Simon said with a sorrowful hiss. "Most people have the impression that working for the IRS is a boring job for angry bean counters that get off on sticking it to people. And you know what? They're kinda right. Most of us do it because we lack drive, ambition, and imagination. We resent people who have those things. We're bitter. I'm bitter—"

"I'm bitter, too," Jennifer asserted, as if this were one of their inspired martini lunches.

Simon laughed. "Not for the same reasons as the rest of us are. And you know why? Because you're not one of us. Never were. You have more drive, ambition, and imagination than you know what to do with, and you joined this crusade because you couldn't get over the disappointments in your past. It's time for you to let them go. I did you a big favor today. I set you free… You're welcome."

She looked shell-shocked. "Are you serious?"

"Serious as the heart attack you gave me when I saw you lurking in the corner."

"Nothing I can do or say?"

"Nope."

"We can discuss it over a few rounds of real whiskey at Delmonico's, I'm buying."

"Relentless!" Simon pointed his remote control toward the front door. "Now get the hell out of my house before I call the cops."

She got up and walked out without saying another word.

After the front door shut behind her, Simon cried for the first time since his wife left.

CHAPTER 6

J ENNIFER DROWNED HER SORROWS at the bar at Delmonico's, a Financial District steakhouse favored by an after-eight lower Manhattan crowd; dealmakers and deal breakers on the move, and on the make.

She sulked, half crocked, watching CNN replay the Max Culpepper story, ad nauseam. Kelly Keefer, a beautiful blonde correspondent known for her unbridled love of transparency, had gone on a tirade about how major loopholes in international banking allow people like Culpepper to game the system. When she replayed the clip of Jennifer in front of the courthouse, some of the Delmonico's patrons took notice.

Jennifer wanted to hide in a ditch somewhere.

Instead, she pulled an amber container from her pocket, popped a Vicodin, and washed it down with her last swig of Macallan. She glanced at the label and moaned, "Alcohol may intensify this effect."

Perfect.

"Another round, Frankie?" Jennifer waved her empty Scotch on the rocks at the bartender, hoping that one more fill would help her stay unconscious throughout the night. "And for the love of God, will you change the channel? Aren't the Rangers playing tonight?"

The bartender flipped through the stations and found a game. "Islanders and Blackhawks okay?"

"Go Isles."

As he delivered another two-finger pour, a square-jawed man in a stylish suit sidled up next to her. The piano player in the corner smiled and began playing a hollowed version of "Mr. Lucky."

The man was a trial lawyer. First name was Mike. Jennifer never knew his last, and that was part of the reason for his acerbic pitch. "Must have been one hell of an investigation, otherwise I'm sure you would have returned my calls."

"I thought we had an understanding," Jennifer said with a lecherous smile, relieved to have company other than the calm of Mr. Vicodin and the rage of the Islanders to break up the monotony of her wallowing thoughts.

"Well, then, let me redirect this line of questioning." Mike placed his hand on her knee. "How does a guy get a second chance with you?"

Jennifer hastened to explain to the luckless fellow who fell victim to her boundless inaccessibility and replied dismissively, "Second chances are usually repetitive, don't you think?"

"Ouch. You're not going to play the commitment-phobe card, are you?"

"I didn't think insanity would fly. I told you I wanted to keep things light. Most guys would gladly accept such a generous deal."

Mike glanced back at a table of his friends signaling for him to return. "It's my own fault," he told Jennifer. "I knew all about your reputation, even before I approached the bar—"

"Objection. Hearsay!" Jennifer played along. "Rumors won't hold up in court."

"But they're usually true."

She shrugged. "Good point."

"Shame, too, 'cause I really thought there was a nice girl behind that iron curtain."

"Nope. Just little ol' me."

"Blow off every guy that gets to know you and you're going to stay single a very long time."

"Objection!" Jennifer pounded the bar mockingly. "I like being single."

Mike said, "I'll rephrase," the trial joke long played out, "keep acting like a cold bitch and you're going to end up all alone."

The piano player finished his rendition of "Mr. Lucky." Jennifer revealed a dazzling smile, her last defense. And Mike made his exit.

Jennifer turned back to the bar and looked up at the TV, hoping to see someone from the Blackhawks take a hit, anybody but her.

Could this day get any worse?

Just then, a woman's voice chimed in, also uninvited, "Men today are a bit too sensitive for their own good, don't you think?"

The lady was in her mid-sixties, strikingly beautiful, albeit hardened and worn, with a sinewy shape that revealed a compulsive running habit or eating disorder, maybe both.

Jennifer revealed a hint of a smile. "We *metooed* them into submission."

The lady crackled, "When we took their jobs, we took their balls." She raised her glass. "I'm Roberta Coscarello."

"Jennifer."

"I know who you are, Jennifer Morton," She lowered her voice, "I'm with FinCEN."

Jennifer waited for her to elaborate.

"Financial Crime Enforcement Network," Roberta said. "We combat high-profile financial crimes, money laundering, tax fraud—"

"I know what FinCEN does... You didn't come here for a drink, did you?"

Rhetorical.

"Information from every federal agency funnels through us," Roberta continued. "Every time you monitored an SEC probe, piggybacked a CIA tap, traced a DEA bust, we knew about it."

"Shouldn't my lawyer be present?"

"That's not why I'm here," Roberta explained. "I'm going after Max Culpepper and I want your help."

"I have no idea where he is."

"I do. When he transferred his boat's title to the Panama Registry in a corporate name, we planted a tracking device."

Roberta held up a tracking app on her iPhone. A red light blinked along a map of the Caribbean Sea. "He's docked in a harbor on Grand Cayman."

"I'm not a bounty hunter," Jennifer said, realizing how ludicrous she must have sounded to Simon when she told him that she wanted to go after Culpepper herself. Even if she could find him, he was likely in a country that would refuse a US extradition request. "If he really is in the Caymans," Jennifer said, "he's free as a bird."

"That's why I need a girl like you, who will do whatever it takes to make sure justice is served."

Did she read my psychological profile, too?

Jennifer wished the fog in her head would lift.

"I started out at the service, too," Roberta said. "In fact, I remember your father, one of the cleverest tax avoidance strategists I'd ever seen—"

"I know all about his reputation."

"Of course you do."

The mention of her father caught Jennifer off guard and left her feeling defensive.

It must have shown on her face because Roberta backed off. "I didn't bring up your father to upset you—"

"Then why did you?"

Roberta's eyes shifted, like she was making sure no one around them was listening.

Jennifer's pit-bull instincts kicked in and she leaned in inches from Roberta's face and whispered, "Does anyone else know you're soliciting agents at a bar?"

Roberta leaned back. "Excuse me?"

"You're uneasy about this… I'm trained to notice nervous traits."

"And I'm trained to notice when somebody's slurring their words." Roberta said as she scribbled her phone number on a bar napkin. "When your head clears, and you realize that no one else in the public or private sector will ever hire you again, give me a call. Shame to let a girl like you go to waste."

—

JENNIFER'S UBER DROPPED HER off in front of her walkup. The back door of a van opened, and crusader reporter from CNN, Kelly Keefer, and her camera crew swarmed like bees.

"Ms. Morton," Kelly Keefer began, pointing a microphone. "Just a few questions—"

"Not now."

"I'm doing a follow-up piece—"

"Good for you."

"You got Max Culpepper convicted on fraud charges. He fled. You were let go. Would you like to comment?"

"No."

"When the IRS fires someone who got results, I have to wonder."

You and me both.

"My sources say Culpepper got away with money the courts knew about..."

Good news leaks fast.

Kelly Keefer checked her notes. "...north of eight hundred million. Can you confirm?"

"No, I cannot."

Kelly Keefer waved her cameraman to stay back. "We can do this off the record, but I want to give you a chance to tell your side."

Jennifer wanted to tell the world that she was just a sacrificial lamb, but she knew that she was partly to blame. She had crowed to the press, didn't play by the rules, and Simon had always added the disclaimer "As long as you don't get caught" because he wouldn't be able to save her if she did. "There's no point," Jennifer said.

Kelly Keefer pressed, "The IMF says Americans have seven trillion dollars in offshore accounts, don't you think that is a real problem—?"

"I think their projections are low," Jennifer said.

"Then you agree that something must be done."

"Of course I think something should be done but I'm no longer in a position to do anything about it, as you well know."

Kelly Keefer stepped closer, so her crew was out of earshot. "I'm working with a consortium of investigative journalists... we have collected thousands of electronic documents relating to offshore investments in shell companies set up by shady law firms—"

The fantastic offers just keep coming. "You can't get that information...legally."

"If names of people and companies came from an unknown source..." Kelly Keefer winked conspiratorially. "Doesn't matter how we expose them. The end justified the means..."

Preaching to the choir, sister.

"The Panama Papers and Paradise Papers just scratched the surface. I'm talking about a data leak that would go way beyond..." Jennifer started for her front steps. Kelly Keefer followed and continued, "Offshore banks have a sanction list of people they're not supposed to be doing business with—drug cartels, terrorists, arms dealers, convicted financial criminals—but we know they do it anyway. If we can lift the lid, we could blow the entire system up. Seven trillion...can you imagine?"

Jennifer unlocked the front door to her building. "I wish you luck with that," she said, finally heeding Simon's advice about avoiding the media. "I'm sorry, I can't help you. G'night." She shut the door on Kelly Keefer, hiked three flights to her studio apartment, ripped off her clothes, and slipped into bed. Mr. Vicodin sent his last wave of benumbing respite through her brain, at last, and she finally escaped this God-awful day.

When she drifted off to sleep, she had one of her recurring dreams where she was submerged under water. In this one, she was lying on the bottom of the ocean floor staring up at pieces of a boat she must have fallen from.

When she woke up in the morning, her new reality felt a lot like her dream; she wondered if she had the strength to ascend back to safety or if she should just let go.

She winced at the thought, climbed out of bed, and set out to pay her mother a visit.

CHAPTER 7

J ENNIFER TOOK THE MORNING commuter train back to Westchester County, nursing her hangover with a Starbucks Venti Red Eye and a bland version of an egg McMuffin. She got off at the Larchmont station and weaved through the rush hour throng. Her clothes suited her newfound unemployment: torn jeans, well-worn sweatshirt, Rangers cap, bomber jacket. The copious gray winter clouds hovering over the swanky exurb reflected her mood: cantankerous, ornery, dark, gloomy.

Sometimes you need to look back at the past to find out why your life went off the rails, she thought as she waited for the train to pass and reached for the vial in her pocket. She was running low on her supply of chill pills, but this was not the time to be thrifty. She popped one before she trekked down Stoneyside Drive, a winding road of Victorian homes covered in a blanket snow—Norman Rockwell utopia, a seemingly idyllic place to grow up.

But not for Jennifer. Her body shuddered as she approached her mother's fortress: Jennifer's dystopia, and the house of lies that left her cold.

The door was ajar. She went inside and heard an all too familiar shriek coming from the kitchen, "Take off your shoes, for Christ's sake, I just had the carpets cleaned!"

"Yes, Mother, I'm taking them off now."

Vera appeared in the hallway, a ball-breaking narcissist wearing haute couture, dripping pearls and diamonds. She was pushing sixty, and sixty was pushing her. If there were collagen treatments that could eliminate a wrinkling spec of skin, she had been injected; if there was a diet to eliminate an ounce of unwanted fat, she had tried it; if there was a retreat that promised youthful rejuvenation, she had been there.

Jennifer conceded to her mother's affected double-cheek kiss. Vera took a step back, looked over her daughter's casual grunge, and exhaled a stupefied sigh. "My how the mighty have fallen."

Jennifer entered the lion's den. "It's nice to see you, too, Mother."

"Jesus, Jen, how does someone get canned from a government job?"

Jennifer knew her mother would attack first—a starved lioness that feasted on belittling her young—but she had promised herself not to be lured in. She reminded herself to stay Zen, get what she came for, and make the visit short. "I'm already fielding offers."

"I hope so because I can't support you while you're floundering."

Jennifer felt her blood pressure soar. "I would never ask you to part with your beloved money." She looked Vera up and down in the same scrutinizing way. "You look great, Mother. Seriously. I see the latest round of fillers are kicking in nicely… Where's Melvin?"

"His name is Marvin."

"Sorry. Hard to keep up with all the husbands."

"Incorrigible…" Vera ducked into the powder room to examine her face. Aging had made it hard on the witch, who had always depended on her looks to lure.

Jennifer took the break to recompose. She opened the front room curtains, looked out at the illusory winter wonderland of Stoneyside Drive, and recalled a memory of her twelve-year-old self, slugging through mounds of fresh snow and the painful details that Norman Rockwell never could have painted—the cuts, bruises, and trail of blood that proved little Jennifer Morton couldn't get along with others. If the principal had told her mother about her inability to fit in, or about the schoolyard brawls, she never knew. But Vera believed that her daughter was different, and those differences had to be fixed so they wouldn't reflect back on her. But sending Jennifer to a psychiatrist backfired on Vera. Jennifer remembered the man with a thick gray beard, who always smelled like potato chips, and how he immediately pegged her mother as a "Borderline Witch," to explain why she was so manipulative and vindictive. Jennifer decided then that it would be best to separate herself from Vera, and she took to independence like a Daughter of Liberty, living on her own island, disengaging from anyone who tried to get close. Jennifer was left with an inability to forge intimate relationships; Vera was left with Vera.

But the doctor had also concluded that Jennifer's more severe problems—including her aggressive preteen behavior—was mostly due to the lack of a father figure.

Jennifer glanced at the front entrance and a memory flashed back to when she was five years old, the day her father left:

"Daddy has to go away on a business trip," he told her.

"You have to take this with you for good luck."

Little Jennifer reached in her back pocket and gave her father a rabbit foot keychain. He took it, smiled dolefully, and walked out the door for the last time.

That scene played through Jennifer's head every time she visited. It still haunted her. Her father was her *raison d'être,* her anchor, the only protection she had from her mother.

And then he was gone.

Jennifer closed the drapes looking out to the front yard, as if she were closing a chapter of her life, and then moved through the living room like a detective seeking clues to a crime, wondering where her mother had hidden the missing pieces. She stopped at an old painting, a distorted caricature of a woman with half of her face colored purple and green, the other black and yellow.

Vera came back into the hallway. "You have good taste," she said, "I'll give you that."

Jennifer stared at the painting. "This was my father's."

"His mother's, actually." Vera reached around Jennifer's back to straighten it, one of the few souvenirs that survived Vera's makeovers between husbands, and for good reason: it was an original Matisse. "Please don't touch. It's quite old. And expensive."

Jennifer rolled her eyes.

Vera sneered. "You could have worked on Wall Street. You could have used your talent with numbers to make real money instead of making slave wages at the IRS."

"I didn't want to work on Wall Street."

"Did marriage ever cross your mind?"

"Not as often as it crossed yours."

"That's funny, smartass... Did you come here, dressed like a hobo, just to insult me?"

"I came to get my hockey stuff from my old room," Jennifer said as she headed for the stairway. "I'll be out of your hair in a minute."

Vera scoffed, "You're playing hockey again?"

"I'm going to join an over-thirty league, while I have the time off."

"I thought you were banned."

"That was the over-twenty league."

Vera gleamed malevolence. "Sorry, hard to keep up with all your screw ups."

"Good for you, Mother. That was witty." Jennifer reached her Zen limit and jogged up the stairs to get away before she'd say something she'd really regret.

—

JENNIFER PULLED HER HOCKEY equipment from the closet in the upstairs study, which once served as her childhood bedroom—but that wasn't the only thing she had come for.

She climbed into the attic, a dusty place her mother would never go even if she thought it was packed with diamonds, or single men. Behind some old suitcases she found the box exactly where she had left it. Her box of facts. Everything her grandfather had given to her about her father—the unsolved mystery of Michael Morton. She opened it and sorted through newspaper clippings, legal files, memorabilia. It was all there. Still. Pandora's Box. Waiting for her to return. Simon Brisco said that she had become an unrestrained justice seeker because she couldn't get over her disappointments. Could it be that simple? Maybe she needed to reopen the case of her father, review the facts, and see if he really deserved to have that kind of power over her.

She stuffed the box inside the hockey bag and headed out.

—

Vera was waiting by the door prepared for one last squabble. "Leaving so soon?"

Instead of responding, Jennifer kissed and held her mother, surprising them both. A wave came over Jennifer. It wasn't from the Vicodin, nor was it from feelings of guilt, remorse, or another passive-aggressive response. It was something entirely new.

It was compassion; compassion for the Borderline Witch.

"I know you did the best you could," she told Vera.

"You have some nerve—"

"I'm not trying to start a fight," Jennifer cut her off. "I want to say that I'm sorry for all the tension we've had. I wasn't an easy kid and you had your own struggles to deal with."

Vera snickered, and her forehead crinkled, where her last shot of Botox hadn't taken effect.

In a flash of madness, Jennifer confessed that she needed to share some of the blame. She had been as stubborn as she was obstinate, as distant as she was aloof, and as bitter as she was resentful. She remembered what psychiatrist number one once told her: *"Apples don't fall far from their trees. Your first order of business is to understand your parents. Your second is to forgive them. Your third is to learn not to repeat their bad behavior."*

"I'm sorry for my part."

Vera's eyes shifted away. "Okay."

"I love you, Mom," Jennifer said for the first time in over twenty years.

Vera retreated. "I know."

In the same doorway that Jennifer had given the rabbit foot keychain to her father and said farewell, she gave her mother a hug and said goodbye. She had a strange feeling that it would be a long time before she saw her mother again.

In fact, it would be her last.

CHAPTER 8

BACK IN JENNIFER'S BROWBEATEN far-East Village walk-up, she sorted through the miscellaneous keepsakes from the box of facts—all the leftover crumbs from her earliest detection work. Her heart tugged, and her belly growled, both empty.

She helped herself to an energy bar and a pour of Macallan, neat, and then sorted through the remnants of Michael Morton's life, all the articles of his high-profile clients, the accusations about him helping them hide money in offshore banks, and the trial. It had been years since she had dug into this, and, just for kicks, she Googled and Binged and Yahooed to see if the Internet would find something else, something she hadn't seen before.

And it did.

From a search of an offshore bank listed in the court minutes of her father's final trial, she found a YouTube video of a *60 Minutes* interview that had never aired. The link was titled "The Briefcase Affair." A chill ran through her entire body. The date on the video was a few days before her father supposedly died.

She hit play.

A young Mike Wallace reported: "Since the IRS had no way of knowing if income was being reported, or even if it existed in this Caribbean bank, they set up Operation Haven..." His voice continued under artist sketches of a sexy woman and a bank executive in a Key Biscayne nightclub; a briefcase left alone in a Miami hotel; the same woman giving testimony in court.

"...An IRS operative posed as a high-end prostitute. While she escorted a Nassau Bank vice president for a night on the town, other agents snuck into his hotel room and copied documents from his briefcase, exposing Americans with offshore accounts—"

Jennifer scrolled back to the rendering of the young and pretty undercover IRS agent posing as a high-end hooker and paused. This woman looked familiar. Very familiar. Jennifer tried to imagine what it would have been like for a woman agent back in the day—a kindred spirit—and then she hit play again.

The video continued with a TV studio interview. Mike Wallace was sitting across from a man with his face blurred and voice filtered. Jennifer sat up and stiffened. She knew it was her father.

Mike Wallace said, "The three hundred and fifty high-profile Americans in question have one thing in common: they're all clients of yours, sir. The IRS believes you are the mastermind behind this entire tax avoidance scheme, that you may have ownership in this Bahamian bank, and that you are helping these people cheat America—"

The blurred man grew angry, his voice boomed through a Darth Vader filter. "It's not illegal to have a bank account in a tax haven—"

"As long as you report its existence," Mike Wallace interrupted, "I suppose that's true, but the IRS claims that these banks, trusts, and corporations are nothing more than schemes to avoid taxes on income earned in the United States, the reason they have initiated an investigation into these affairs, Project Haven—"

"Project Haven is nothing more than a witch hunt."

Mike Wallace looked annoyed. "In my experience, people that call investigations witch hunts are usually hiding something."

The body behind the blur stiffened and the deep voice snapped back, "And in my experience, journalists that editorialize have no credibility."

"Shouldn't wealthy Americans be held accountable for not paying their fair share?"

"Fair share? The top one percent pays more than ninety percent of the tax revenue in the United States. Shouldn't they be rewarded for their success? And shouldn't the IRS be accountable for violating search and seizure protocol?"

Mike Wallace turned toward the camera to explain: "The courts will now decide if the evidence should hold or be dismissed since the IRS agents did not have a warrant when they broke into the bank executive's hotel room—"

"If they are not," the blur concluded, "it will be such an erosion of our constitutional rights, I won't know what to tell my five-year-old kid when she grows up."

Jennifer's heart thumped. She was that five-year-old. She paused the video and stared at the fraught expression on her father's face, through the blur. She thought of the special times she shared with her father, the joyrides on his Chris-Craft Capri, how he always came back from business trips with gifts, and how she sent him off on his last with her lucky rabbit's foot. She had adored him once, vowed to become just like him, and treasured his memory as a blessing.

Until Grandpa Leonard told her what her father had done.

She spent her winter holidays with her Grandpa Leonard— her mother's father—in Jupiter, Florida, whenever Vera would fly away to some quixotic getaway with whomever she was romantically involved with at the time. Grandpa Leonard was a former litigator with too much time on his hands, and boorishly outspoken due to an increasing senescence of Alzheimer's.

The last time Jennifer saw him was winter break of her junior year of high school, and she vividly remembered how the subject came up. He had asked her what she wanted to do with her life, and she told him, "I want to do what my dad did. I take after him, you know. He's the reason I'm so good at math."

"God forbid!" her grandfather snapped, as if Jennifer had wished a disease upon herself. "Your mother isn't doing you any favors by keeping you in the dark."

"You asked me what I want to do," Jennifer reminded her grandfather, used to his frequent crabby quips, "and I'm telling you that I want to be a tax attorney, just like my dad."

"Your father was a crook!" Grandpa Leonard shouted.

"My father was a brilliant lawyer," Jennifer objected, this being the first time she had heard such slander. "His only crime was that he loved boats and couldn't stay off of them. He shouldn't have gone out in a storm, but he did—"

Grandpa Leonard cut her off, "In my desk drawer, there's a collection of facts that prove otherwise. I saved everything, so you would one day know the truth. This is that day."

Jennifer read about the allegations against her father, and all her illusions about having one respectable parent started to shatter. The articles painted a picture of Michael Morton as a man who bent, broke, and completely disregarded the rules to help the mega-rich cheat the system, and it tarnished the idealized image she had of him. Then her grandfather took it further. He told her that his collection of facts proved that her father had fled the country in the middle of his trial to save his own ass. It was the first time she learned that they never found his body, or the boat. Of course her mother denied it all, most likely well compensated to keep her lips sealed.

And it broke her heart.

All the lies, cover up, deception, and the abandonment.

Mostly the abandonment.

That's when the tides turned for Jennifer, when she decided to pursue a career where she could punish the cheaters and schemers, a thorn in her paternal ghost's side, a tax attorney's worst nightmare: the most ruthless IRS agent anyone had ever known.

And this is how that turned out.

She rested her head on the kitchen table and stared at the faded newspaper clippings. There was one article about the final trial with a photo of her father standing with other lawyers from his firm. She had seen the clipping before, but now she recognized one of the lawyers, the third from the right—a tall, lanky man with an eighties Chevron mustache.

She sat up, grabbed the clipping, and took a closer look. She tried to imagine the man without the mustache, thirty years older, and with more girth.

She realized who it was, and the caption below confirmed it: Barry Lynch.

The lawyer who defended the GCA scumbags knew my father?

Maybe reopening the box of facts was good idea, she thought. Maybe she just needed confirmation that her grandfather was right. For so long, she had been in the middle of a war, fighting an enemy that couldn't fight back, attacking surrogates and proxies to fill the void. In the morning, she would pay him a visit.

Jennifer closed her eyes and fell asleep. Once again, she had a dream where she was trapped under water. In this one, she was inside some kind of vehicle, sinking. Someone was watching her through the window. She couldn't make out who it was, but the person wasn't there to help.

CHAPTER 9

B ARRY LYNCH KEPT HER waiting in the lobby for almost forty-five minutes. She knew that he wasn't about to move mountains for the girl that had been nothing but a thorn in his side. She didn't mind. She had no place to be anyway.

When the receptionist finally sent her in, she found him perched behind a large maple desk, his head buried in paperwork, and he didn't look up when she entered.

"Thanks for making time for me," she said.

He glanced at his watch. "I have to run to my staff meeting in a few minutes."

"I know you're busy—"

He finally made eye contact and asked, "What can I do for you, Ms. Morton?"

Jennifer took a seat. She felt nervous. "I don't know if you heard but the IRS let me go." News like that gets around fast in this circle. She assumed he already knew.

"Sorry to hear that," he said.

Jennifer let out an acerbic laugh. "No, you're not."

"You're right," Lynch agreed, gleaming a smile. "You know what we say the IRS stands for in our office? Internal Rotten Scoundrels. Internal Rectal Service. Infernal Revenue…"

"Infernal Revenue Service is my favorite," Jennifer piped in. "I've heard them all."

"At least now you can be in on the joke... Have you started looking for work?"

"Is that a job offer?" Jennifer joked.

Lynch's smile faded. "Not a chance in hell."

"The reason I'm here..." Jennifer straightened in her seat. "You knew my father..."

Lynch's expression didn't change.

"...Michael Morton."

"I know who your father was," Lynch said. "We started out at the same firm."

"I know," Jennifer told him. "You worked on his last case. Several of his clients were accused of hiding money in an offshore bank."

"That was a long time ago," he said with a shrug.

"Nassau Bank & Trust. You must remember the trial," Jennifer pressed. "There was a pretty woman, an IRS agent who went undercover as a hooker—"

"Oh, yeah," Lynch said, his grin returning. "She was hard to forget."

"She exposed all the investors that were hiding money offshore."

"She was also the reason the evidence didn't hold... She told the court everything: how she took the bank executive out on the town while IRS agents broke into his hotel room, stole his briefcase to get names of people with offshore accounts." Lynch laughed. "She admitted the entire thing."

"Why—?"

"Who the hell knows, maybe she grew a conscience!" Lynch leaned in. "Doesn't surprise me that an illegal search and seizure is hard for you to comprehend, though...the evidence was tossed because it was stolen, just like the bullshit you came up with in the Culpepper case. Did you come here to confess?"

Jennifer disregarded Lynch's umbrage. "If the evidence was thrown out, then they all got off."

Lynch snickered. "You bet they did."

She asked, point blank: "Then why did my father leave?"

Lynch face turned sad. "You must know about the boating accident—"

Jennifer's entire body stiffened. "They never found the boat, or his body."

Lynch leaned back in his big chair and nodded and he softened. "So you've been hanging on to that... The loss of a parent is hard to accept, and you were very young—"

"There must be another reason he fled," she said, cutting him off, anxious to discover more about her father and his last case from someone who had been there. "If he was going to get off, he must have been running from something else, or someone else."

Lynch sneered. "Or he actually died in a boating accident."

She glared back at him.

"I'll tell you what I do know about your father," he said, leaning in again, like he was about to reveal something important. "Heaven, hell, or somewhere in between—wherever he may be— he'd be glad that you're no longer doing what you were doing, that's for damn sure. Getting booted from the service is the best thing that could have happened to you. Now you can do something productive with your life."

"Like you?" Jennifer snapped. "Defender of the schemers and cheaters."

"Sticks and stones," he said, checking his watch again.

She softened, tried another approach. "I wanted to make a difference..."

"I remember," he said mockingly, "you could no longer allow people like Culpepper to cheat America and force honest tax payers to pick up the tab."

Fuck another approach.

She snapped, "How do you live with yourself?"

"You mean, how do I advise and counsel my clients about their legal options and represent them in the court of law—?"

"No, I mean how do you help someone that screwed so many people escape?"

"You have some nerve."

"And you have no shame. I know where Max Culpepper is. And I know you helped him get there."

Lynch was fuming. "Then why don't you tell someone who gives a shit?"

"Aiding and abetting a fugitive is against the law—"

"Aiding and abetting?" Lynch stuttered, his face turned blood red. "You're insane—!"

The phone rang, seemingly on cue. Lynch picked up. His receptionist reminded him that his next meeting was about to begin. "I'll be right there." He slammed the phone down, stood up, and seethed, "If you'd excuse me, one of us still has a job."

—

JENNIFER SPENT THE NEXT few weeks in a state of stagnation, a span of world-weariness, drowned in boredom, depression, and alcohol. She tried to take out her aggressions as the midseason replacement on the over-thirty women's hockey team affectionately called "Chicks with Sticks," but she was told not to return after she came down on a brawny six-foot defenseman they called "The Hammer" and broke her nose.

Most nights were spent alone, pondering her murky past and strategizing a way to jump-start a new career path. She searched for civilian jobs on the Internet and phoned all the business contacts that would still take her call, but she had made many enemies over the years. The few IRS friends she had either didn't have any clout in the private sector or didn't really want to help. Jennifer concluded that she would have to create a job, maybe start a business of some kind, build from scratch and reinvent herself. But coming up with a good business idea wasn't as easy as she thought it would be. Committing to one was even more challenging, which was no surprise to Jennifer given her track record with commitment. For a while she thought the problem was that she knew too much. She had seen so many businesses from the inside out and she knew why most ventures failed, which gave her a bad case of analysis paralysis, and she talked herself out of any promising idea.

Money was getting tight, too. She thought about bartending or waiting tables, but it would only be a Band Aid. She would soon have to give up Manhattan and move to a cheaper borough. And then what?

One evening, she tried to lift her spirits by blending into the winter festivities at Rockefeller Center—watching lovers circle the ice-skating rink under the multihued lights, enjoying the omnipresent scent of roasting chestnuts—but she couldn't ignore the fact that she was wallowing, detached, and unimaginably despondent. She reached in her pocket for her amber container. It was empty. She felt a wave of panic overcome her.

No more Vicodin. No more fluff. No more chill.

Then she saw something that gave her the answer she was looking for. Behind the Prometheus statue, there was a lovely little girl sitting between her parents, sipping hot chocolate, having the time of her life. It was a sweet vision of felicity; the warmth Jennifer had missed; the childhood she wanted. It should have made her feel more bitter, sent her over the edge, maybe over a ledge.

But it didn't.

It helped her realize that she couldn't change the past any more than she could change who she had become. Whatever had turned her into an overambitious sleuth didn't matter. This is who she was. If no one else in the public or private sector would ever hire her, justice could still be served. She decided to finish the job she started, whatever it took.

Max Culpepper got away, and she was going to make him pay.

The next morning, she pulled out the Delmonico's bar napkin with Roberta Coscarello's number, called her, and asked, "Is your offer still on the table?"

Roberta sounded like she had been expecting Jennifer's call. "The position is still available," she said. "Would you like to come in and discuss?"

CHAPTER 10

THE COBBLESTONED TRIBECA STRIP just west of Broadway and south of SoHo was laced with world-famous restaurants and multimillion-dollar lofts. Jennifer confirmed the address Roberta had texted her and looked up at a ten-story nineteenth-century commercial warehouse that had been converted to postmodern luxury apartments.

Not your typical government building.

The name on the bell was even more innocuous: Tenant in Unit 8A.

Jennifer was buzzed inside. It was another blasting cold day and she welcomed the warmth, but in the elevator, she wondered if Roberta Coscarello was really who she said she was, or if she was walking into some kind of trap. When Roberta came to the door wiping her hands with a kitchen towel and hugging her like a long lost relative, Jennifer felt at ease. "So glad you're here," Roberta said. "Excuse the mess."

Jennifer went inside. It wasn't messy by anyone's standards. It was a charming home. Jennifer came through the foyer and saw a tidy living room and an adjoining den, which had furniture pushed aside to accommodate a large computer station with several tracking-device monitors. The doors to the bedrooms and other living spaces were shut.

Jennifer heard a male voice from behind one of the computer screens. "Is she here?"

"She is," Roberta said, "come say hello."

A twenty-something dude with long hair and tattoos all the way up his arms emerged and greeted Jennifer with a fist pump. "I'm Marcus. Nice to meet you."

Marcus's deep-set gray eyes, inviting smile, and cool manner put Jennifer at ease even more. Something about him looked familiar. "Have we met before?" she asked.

"Nope." He seemed rather certain.

"What's your role here?"

Marcus glanced at Roberta, as if asking permission.

Roberta answered for him. "Marcus will be your digital forensic technologist. He'll provide support and information. You will take orders from me, and only me. You will have no contact with anybody else."

Jennifer thought it was presumptuous of Roberta to be laying down conditions, as if she had already accepted. Then again, Jennifer couldn't imagine why she wouldn't accept. All she wanted was a way to go after Culpepper and this woman was making that possible. "I think I get it," Jennifer said. "Marcus will have his ear to the ground but you're in charge."

"I told you she was sharp," Roberta said as she headed into the kitchen. "I'll bring out a little something to snack on and then we can begin."

Jennifer moved into the living room and scoped out the place. "Smells good," Jennifer said to Marcus. "What's she making?"

"If you're really so sharp," Marcus said playfully, "you tell me."

Jennifer played along. "That's a high-end chef's kitchen with a *Cucina Bella* sign on the door. My guess is her 'little something to snack on' is going to be a spread that would put Mario Batali to shame."

Marcus was amused, "Nice, Italian mothers can't help themselves."

Roberta reentered with a tray of bruschetta, roasted fig salad, and grilled basil, tomato, and cheese paninis. "Please, help yourself."

"Thanks." Jennifer grabbed one. They looked and smelled delicious. "This is your home, Ms. Coscarello, and it's lovely, but it isn't a FinCEN office."

"Another good observation," Roberta said as she pulled two seats up to the computer station where Marcus was working.

"And Marcus doesn't look like he works for the Treasury Department," Jennifer added as she sat down. "He doesn't even look old enough to have a job."

Marcus flipped Jennifer the bird behind his chair and Jennifer returned the gesture, like teasing siblings, or peer buffoonery.

"You're doing this on your own," Jennifer said to Roberta. "Why?"

"I can't investigate or arrest Culpepper through FinCEN," Roberta explained. "Privacy laws in safe harbors are immutable."

Jennifer had been hoping that the financial crime unit had rules of their own, that she would at least have their backing. "Then how do you expect me to do anything?" she asked.

"You're no longer affiliated, and you're motivated. That's a vicious combination."

"You mean I'm disposable."

"You're angry, just like I am," Roberta said, her voice rising with a hint of fervor. "People like Culpepper get away all the time. Even when we know how they do it, we've never been able to do a damn thing about it. I want to change that. And so do you. But we can't do it if we play by the rules. We have to find another way to bring Culpepper to justice, so it will send a message to others…"

Music to Jennifer's ears. She thought about her plea to Simon Brisco: *Think about how effective I can be without having to play by the rules.*

Roberta tapped Marcus's shoulder. "Show her—"

Marcus called up a GPS map. A bird's-eye view homed into Grand Cayman and landed on a two-story corporate structure swathed with tropical landscape.

"Flamingo Enterprises is a privately held company that owns Caribbean real estate, resorts, casinos. They also shelter thousands of American businesses. If the Caymans are the most well-known tax haven, Flamingo is their best kept secret, the Holy Grail."

"I've never heard of them," Jennifer admitted.

"It's only shared among very exclusive circles," Roberta said. "The savviest money manipulators are good at keeping secrets about places that hide assets. Flamingo only does business on islands with shelter provisions."

"This is their headquarters," Marcus said as he called up an animated CAD image that toured through Flamingo Enterprises, tracking a survey of the corporate building's alarm systems, dead bolt locks, infrared passkeys.

Jennifer asked, "This is where they shelter money?"

"And people," Roberta added. "They harbor the largest network of wealthy expatriate fugitives in the world, changing their identities, laundering their assets, helping them purchase property in impenetrable safe havens all over the Caribbean, throughout the Pacific, off the South American and European coasts, all around Asia, and Australia, too."

Marcus called up another bird's-eye view, this one landed on a storefront office space on a busy town center street, between a dive shop and a travel agency. This is Flamingo Properties. Looks like an ordinary real estate office that sells homes, right?"

Jennifer nodded.

"Because that's what they want people to think," Roberta said. "Flamingo Properties buys and sells over a billion dollars' worth of residential properties at any given time. And that's just what we can track. There's probably more."

"That's no ordinary real estate office," Jennifer agreed.

"And they don't sell to just anybody," Roberta said. "All buyers come through Flamingo-approved real estate investment firms, or private referrals."

"Probably through lawyers representing affluent clients under investigation," Marcus chimed in, "or worse."

Jennifer got their point. "Like Culpepper."

Roberta nodded. "A lot of people want to escape a bad situation—the law, a business gone bad, a spouse from hell, but only the very rich can afford this…"

Marcus called up a list of spectacular Flamingo residential properties and the outrageous prices they sold for.

"We believe that buying property through Flamingo gives access, immunity, and protection," Roberta said. "Their motto is, 'Ownership has its privileges and privacy is king'."

"Nirvana for the ones that got away," Marcus added.

Jennifer got the drift. "Culpepper found his peeps."

"The most cunning escape artists in the world," Roberta said. "You're going to go there and become one of them. That's how you're going to get to Culpepper."

Jennifer felt her face smile without giving it permission. "I'd need an ironclad cover with a huge net worth."

"Yes, you would," Roberta tapped Marcus on the shoulder. "Show her Concord."

Marcus's fingers floated over the keyboard and images of stunning destination hotels appeared on the monitor.

"Concord LLC owns and operates exclusive boutique hotels in eighteen countries," Roberta explained. "They're quite successful and family owned."

Marcus blew up a portrait of the Concord dynasty, a family of obvious prominence and privilege. Roberta pointed to a young woman in the center, looking off with an ethereal expression. She was close to Jennifer's age, same build, same dimpled chin and sea-glass eyes. The only distinctive differences were her short, blonde hair and glasses.

"Eloise Concord was the eldest daughter," Roberta said. "She was poised to take over the business until she had a falling out with her father. They never spoke again, but Eloise still had full access to her trust funds, and she sure knew how to use and abuse them."

Marcus flashed some tabloid photographs of Eloise Concord seen partying with celebrities. "Here she is jetting around the world like a rock star—fancy cars, fancy men, fancy drugs—"

"Unfortunately," Roberta cut him off, "the lifestyle caught up with her."

"Usually does," Jennifer said. "Overdose?"

"Car accident."

Marcus called up police snapshots of a Maserati wrapped around a tree.

Roberta said unabashedly, "We paid off the coroner's office to keep her corpse on the unidentified list."

Jennifer felt a sudden chill. "Her family doesn't know?"

"She was dead to them anyway."

"You want me to go undercover as a dead girl?"

"It's the perfect cover…" Roberta opened a folder and showed her Eloise Concord's financial statements, "with a huge net worth."

Jennifer's jaw dropped. "That's a lot of money."

"If we're right about buying property through Flamingo giving you access, then you'll need proof of assets."

"So Eloise Concord can start her new life in the Cayman Islands?"

"Exactly. Think you could pull of an angry young lady who resents her father for everything he stands for?"

Jennifer had wondered why Roberta mentioned her father when they first met at Delmonico's. Now she had a pretty good idea. If Simon knew about the residual anger she harbored, so would Roberta; they were all trained to learn things that motivate people, and a corrupt dad ranked high. "I get it," Jennifer said. "It wouldn't be a stretch."

"I almost forgot…" Roberta reached for a box on the desk and pulled out a rose gold Sky Dweller Rolex. "Eloise Concord never went anywhere without this."

Jennifer took the aureate watch and looked it over. On the back was an engraving. Jennifer looked up. "Love Dad?"

"Ironic," Roberta admitted. "I know."

Jennifer took off her Fitbit and tried it on the elegant rose gold timepiece. She could understand why Eloise Concord never took it off. It was lovely. "She traveled light."

"Not really." Roberta got up, opened a closet door, and rolled out a large Louis Vuitton suitcase. Marcus helped her lift it up onto his desk. "You look like a size two," Roberta said as she displayed an eye-popping assortment of party girl accessories—fancy clothes, copious jewelry, and risqué lingerie. "You'll need to live believably in the lifestyle of Eloise Concord." Roberta unzipped the interior liner and revealed stacks of cash, enough to make Jennifer's eyes bulge.

Roberta grinned. "So are you on board?"

There was nothing not to like. Roberta was providing everything Jennifer needed to go after Culpepper, no strings attached, without the usual politics or any real authority, and playing by the rules was never really Jennifer's thing. All that mattered were results, and now she would be free from almost all restraints. Jennifer's heart beat heavy, her blood pumping. She felt alive again. She stood up and said, "Let's do this."

"Fantastic." Roberta gave her a big hug.

Jennifer felt her warmth and it was comforting. She trusted her.

But did Roberta trust her?

As Jennifer reached for the Louis Vuitton suitcase, Roberta grabbed her arm gently. "Just remember who you are and what you're there for," Roberta said. "There will be temptations with an assignment like this. Even the best of us can get caught up and forget that our covers are temporary—"

"You don't have to worry about me."

"Good to hear, but just to be clear: Everything must be accounted for and returned. Including you. If you get compromised, you come home. If you get caught, we never met. *Capiche?*"

Jennifer understood completely, but all she cared about was getting a second chance at Culpepper, and she assured Roberta with all the verve she could muster, *"Capiche!"*

CHAPTER 11

ROBERTA AND MARCUS PROVIDED Jennifer with Eloise Concord ID's, a passport, and an iPhone with passwords installed to give her access to her trusts, shelter provisions, and transfer of deeds—everything she would need in order to buy a Flamingo property. Jennifer spent the next few weeks studying every detail of Eloise Concord's short life, inside and out, all about her childhood, family, and family business. She practiced every nuance, from her upper-crust Boston accent to her low-cut dresses and tops. She turned her long dark curls into a short bleached blonde bob, changed her bland, basic garb into Gucci *au fait*, and replaced her purple Fitbit wristband with the rose gold Sky Dweller Rolex Eloise Concord never went anywhere without. Once she familiarized herself with the custom features on the iPhone that Marcus prepared for her—with the latest and greatest search and detect apps, encryption to ghost all of her emails, texts, and calls, and a GPS guard that made it impossible for anyone to track her—she was good to go.

With a thick envelop of cash in her pocket and a large Louis Vuitton suitcase in tow, Jennifer left her grungy walk-up behind, realizing she could easily walk away from her entire life and no one would know, or care. But she didn't mind just then. It didn't matter that upon her return nothing would be different; she would still be lacking a job, money, and love. For now, she had purpose. She was going after the one that got away, to find a way to make him pay, and she had an impassioned, likeminded partner providing resources, the perfect cover, and very few restrictions.

She took a limo to JFK Airport, champagne glass in hand, and left New York City as Eloise Concord. When the job was over, Jennifer Morton would have to return, but she didn't worry about that just then. Operation Culpepper was on and that's all that mattered.

—

A FORTY-FOUR-FOOT SWAN—THE ROLLS Royce of sailboat racers— was leading the pack of the Flamingo Sailing Club. Manning the boat was a former New Yorker and SEC villain of the year, Max Culpepper, although he was no longer using that name. He was now Rupert Reynolds, a tanned, retired billionaire who didn't have a care in the world.

Accompanying him was an exquisite Brazilian companion with a bikini-clad Venusian body who had thrown herself at him at the Flamingo Yacht Club the night before. Despite her obvious intent of scoring a billionaire, he had a hard time resisting. He was only human, God knows.

She rubbed her skipper's shoulders and whispered in his ear, "You are amazing, sailor. I am so very impressed."

"I told you," he trumpeted, "I never lose."

She giggled. "You promise me romantic dinner if we win race, no?"

The former Max Culpepper drew an inhale from his big Cuban stogie, tried to remember where he packed his Viagra, and moaned like the cat who ate the canary, "Get ready for the night of your dreams, Sugar Pie." The evening promised to be epic.

Plan B was never meant to be a punishment or even a lesser lifestyle. In fact, he had designed it to have plenty of upside, like all great deals. As Rupert Reynolds, he was relieved from all ties to Max Culpepper. He no longer had to manipulate his schemes, cover his lies, manage his demanding clients, or coddle his bloodsucking employees, and he was finally free from his thirty-five-year marriage he would have left long ago if he could have stomached the financial loss, which was worse than the discomfort of getting caught embezzling.

He believed it was his turn to enjoy the fruits of his labors with every newfound liberty that presented itself, beginning with this willing Brazilian goddess. His mast shimmered as his sail caught the perfect breeze and his beloved Swan careened the luminous coast peppered with speedboats, wave-runners, and colorful parasails, and raced for the finish line. He had never been happier in his life. He looked up at the sky and literally roared. That's when he noticed the transatlantic flight rumbling above them, preparing to land at Owen Roberts International Airport, just beside the coastline of the North Sound. He shouted up to the plane, "Welcome to paradise!" completely unaware that it was bringing a passenger who was coming to destroy him.

—

JENNIFER TOOK HER TIME to get acclimated. She immersed herself in island life, mingled with tourists, frequented restaurants, shops, clubs, and beaches.

But she spent most of her time at Hotel Flamingo. If Roberta's assessment was valid and Flamingo Enterprises was a front, then their flagship hotel would likely be the epicenter. And if it was a façade they allowed the world to see, used to deflect the deception, then Jennifer was sure it would have a few cracks and leaks. She just had to find them. She chatted up other guests in the hotel lobby, participated in the beachfront activities, and roamed the grounds, looking for a crumb of a clue. Something. Anything.

Jennifer had heard that spy work is 90-percent boredom and 10-percent terror, but in a paradisal place like this, the downtime was inspired. The scenery was lovely, and she was never alone. In the evenings she hung out in the hotel bar, and that's where she met Alex the bartender, a young American who had worked there long enough to know the ropes, and seemed slippery enough to be bought off.

"Macallan?" Alex called out when he saw her hopping up on a stool.

"Thanks for remembering," she said, "but I'll switch to Glenfiddich tonight."

"Eighteen or twelve?"

Eloise Concord would favor the good stuff. "If you have to ask—"

Alex smiled, reached for the top shelf. "You have good taste, Ms. Concord."

"You know my name. I'm impressed."

"Don't be," the bartender said as he pointed to the iPad sticking out of her bag with Eloise Concord's name engraved in the leather cover. She giggled, postured, and pointed back at the nametag on his vest. "Thanks, Alex."

He grabbed a glass from the dry rack, scooped ice, and poured her drink. "How long will you be staying with us?"

"Haven't decided yet."

This piqued his interest. Who doesn't know how long they're staying at a five-hundred-dollar-a-night-and-up hotel? He gave her a very generous pour and said, "This one's on the house."

"That's really sweet. Thank you."

He grabbed another glass, poured a little for himself, took a swig, and added, "Anything you need during your stay just let me know. Anything at all, Ms. Concord."

Jennifer noticed that his voice elevated when he said, "Anything at all, Ms. Concord," like he was either offering items that weren't on the menu.

"Call me Eloise," she said, "since we're about the same age and all." And since she thought that Eloise would be even more flirtatious, she asked, "Do you have a girl, Alex?"

The bartender's face tightened. "House rules. I have to address all guests as 'Mister' or 'Miss.' Unless, of course, a more prestigious title is required...and yeah, I have a girlfriend," he admitted sheepishly, almost like an apology, or a regret.

Jennifer chuckled. "Call me Ms. Concord then. How long have you been living down here, Alex?"

"Couple years."

"Like it?"

"What's not to like?"

"I could imagine, a young, good-looking guy like you must be crushing it down here."

Alex blushed, and it wasn't because she embarrassed him, but because a lady in a Flamingo uniform walked by, eyeballing the bar. "'Scuse me a sec," he said, moving back down the bar to check on another customer.

Must be his boss, Jennifer thought. *Or girlfriend. Maybe both.*

Once the Flamingo uniform disappeared into an elevator, Alex returned with another pour of the good stuff. For both of them.

"They keep you on a short leash," she said. "Lots of rules, huh?"

"It's a wonderful organization to work for," he said like an obedient soldier.

She tried another approach. "Where are you from, Alex? Do I detect a little Queens in your voice?"

"Jersey," he told her. "And you? Manhattan or Brooklyn?"

If this were a game of rock, paper, scissors, Long Island smothered New Jersey. Manhattan and Brooklyn could squash the rest of the Tri-State area.

"I've been living in the city," Jennifer admitted, trying not to sound superior. "But I'm originally from the Boston area." She wondered if he would expect more of a Boston accent, but she decided it was safer to stay neutral, in case she slipped or wasn't believable.

"Boston's nice," he said, glancing down the bar to see if he was needed.

"Truth is," she lowered her voice, "I'm thinking of staying down here. Permanently."

Alex looked as if he wanted to ask her for more details, but he restrained.

"I'd love to meet some of the others," she added.

Her words seemed to hang in the air. He looked at her like she was a customer at an Italian restaurant asking to meet the mafia. "What others?" he asked.

She decided to back off the pedal a scooch. "You know...other people looking to get out of the rat race, live on the island, and hang out with other compatible expatriates."

She was really only putting it out there, but vaguely, to see how he would react; she knew how to read a face, and that would tell her if he was in the know. But it wasn't his shifting eyes or tense lips that gave him away. It was what he said when he leaned in and whispered, "Club Flamingo is private, but sometimes they let in some eye candy...like you."

"I'll take that as a compliment." Jennifer said, revealing a grateful grin. She dropped two $100 bills on the bar and waited to see how he responded to a little extra incentive.

Alex pocketed the cash and confirmed that she had paid the right fee for such a favor. "You want to party with Flamingos..."

They actually call themselves Flamingos!

He winked again, this time with an assuring nod. "I got ya covered."

She had in fact found a crack in the wall and Club Flamingo would be her first peek inside the labyrinthian Flamingo fold.

CHAPTER 12

THROUGH THE YACHT-LADEN FLAMINGO marina, across from the streets peppered with elegant boutique shops, down the shore, and past a gated community of designer homes nestled into the hills of this Kingdom Come, Jennifer came to the secluded entrance of Club Flamingo, an over-scaled Mediterranean-style edifice surrounded by tall palms.

Jennifer checked in with the bouncer at the door as Eloise Concord. She was on the list, as Alex had promised, and she entered a large ingress and looked around the sprawling hideaway. Like a modern-day Rick's Café, it was a multipurpose venue—cocktail lounge, supper club, gaming room, and dance hall—bustling and crowded, but not uncomfortably so. A local Reggae band filled the room with a loyal rendition of Ziggy Marley and the Melody Makers' "Tomorrow People," and Jennifer moved through the throng, observing, trying to listen to snippets of conversations. It seemed they were all expatriates, mostly from America, but she also picked up accents from Australia, Ireland, Singapore, Dubai, and one loving couple speaking Castilian Spanish. They all seemed emboldened, entitled, debauched, indulgent, and dissolute—discussing their paradisiac lives in the Caymans and their high-class problems like too early tee times and limited number of Michelin three-star restaurants on the island. Jennifer marveled. Were they all kings and queens of fraud—former inside traders, corporate embezzlers, Ponzi schemers, insurance scammers,

money launderers, tax evaders—the ones that got away. It made
sense that they would converge in a private club where they could
meet others just like them without the risk of being exposed.

Will I run into Max Culpepper?

She studied the room, wondering if Culpepper would
recognize her in this context. He had only seen her once, at his
trial, and she hoped that her transformation into Eloise Concord
was extreme enough. If she did see him, she decided, she would
have to keep a safe distance.

She took a seat at a thousand-dollar-minimum blackjack
table. The dealer nodded, and the other players took notice. She
reached into the Lana Marks ostrich pocketbook she bought at
the hotel boutique—in true Eloise Concord fashion—and peeled
off ten thousand dollars from a thick wad of cash. Even though
the remainder of Eloise Concord's money had to be returned
in the end, she was expected to use her discretion, and it would
be prudent to show off a blatant disregard for cash, she figured.
Jennifer wanted these people to see Eloise Concord not only as
eye candy, as Alex the bartender had referred to her, but also as
one of their own; she needed to fit in to get in. And Jennifer could
definitely hold her own in a gaming room. She once audited a
three-time World Series of Poker champion, who taught her how
to beat Vegas every time, and whom she taught how to pay his
fair share of taxes. She also had a nearly photographic memory
when it came to numbers.

"You shouldn't hit," Jennifer whispered, to lady next her, trying
to make a friend.

"Are you sure?" the lady asked, a Southern belle, appreciating
her help.

Jennifer noticed a five-karat diamond on the lady's finger, the
likes of which she had never seen before, and tried not to stare.
Eloise Concord would have seen bigger rocks. "Yeah," Jennifer
explained, noticing she was already at sixteen. "Dealer's got a four
facing up. Let him bust."

The lady looked confused but smiled at the dealer like she had already beaten him, waving her hand with the big rock like an exclamation point. "I'll hold!"

The lady started counting her chips, laying them out by her cards, and the dealer didn't say anything. Jennifer knew why. Five Karat was a Flamingo and the rules didn't apply; Flamingos paid to play; etiquette was optional.

The dealer flipped over his jack, dealt himself a ten, and then acted as though he couldn't believe his bad luck. "Busted!"

Five Karat cheered.

"Well played," the dealer told her, as he collected all the cards for a reshuffle.

Jennifer looked up and saw a vision more striking than the five-karat ring: an elegant young man with olive skin weaving through the crowd, shaking hands with everyone he passed. She could see that he was well-known and well-regarded.

Five Karat noticed Jennifer's gaze. "He's quite breathtaking, isn't he?"

Christ, I'm staring. "I hadn't noticed," Jennifer said with a smirk.

Five Karat giggled. "All the young ladies go gaga over Jack Martin. I've seen some standing in front of Flamingo Properties just to get a glimpse through the front window.

The handsome young guy is Jack Martin. Works at Flamingo Properties.

"Nice-looking boy," Five Karat said approvingly, "but Marshall Shore's more my flavor of gin..." Her spine straightened, and she beamed, "Speak of the devil—"

Jennifer saw that Five Karat was salivating over a distinguished-looking man entering the room. He had a graying, trimmed beard that framed a tanned face and piercing, translucent eyes that were anything but kind. "Marshall Shore?" Jennifer asked.

The five-karat lady turned beet red. Jennifer realized that she had tipped her own hand and revealed that she was an outsider. She should have known who Marshall Shore was. Five Karat looked around nervously, as if making sure no one had heard her, and then looked down at her cocktail and mumbled, "I think I had one too many tonight."

Flamingos only discuss Flamingo business with other Flamingos.

The dealer finished shuffling the cards and started to deal another hand.

Jennifer watched as people approached Marshall Shore, greeting him like royalty. He had an air about him, like he owned the place. For all Jennifer knew, he might. He moved like a proud emperor, this one in designer clothes, Issey Miyake's finest. Jennifer would do her diligence on His Highness Marshall Shore, and the hottie, Jack Martin, as soon as she got back to the hotel. She searched the room for more standouts.

"The dealer's waiting," Five Karat said, bringing Jennifer's attention back to the game.

Jennifer waved her hand. "I'll stick."

"Good choice," the lady told Jennifer. "Sometimes it's best to stay out of the game."

Was that friendly advice or a warning?

—

JENNIFER'S DUE DILIGENCE ON Marshall Shore found absolutely nothing: nothing online, nothing in any public records relating to Flamingo Enterprises or any of their subsidiary businesses. From the reaction of the five-karat lady, he clearly played an important role, but only people inside knew what it was, and they weren't allowed to discuss it. As Roberta had suspected, privacy was king.

Jennifer switched her focus to Jack Martin—the tall, dark, and handsome younger man she had seen in Club Flamingo—and he did have a public profile. He headed up Flamingo Properties. If Roberta was right and owning Flamingo real estate was the way in, then Jennifer would have to find a way to get to Jack Martin. She knew their office had storefront office space on a busy town center street, like an ordinary real estate office, but she had been warned that they didn't take people off the street. So Jennifer tried cold-calling Jack Martin's office and telling the assistant that answered his phone that she was referred to him by her attorney. The assistant directed Jennifer to a link on their website, which was the first step in their vetting process. The link led her to a personal profile form, and it was unusually extensive and detailed. They wanted to know about family background, professional associations, and net worth. They asked for names, addresses, phone numbers, and every component that would lay out a complete financial picture—every investment, trust, account. Everything.

Luckily Roberta and Marcus had provided Jennifer with all of Eloise Concords details, and she was able to fill out the form completely, evincing an ideal applicant—a cash buyer with a reason to run. *The perfect Flamingo* Jennifer thought, prepared to buy in. She just had to get through the pearly gates, and Jack Martin.

The thought excited her.

CHAPTER 13

JENNIFER GOT A MEETING.

She arrived a few minutes early and waited in the reception. There were miniature models of their developments, constructions, acquisitions, and renovations; a "Sold Out" sign on every one. Seemed like a typical real estate office. But Jennifer knew better.

A poised young lady in her mid-twenties introduced herself as "Mr. Martin's assisant," and escorted Jennifer upstairs to the private offices. At the end of the hall was a large corner office. "Have a seat and Mr. Martin will be with you shortly," the young lady said as she handed Jennifer a chilled bottle of water and left.

Jennifer took a seat on one of the wicker chairs across from a cluttered L-shaped desk. The office was well-appointed with a simple, tasteful Caribbean flare. Jack Martin was a busy guy with good taste and a lot of responsibility, but Jennifer noticed something else: there were no pictures, no personal items. She wondered about the possible implications of that. There was a small plaque behind the desk with a Flamingo Enterprises logo. She leaned forward to read the words: "Ownership has its privileges and privacy is king." Roberta had gotten that right. Jennifer wondered if it applied to the people selling the properties as well as the buyers, and if that may be the reason that nothing personal was displayed.

Handsome Man entered just then. He introduced himself with a warm smile and firm handshake. "I'm Jack Martin. Pleased to make your acquaintance."

He was just as striking in daylight, Jennifer thought.

Maybe even more so.

"Pleasure is all mine," she said, spilling her water as she stood up.

He didn't seem to notice the spill, or her jolt of nerves, probably because the low-cut, bright-red halter dress that she wore like an assault weapon required his full attention, just as she had hoped it would.

"Please, have a seat," he said politely. He was holding a printed copy of the twenty-some page form Jennifer had sent in. "I hope you weren't waiting long."

"Not at all," she told him.

"Great." He sat down and reviewed her profile. "Let's see what we have here..."

She detected a gentry British accent. With his olive skin, emerald green eyes, and exotic island looks, she had expected a Shetlandic dialect like she had heard from the island locals. "Are you from London?" she asked.

He didn't answer, didn't offer where he was from, and looked up from the form. "Says that you were referred by Lynch, Arnold, Heller, and Gold?"

"That's right," Jennifer lied, sensing that he approved of their endorsement. "The firm has represented my family on various occasions, and I confided in one of the lawyers." She lowered her voice and said, "He told me about Flamingo."

Jack seemed satisfied, and Jennifer decided that she had been right to accuse Barry Lynch of helping Max Culpepper flee; at the very least he must have recommended Flamingo to him and other clients that were out of options.

Jack turned the page and reviewed her real estate request. "You're interested in property on the west side?" he asked.

"I hear it's the best."

"Then you must be a diver."

She wasn't, but she had done her homework. "Isn't everyone who comes to the Caymans? All the remarkable access to reefs, wrecks, and walls, warm waters with crystal visibility are like no other place on earth."

"That's true," he said, "but the best dive sites are also close to our most crowded resorts, and Flamingo applicants are often looking for privacy, sometimes seclusion. Even anonymity." He looked at her hard and asked, "How important is privacy to you?"

"Very." Jennifer's voice dipped. "Let me put it this way: no one knows I'm here right now and I want to keep it that way."

Jack got up, crossed the room, and opened the plantation shutters. A warm breeze flowed through. "Are you able to tell me why?"

She looked past him, out the window he had just opened, as if she were deciding if she could trust him. She wanted him to really believe in the plight of Eloise Concord. "It a long and complicated story."

He seemed to buy the ruse. "We can't guarantee privacy if we don't know why you need it," he insisted, coaxing her.

"Do you know anything about my family?" she asked.

"I know of the Concord Hotels. Isn't there one on St. Lucia?"

"St. Croix," she corrected him, unsure if that slip of information was a test, "one of our nicest resorts."

Jack nodded, encouraging her to continue.

"My father groomed me to take over when he stepped down, but I'd rather die."

"You don't like the hotel business?"

"I love the business, but I don't like... It's my father...he's controlling, and cruel."

"You could work somewhere else."

"Therein lies the problem. He won't let me leave. He thinks of me as an investment that keeps trying to get away. He'll eventually come looking for me. I can't have him find me this time..." She paused, feigning difficulty, and then told him, "The lawyer that told me about Flamingo said it was possible to buy a property under a different name."

Jack walked back to his desk and asked, "What else did your lawyer say about us?"

"Just that…" She glanced at a Flamingo plaque behind him and sang it like it were a jingle from a beer commercial: "…Ownership has its privileges and privacy is king."

Jack laughed and pat the plaque like a favorite child. "Our mantra."

They brag about what they do; they don't talk about how they do it.

"My lawyer said Flamingo helped a client of his start over. Completely. Was he right? Can you do that?"

"Anything is possible."

"And what about my money?"

"What about your money?"

"I have a lot of it."

He laughed and regarded her twenty-some page profile, which detailed Eloise Concord's notable financials. "I can see that."

"If I were able to buy a property under a new name," she pressed, "how would I transfer my money here?"

"That wouldn't be a problem."

"Without it being traced?"

"Asset protection is something Flamingo does better than anyone."

"Because you have relationships with the banks—?"

He shifted in his seat. "Let's not get ahead of ourselves."

She was pushing too hard, too fast, and she just then realized that Jack's British accent was slipping in and out; when it was out, he sounded more like a local. She wanted to ask why but she knew better.

Privacy is king.

There was a knock at the door.

An older man was holding up a contract for Jack to see. "Would you excuse me—?"

"Of course."

Jennifer watched Jack head down the hallway with the man. Once they turned the corner, she reached for his computer and typed "Max Culpepper" into the Spotlight Search. Nothing came up, so she tried, "Clients," "New Clients," "Transactions," "New People," "New Applications," "Sold Properties…"

She found nothing.

She looked through the computer's history, cookies, extensions, everything. Still found nothing.

Nada.

Either they had a cyber security she hadn't seen before or they didn't keep client files on their computer—the best way to prevent getting hacked.

Then she noticed a cabinet door behind Jack's chair with a pink flamingo logo.

Jennifer checked to make sure that Jack was still out of sight. She kneeled down and opened it. There was a safe inside. A hefty one, likely bolted down to the floor and cabled through the walls. She could crack it if she had the right tools, and enough time, but she had neither of those. She would have to come back after hours. She looked around to see what kind of alarm system they had, and it was a gnarly one. She'd need a passcode.

She saw Jack turn the corner, heading back, and swiftly sat back in her seat.

When he entered she acted like she had been checking emails on her iPhone.

He didn't seem to suspect anything. "Sorry about that," he said apologetically, "we're in the middle of a deal that needs to close by noon." He sat back in his chair. "So now that I understand what you're looking for, I'll talk to my team and we'll go from there."

"Anything I can do to move things along?"

"Not a thing…" He grabbed her application and leaned down to the cabinet she had just been looking through. He opened the door and punched a code into the keypad. His body blocked her view of the passcode.

There was another knock at the door.

Jack spun back around, looking irritated.

Another associate waved him over, a younger employee who looked embarrassed for interrupting.

"I'm really sorry," Jack said as he headed out again. "This'll just take a sec."

"No worries," she assured him, "I'm in no rush."

As she watched him rush down the hall, she heard a noise, a creak. It came from behind his desk. She leaned over to see.

The cabinet door with the flamingo sprung open. She made sure Jack had turned the corner and took a closer look. The door on the safe was ajar; it hadn't caught its latch.

She kneeled down, opened the safe door, and looked inside. There was a neat row of folders. She searched the labels. No names. Just numbers. She went to the first folder, hers. She was applicant F-659. She looked inside the next, F-658. It was thicker. It not only had an application, but also copies of financial statements, bank account transfers, and closing papers on a condominium.

Bingo!

The folder belonged to the former Max Culpepper. And it had all the transformation details since his arrival. Including his new name: Rupert Reynolds.

Rupert Reynolds!

Jennifer felt the floor vibrate. She looked up at the door.

Jack was coming back down the hallway.

She moved fast, slipped the Max Culpepper file into her shoulder bag, snapping it shut, and got back to her seat just before Jack reentered. He looked harried.

She glanced the cabinet and saw that the safe door hadn't caught the latch for her either.

Shit.

Jack noticed right away and knelt down.

Her heart beat heavy.

He slammed it shut, like he was used to the stubborn door.

She felt relieved.

He didn't sit back down this time. He was ready to wrap things up. "So I'll be in touch soon," he said.

She took the cue and stood up. "Terrific."

He walked to the door. "Are you enjoying your stay at our hotel?"

"Yes. It's lovely. And the staff is amazing."

"Great to hear. I'll leave some passes for the spa at the front desk." He lowered his voice like he was telling her a secret, "And I'll get you into our private club."

Already been there.

"We have a terrific new chef in the main dining room, an amazing band... I think you'll have a great time, girl like you."

He must have pegged her as a true *bon viveur*, which is exactly what Eloise Concord was. Jennifer Morton would have played it cool with a guy this hot, make him work hard, and then back away if he wanted any kind of commitment. Not Eloise Concord. She would get as close as she could, as fast as she could. Jennifer shifted so her low-cut dress gave Jack a good angle and asked sweetly, "Was that a dinner invitation?"

Jack looked surprised. "Oh...I...I'm sorry, Ms. Concord, I didn't mean to imply...I don't date my clients. Flamingo policy."

She blushed. "Lots of rules here, huh?"

Jack laughed, flashing his heart-stopping smile. "You have no idea."

Did he think that was a good thing or not?

Either way, she decided Handsome Man must be high enough on the food chain to break a few rules if he wanted to. She would just have to figure out what would get him to want to. She leaned back, crossed her arms, and said, "I wasn't looking for a proposal, just a friend, being new in town and all. Does Flamingo allow you to have friends?"

Now he blushed. "I'm sorry, that was presumptuous. Of course we can be friends. And I would be honored if you would join me for dinner."

CHAPTER 14

THE FORMER MAX CULPEPPER was enjoying a post-coital cigar as he glanced over *The Wall Street Journal* headlines, gloating. Unemployment was creeping up. Europe was sluggish. The Feds were still raising interest rates, forcing bond yields down. Equities were erratic. Nothing new. But for the first time in his life, none of it affected him. His money was secured in an untraceable bank, locked into TIPS—inflation-protected securities—the safest play. He no longer needed to beat the market. He was done growing his fortune. He couldn't spend it all in this lifetime if he tried. He had a new life, a new name, and he was banging a sexy Brazilian woman in a stellar penthouse with a spectacular view of the Caribbean Sea.

She was in the kitchen singing a Portuguese version of Madonna's "Justify My Love" while she stirred mimosas with fresh-squeezed oranges and generous pours of Grande Cuvée Brut left over from their foreplay the night before. He was savvy enough to know she was bidding for an invitation to stay, and he was prepared to deflect any attempt.

"Last night was incredible," she told him, "you are tiger in the bed."

"Thanks."

"How long have you had this place?" she asked.

"Not that long."

His answers became more abrupt, never looking up from his newspaper, to send the message that he was satisfied, satiated, and ready to enjoy a quiet Sunday. Alone.

"This was an exquisite holiday," she said. "I loathe idea of leaving."

"All good things must end."

She crossed the room slowly in her see-through negligee, so he could watch her provocative delivery of a mimosa she made with freshly squeezed oranges and croissants baked from scratch.

When that didn't get much of a response, she tried again. "Do you miss your home?" she asked as she sat on his bed and rubbed his feet.

"This is my home."

"But you're not from here—"

"I'm trying to forget where I came from."

"Why would you do that?"

He finally looked up from *The Journal*. "Do you need a ride to the airport?"

Her forehead burrowed.

"I'll call you a car." He reached for his phone on the bed stand and made the call, just to be clear: her time with this billionaire was over. He was not going to be her sugar daddy, free ride, or lover. Max Culpepper had had a lot of baggage; Rupert Reynold would travel light with only his Swan and his TIPS, and his hundred-thousand-dollar plus wrist watches. No other attachments, wives, live-in girlfriends, or better halves. He was free agent.

"I'm going to the loo," she said, the mimosa spilling on him as she stormed away in a huff. "I'll leave after shower."

"I hope that was an accident," he joked, wiping himself off with the sheets.

Clearly it wasn't. He could tell that she was not used to rejection. She came here to bag an elephant and she wanted to leave with some dignity. Rupert didn't know then that she was also about to leave with his Patek Philippe, Hublot Black Caviar Bang, and Breitling Navetimer World GMT, the pricey indulgences he kept on the bathroom counter.

She showered, dressed, packed her bags, and headed for the front door. When she passed the large bay windows, she noticed a blonde girl on his precious Swan, and scoffed, "Your next bimbo is here."

That got his attention.

She slammed the door as she left and affectionately shouted, "*Capullo!*"

He choked out a billow of cigar smoke, grabbed his binoculars, and ran to the window. Sure enough, someone was climbing onto his sailboat.

He paid damn good money for Flamingo security. Maybe the person on his boat was there for his protection, part of the service. But he hadn't been informed of anything. If fact, they had told him what to do if he ever suspected that his newfound privacy was in jeopardy.

So he pushed the red panic button they had installed behind his bedside table.

During business hours, the signal would go to Flamingo Security. But since it was so early in the morning, the CIA was notified first. They had better surveillance capabilities, and someone was on duty around the clock.

—

THE CIA BASE WAS housed in a nondescript office space above a local bank in George Town, in the heart of the Grand Cayman's financial district. The operative who first heard the request shouted, "Alarm's been activated! F-658. That's foxtrot six-five-eight!"

Rupert Reynolds was Flamingo number 658, but all this agent knew was that he was a resident in Flamingo Towers, penthouse number seven, parking space number six, and boat slip number fifty-eight. He also knew that any Flamingo with a number needed protection. The agent didn't know why. He just knew that they were supposed to search their properties and report any unusual activity to their senior field agents immediately.

—

ULTRAVIOLET LIGHTS GLEAMED DOWN from a satellite 150 miles above the earth, and microphones positioned on top of the tallest buildings recorded the cacophony of sounds. Miniature unmanned aerial vehicles probed every corner of Flamingo Towers—including invasive angles of Rupert Reynolds' condo, the garage where his Bentley was parked, and the harbor where his boat was docked.

—

THE OPERATIVES BACK AT the base watched the video feed on their monitors and honed in on the man in penthouse seven looking out his window through binoculars, and a female form moving about his boat. One of them radioed their senior field agents and reported, "Intruder has been identified on the boat, female, thirty to thirty-five, short blonde hair…"

The senior field agents notified had been in the Grand Cayman branch for years now, both former Virginians relocated to the Caribbean assignment with no plans of returning to the States. Ever. They had it too good here and had opportunities for advancement they couldn't get back home.

Agent Dick Perretta was a disheveled, unshaven, Tommy Bahama–wearing spook, and the nicer of the two. Agent Kirk Shannon was considerably more polished, but a sardonic dick. He was the one that answered the call.

"…I repeat…red button activated at F658. We've spotted a woman on his boat—"

"For fuck's sake, mate, I heard you the first time," Shannon mumbled through a mouthful of flapjacks, his peaceful breakfast watching a magnificent sunrise glowing off the placid seaway interrupted, "We're on our way."

CHAPTER 15

A WHITE-BELLIED MARTIN FLAPPED nosily as it dove into the water for its morning meal.

The splash startled Jennifer. She peered out from the back of Rupert Reynolds' Swan, saw the large swallow, and was relieved that she had not been spotted by harbor security. Not a soul in sight, she mused, and the solitude felt extraordinarily refreshing. She hadn't left New York—except for a few assignments—since she started working for the IRS over a decade ago. Now she was rocking in a quay, taking in a beautiful view from her target's luxurious sailing yacht—prepared to taste the sweetness of trapping a real vulture.

She leaned over the stern rail to check out the new moniker Culpepper gave his lovely Swan: *The Getaway*. She used a penny to scrape the letter "y," to be certain it had recently been painted over.

It had.

These guys love to tip their hats, she thought, remembering the name of her father's beloved Chris-Craft Capri speedboat, *The Great Escape*.

She then checked out the HID (Hull Identification Number)—the boat's fingerprint—to confirm that they too had been altered.

"Not bad work," Jennifer mumbled, as she scraped away the last digit.

It felt nice to be in a harbor again, surrounded by beautiful boats. Her best memories of her father were on his boat. And years later, when she would visit her Grandpa Leonard, she would sit for endless hours on his screened-in balcony, staring out at the Intracoastal, watching all the watercrafts trek out to sea. She thought back to the day that had changed everything, when she learned the truth about her old man. Max Culpepper was most like her father, she imagined, a mega-cheat that got away, and she badly wanted to catch the big fish. The file she stole from Jack Martin's office proved how he transformed into Rupert Reynolds. He bought a Flamingo property. And he she found his getaway vessel docked in their harbor. But as she ducked into the cabin to sort through the closets and storage compartments, she was reminded that she didn't have any way of dragging the newly minted fraudster back to the States. She started wondering if she was chasing another ghost. She took the time to run a few searches on her phone for Rupert Reynolds, to learn what she could about who Max Culpepper had become, but she came up empty. Did Flamingo just make up a new identity or was Rupert Reynolds a real person? she wondered. FinCEN could easily pull up every Rupert Reynolds that had entered Grand Cayman, and so she texted Marcus: "What can you tell me about Rupert Reynolds?"

Just when she hit send, a voice bellowed from above: "Come out with your hands on your head!"

Jennifer emerged from the cabin and saw two men. She shielded her eyes from the bright morning sun and smiled unabashedly. "Is this your boat?" she asked them, knowing they were there to ask her to leave, that someone had noted the intrusion.

Shannon lifted his windbreaker to draw attention his gun. "This is private property."

"And you're trespassing," Perretta added. "Let's see some ID."

"You first," Jennifer said, knowing they weren't local cops or guards based on their American accents and bad sense of style.

Shannon revealed a CIA badge and a fuck-you smirk. Jennifer could have called foul, but she kept her cover. She pulled out her Eloise Concord FinCEN-forged drivers' license and handed it to Shannon.

"Here on vacation, Eloise?" Shannon asked.

"Hoping to stay permanently," she said, hoping that Roberta's charge about buying property through Flamingo provided access, immunity, and protection was correct. "I'm looking to buy a place."

It seemed to have some effect. The agents shared a look. Shannon handed her license back. Perretta reached for her hand.

"I was just admiring it," she told them, as she hopped out of the Swan, "I'm considering getting one."

"Next time try a boat shop," Shannon retorted.

"I think she gets the point," Perretta said as he urged his partner away. "Enjoy your day, Ms. Concord."

—

ONCE THE AGENTS DISAPPEARED into the parking lot, Jennifer snuck down to the lighthouse where she had parked her rented Vespa. When the agents drove away, she followed them, wondering if the federal agents were protecting Max Culpepper, or if they too were here to nail him.

She trailed agents Peretta and Shannon to George Town and watched as they pulled up in front of a bank and got out.

Jennifer parked across the busy street and saw them walk up a stairway on the side of the bank building, leading into an unmarked door on the second-floor door.

She texted Marcus and asked him to confirm that this was a CIA outpost. If the CIA's involvement was on the up-and-up, Roberta should know about it through FinCEN.

He texted back right away: "It is."

She asked him what operations they were there for.

He answered: "Classified."

Did that mean he didn't know or couldn't tell her? After all, Operation Culpepper was being run out of a Tribeca apartment. She decided not to press the request. Not yet.

She waited for a while more, but the CIA agents didn't leave the building.

She headed back to the hotel and made a mental note to mention the CIA security guards when she gave Roberta her first update on the pursuit of Max Culpepper.

—

THE CIA BASE IN the financial district of Grand Cayman served mostly as banking watchdogs, making sure banks in the Caribbean didn't violate international law by doing business with UN, EU, and US enemies. They also helped stabilize nearby economies by bumping up State-run industries in places like Havana and Caracas, which in turn served US interests.

That's an old story.

Operatives in this office also did a little moonlighting that had nothing to do with US interests and no one back in Virginia was aware of such activities. They provided surveillance for Flamingo Enterprises and received cash at the end of the year, like a Christmas bonus. They were helping out the locals and they were getting greased.

That's an even older story.

Perretta and Shannon had been in this office the longest. They were the most senior agents and only they had direct contact with Flamingo security. All the others obeyed their orders. No one ever questioned their intent. And none of them were aware of any additional services they were providing for highly confidential Flamingo business activities.

When Shannon and Perretta came back from the marina, they headed toward their office in the back. As they passed the operators scrolling through surveillance monitors, Shannon asked one of them, "Did you have the footage from the Flamingo Harbor break-in?"

An operative scrolled his surveillance video. "All here. Would you like to look at it?"

"No," Shannon said. "I want you to destroy it."

Shannon and Perretta closed their office door for privacy. They had Flamingo business to tend to.

Perretta logged into his computer to locate one of their United States Predator drones. The sleek robotic flying machine with a bulbous head and plank-like wings was soaring over an oil refinery in Maturin, Venezuela, and sending back surveillance images.

"I have it up on my monitor," Perretta said, "Let's make the call."

Shannon phoned the operative back in Washington who controlled the flight pattern of the Unmanned Aerial Vehicles in their region. Shannon didn't know his name, but he wanted to make it personal, so he always called him Bubba. "I need you to miscalculate our UAV over the oil refinery in Maturin, Bubba."

Bubba recognized Shannon's voice right away, "You're not going to get it replaced," Bubba warned.

"Understood."

The new administration was pulling back on drone usage in peaceful nations and they weren't replacing them when they malfunctioned, crashed, or wore down.

"Just run it off course, like the others." Shannon knew that Bubba was trying to pay off the mortgage on his fishing cabin and wouldn't require too much convincing. "Same deal as last time, Bubba."

"Consider it done."

After they hung up, Bubba programmed the drone to avoid heavy northern winds—which didn't exist—so that it would dip to its lowest setting.

Agents Perretta and Shannon watched on their monitor as the UAV nosedived and scraped roadside telephone poles. Wires sparked. The drone crashed onto the adjacent property and burst into flames, which quickly self-extinguished. A few cows moseyed over to explore the remains.

A surveillance operator pounded on their door.

Perretta shut down his computer and Shannon waved for the operator to come in.

"The Maturin drone was just knocked off course," the operator said. "Should I let Washington know?"

"We already called it in," Shannon lied.

The operator stood in the doorway. His job was to monitor surveillance footage from their eyes in the sky, and those eyes kept falling out of the sky.

"You need something else?" Shannon snapped at the operator.

"No...I just—"

"Thanks for letting us know," Perretta said.

"Yes, sir."

Perretta sent a message to his contact at Flamingo Enterprises, telling him they were now clear to do business at that refinery in Maturin, Venezuela, just like the others. Their business was expanding fast.

Shannon headed over to the coffee machine. "Want one?"

"Two sugars," Perretta said with his first smile that morning. "I like mine sweet."

CHAPTER 16

THE HOTEL LOBBY WAS abuzz. There was a rush of new check-ins, winter escapees anxious to get out to the sunny beaches, and a staff in pink-linen uniforms eager to serve them. Jennifer moved through the fray and headed up to her room, anxious to fill Roberta in on her progress.

"Jack Martin heads up Flamingo Properties," she told Roberta as she entered her room and locked the door behind her. "He diligently screens Flamingo applicants before they even let you see any properties... And he's not too hard on the eyes, either."

"Hold on," Roberta said, as she shut the door to her private office at FinCEN. A large window looked out to the discovery center, so she could monitor the operatives. With one pull on her Venetian blinds, she prevented any fervent subordinates from monitoring her as well. She called up Jack Martin's company profile on her computer and scanned the pictures that were posted. "He's very cute," she agreed. "Just remember what I told you about temptations."

Jennifer ignored the warning. "Do you have any more intel on him?"

Roberta scrolled his file. "He's been on their payroll for nearly twenty years..." She took a moment to blow up the recent photos that came up. "Which seems strange because he doesn't look old enough to have been working that long—"

"He's in his mid-thirties," Jennifer confirmed. "Forty max."

"Is he going to show you some properties?" Roberta asked.

"They're reviewing me first. Hang on a sec…"

Jennifer checked the bathroom to make sure no hotel employees were loitering and listening in. The coast was clear, and she continued, "I checked his computer when I had my interview. He walked out for a bit—"

"That's my girl."

"I couldn't find any information about applicants or people that bought property. I think that's why you never found money trails or purchases when you hacked into Flamingo computers. I don't think they put any sensitive information on their computers at all."

Roberta said, "That's kind of brilliant, but it'll make things more difficult—"

"Not for me," Jennifer said. "Jack keeps files of his new applicants in a safe behind his desk."

"Can you break into it?"

"I didn't need to," Jennifer said, no explanation needed. "Culpepper bought an oceanside penthouse in Flamingo Towers when he got here, a fancy condo building by the harbor—"

Just then Jennifer received a text from Marcus. "I think I found the Rupert Reynolds you're looking for."

"Hold on a sec," Jennifer told Roberta as she opened a link to a *New York Times* article sent by Marcus titled "New York Investment Banker Gone Missing." It was dated three years prior.

Marcus texted her again saying, "The Department of Vital Statistics confirmed that they recently filed a request for a new birth certificate for this guy."

"You're not going to believe this…" Jennifer told Roberta, "Culpepper bought his condo under the name Rupert Reynolds, a banker that went missing years ago, who is likely dead—"

"Flamingo gave his identity to Max Culpepper?"

"Looks that way." Jennifer said, feeling a rush of excitement. "And he also changed his boat name, from *Hedge Fund Joy* to *The Getaway.*"

"*The Getaway*," Roberta repeated, followed by a sardonic moan. "So clever."

"And this was strange... When I found his boat, two field agents were all over me. One of them showed me his ID. CIA. I need you to find out what their assignment is and why they are guarding Flamingo property—"

Roberta cut her off, "They have jurisdiction, you don't."

"Could you get them to back off?"

"No. I can't. When it comes to the CIA, you have to stay away."

"I thought intel from every federal agency flowed through FinCEN."

"It does. But national security overrides everything."

"National security...these guys police the yacht set. What could they be working on, Operation Beach Combers?"

Roberta repeated Marcus's claim, "It's classified."

"Maybe you can help me with this then: Who's Marshall Shore?"

There was a long pause before Roberta said, "That's something you need to figure out."

Jennifer hissed. "Do you really work for FinCEN? I need some proof, because I have to say, I'm starting to have doubts—"

Roberta appeared on Jennifer's FaceTime. "You want proof that I work for FinCEN?"

Roberta opened her blinds, bringing the discovery pit into view. "Our offices are off limits to everyone without clearance, but let me make an exception for you, so you can have 'proof.'" She pointed to her phone so that Jennifer could see operatives searching data, intercepting emails, and tapping phone calls. Roberta turned her camera back and her face filled the screen again. "Convinced?"

"Okay, okay," Jennifer said.

Roberta pulled the blinds shut once more. "I can't tell you about Marshall Shore because he's a ghost. He doesn't exist."

"I saw him!" Jennifer objected.

"I meant that we've never been able to prove that he exists," Roberta explained. "He's the Flamingo puppet master, he runs the show and never leaves a trail. As far as the CIA is concerned—"

"I get it," Jennifer cut her off. "Operation Culpepper isn't going through FinCEN, I know what I signed up for.

"—The CIA branch on Grand Cayman mostly police offshore banks, making sure they don't violate international law. Sometimes they help stimulate local economies."

"Like Venezuela and Cuba?" Jennifer said provokingly.

"Exactly," Roberta confessed. "Those relations fluctuate. Sometimes they have to keep the dictators and petro-dictators in-line. That's why it's classified."

"Right…I just want to know who I'm dealing with—"

"I don't blame you for feeling uneasy," Roberta interrupted. "You've never had an assignment like this, unaffiliated, in a place filled with shrewd people, all with secrets, where nothing is what it seems and everyone you come across used to be somebody else. You don't trust anyone in your life. It's one of the reasons you're so good at what you do. It's one of the reasons I chose you for this job."

Was that a criticism or a compliment?

"Makes sense," Jennifer said. "I started to realize how little I knew about you and I got nervous. Our background speaks volumes about how we approach our job. You chose me for this because I have no ties—"

"That's not the only reason."

"Fair enough," Jennifer said. "Can't blame me for inquiring about your allegiances and motivations."

"What else would you like to know?"

She sounded open, so Jennifer asked, "Do you have kids?"

"Yes."

"How many?"

"One."

"You don't wear a wedding ring—"

"I'm not married."

"Divorced?"

"You know everything you need to know about me," Roberta said.

That was all Jennifer was going to get; that was good enough for now. "Thanks for sharing."

"You can't trust anyone at Flamingo," Roberta added, "but you have to trust me."

"I realize that." Jennifer opened her curtains and looked out at the view over beautiful hotel grounds and stunning beach. When she had traveled on IRS business, she stayed motor inns with views of interstate highways.

Roberta peeked through the blinds at the room full of FinCEN operatives milling about. "No one can know who you are or what you're doing. The only way this will work is if you stay true to your cover. Got it?"

"Got it."

They hung up. Jennifer thought about her cover, taking a good look at her reflection in the mirror. Besides her new short blonde hairdo, she didn't look that much different. But Eloise Concord was careless, indulgent, spoiled, and would make a statement as soon as she came to a place like this. Jennifer decided that she would head out to buy the most expensive un-necessities she could find. She grabbed a stack of cash and headed out for a shopping spree that would make people take notice of the new girl in town.

She was, after all, just staying true to her cover.

—

MARSHALL SHORE DIDN'T EXPECT his staff to treat him like royalty, even though they usually did, but he demanded that they were loyal as dogs. Especially his head of security and head of property management and acquisitions, because they vetted all new Flamingos, and Flamingos were the backbone of Flamingo Enterprises. When they discussed New Deals—people that were vying to join their flock—they usually met on Marshall's boat, out at sea, to be certain that their conversations were private.

And because Marshall loved his boat.

Dark cumulus clouds swirled overhead, but the pending tropical storm didn't spoil Marshall's fun. His long salt and pepper locks flapped wildly as he steered his hallowed Riva Aquariva Super speedboat over the wake of a sluggish cruiser, landing hard, nearly tipping over. He howled with delight, and then looked back, appreciating the elegant, sinuous lines and precious lacquered woods on his million-dollar toy almost as much as the priceless expressions on his two passengers bracing themselves for the next approaching wave.

"Can we get on with this?" Dex Boonyai shouted, managing his put-upon nausea.

Dex was a Jamaican with cocoa colored skin, icy gray eyes, and a permanent frown. He was also perennially skeptical, which suited him well as the head of Flamingo security.

"Soon," Marshall said with a laugh.

Marshall had given Dex the most coveted security position in the Caymans with a salary big enough to own his home outright and send his kids to private school with Flamingo children. He could certainly allow Marshall his indulgences, and endure his frequent antics, mood swings, and outbursts.

"We need to do this," Jack Martin agreed. "I have a showing in a half hour."

After traversing a few more waves, Marshall pulled back the throttle and eased into a slow coasting speed. "Okay then," Marshall said as he turned to face his men. "How many applicants do we have this month?"

"Five," Jack said, fanning his files for Marshall to see.

"How many are worthy?"

"One." Jack handed Marshall the top file. "Her name is Eloise Concord."

Marshall grinned as he skimmed the application. "As in Concord Hotels?"

"Yes," Jack confirmed. "She's the eldest daughter."

"Have you verified these trusts?"

Jack nodded. "Everything checks out."

"I once had some minor dealings with Concord," Marshall told them, "when I practiced law. I met her father a few times."

"He's the reason Ms. Concord wants to get away," Jack said.

"Makes sense. He was a pompous ass when I met him." Marshall skimmed the financial assessment. "Is this everything?"

"That's a lot of money," Jack said.

"It is, but Concord Hotels are worldwide. Their holding company is flush. She might be entitled to other assets."

"I get the sense that she doesn't care about inheritance. She just wants to be happy."

"Famous last words," Marshall groaned. "Find out for sure. Any skeletons, Dex?"

Dex finally released his blue knuckles from the side rails and pulled out his notes. "Looks like your typical blue-blood rebellion. She grew up like a Saudi Princess, went from Exeter to Princeton. Her father groomed her to run the family empire, but she had other plans. She showed up in tabloids for a time, running with celebrities and whatnot."

Jack chimed in, "A lot of pressure growing up rich—"

"And spoiled," Dex said, already suspicious of Eloise Concord. "You can never trust the ones born with a silver spoon in their mouths, especially trust-fund babies. They are forever trying to prove themselves, forever young."

"That's insightful," Jack said. "Aren't you supposed to stick to the facts?"

"Aren't you supposed to keep your mouth shut and look pretty?" Dex snapped back.

Marshall dismissed them both, ignoring the subsurface tension that always seemed to manifest between these two, attributing it to their competitive nature, a healthy thing to encourage within an ever-expanding corporation.

Checks and balances.

"We need to be cautious," Marshall said to validate his head of security, "but we can live with rich and spoiled," he added to validate Jack's recommendation. "Let's move on her."

Marshall didn't allow any rebuttals once he made up his mind. He revved the motor loudly, and their jaunt back to the island was in silence, the humid winds wafting over them. Marshall thought about the empire he built and the people he trusted. He was getting older and he needed to plan for the future. He needed to begin grooming someone to protect his legacy, covet his four golden rules, and make sure his empire thrived. He glanced back at Dex and Jack, two of his best candidates.

Something told him that he needed to choose someone soon.

CHAPTER 17

J ENNIFER MET JACK AT the Club Flamingo entrance and greeted
him with a staid embrace. Since he had been clear about
the policy forbidding him to date his clients, she wanted to act
accordingly. She wore a black backless midi dress, partly because
Eloise Concord always dressed to kill, partly to make him regret
that policy.

The doorman opened the door for her without checking his
list this time. She was clearly with a top Flamingo. "Have a good
evening, Mr. Martin," the doorman gushed.

Jennifer could feel Jack's eyes on her as she entered. It stirred
something she hadn't felt in a long time. Desire.

Once inside, he took her hand and led her past the long line
at the host station. The bar and gaming room were buzzing.
The dining room had an hour and a half wait. But they were
immediately escorted to the coziest corner booth with room for
six and the best view of the entrance.

No one waiting for a table sneered or complained. Jennifer
could see that Jack was a Flamingo force, a guardian entitled to
special treatment and privilege amongst the most privileged.
Jennifer noticed some ladies staring at him, clearly impressed. She
believed that Eloise Concord would acknowledge it.

"Is this seat adequate, Your Majesty?" she teased as the maître
d' headed back to his station.

"It'll do," Jack joked along.

Los Melodicos, a popular Venezuelan band, played before an expansive dance floor, and the audacious attempted the latest merengue moves.

Jennifer sidled close to Jack, to hear him over the din. She looked around. The last time she was at the club was a Tuesday evening, and it was quite busy. Now it was a Friday night and it was twice as jammed.

"Can't imagine what this place is like during tourist season," she said.

"Tourists don't come here," Jack said, with all the implied implications.

Jennifer already knew that you needed an endorsement to get into the club. She thought about how the Wall Street base at Delmonico's tried to be noticed for their prowess; she wondered if Flamingos did everything they could to minimize theirs, to avoid the risk of their pasts catching up with them.

Someone waved for Jack's attention.

"Excuse me," he said. "I'll be right back."

Jennifer watched him join two men in fine suits for a brief powwow at the club bar. She noticed a middle-aged man beside them wearing a modest IZOD shirt, khakis, and running shoes. He looked like he could have been a New Jersey insurance broker on holiday slipping away from the wife and kids for a couple of beers, but insurance salesmen rarely sport an Oyster Perpetual Cosmograph Daytona on their wrist—which cost more than a Ferrari—suggesting he might be slipping away for good.

Then Jennifer saw a skinny woman wearing trendy Bleulab Jeans and a simple T-shirt, which made it look like she was fishing for a new sugar daddy to accessorize her new Double D's, cheekbones, and collagen creases, however, the rock she wore around her neck suggested she was more likely scouting for a boy toy.

Jennifer was turning from "Dark Princess of the Audit" into "Queen of Detecting Bling."

She imagined who these people once were: *former Enron execs over there who were never tried, AIG guys who dipped into bonuses, pension fund managers who bilked investors and supposedly jumped off the Golden Gate Bridge...*

Jack came back. "Sorry about that."

"Don't be. You're a busy guy."

"Where were we?"

"You said that tourists don't come here," Jennifer reminded him.

"I told you on the phone that there were some things we needed to discuss before we move forward," Jack said, taking a more businesslike approach.

"In regard to purchasing real estate?"

"You had inquired about buying property under another name." Jack leaned closer.

"You're talking about privacy?"

"I'm talking about becoming a Flamingo."

She remembered Roberta's claim, *"Buying property through Flamingo gives access, immunity, and protection."*

"Yes, let's discuss," Jennifer said, like a girl whose life depended on it.

"Maybe we should order a round from the bar first. Would you like some wine?"

"Sure."

"Any preference?"

"Red—"

Jack raised his arm. A waiter far across the room raced over, an obedient Labrador. "Yes, Mr. Martin."

"Bottle of Guigal Côte Rôtie La Landonne, please."

"Yes, sir." The waiter said, eager to please.

After the waiter ran off, Jack began, "Every Flamingo has a reason for leaving their former life behind. That's why we offer different levels of service. If a Flamingo is being hunted, we have more extreme options to make sure they're never found: plastic surgery, a gated home, round-the-clock security on a far-off island—"

"I just don't want my father to find me."

"If we set you up here, you'll never see the man again," Jack assured her.

Jennifer simulated a hopeful gaze.

"Was growing up a Concord that bad?" Jack asked.

Jennifer took a long pause to emote the requisite sadness and then told him, "They called me 'Eloise at the Plaza' when I went to school. You know, from those children's books about the little rich girl?"

"Doesn't sound as bad as what they called me," Jack half-joked, "I wore the same soiled shirt for three years."

"Growing up privileged isn't always easy," she lamented. "There are expectations. Demands. My father started teaching me the business when I should have been learning how to make friends. And let's just say he didn't become wealthy by being honest, or nice. When I was old enough to see his true colors, I wanted out. But he wouldn't let me go."

"So you acted out?"

"I was rebellious, yeah. Until I realized that I couldn't change him. I was only hurting myself... And, so, here I am, looking for a new beginning..." she paused to wipe a tear, and Jack put his hand on hers. She noticed his warm eyes and wished she could tell him who she really was. She composed herself and scanned the room again. "It's still hard to imagine how you can guarantee privacy in a place like this."

"We have a remarkable infrastructure and incredible security," he told her. "Cameras and ID scans verify everyone that walks through a Flamingo property—our country clubs, beach clubs, supper clubs."

"But still," she pressed, "if people can so easily become someone new, as if they never existed—"

"It's never easy," Jack said. "Every act of creation is first an act of destruction."

"You have to kill your former self to be transformed?"

"Something like that."

There was a long silence. Jennifer couldn't help feeling that she had passed the introduction phase. She had the right pedigree, enough money, and a good enough reason to drop off the grid, without a hint of doubt or remorse.

"We basically have three plans at Flamingo," Jack told her. "The first is for people all around the world who need to move or shelter money, set up corporations, that sort of thing. We call this plan 'Gimme Shelter.'"

"Cute name," Jennifer said with an ardent smile. "I love the song."

He smiled and continued, "The second plan is for people who have to stay away and disengage for some reason but will eventually go back to their old lives. We call that one 'Unplugged.' We often lease a property to these individuals and provide a fair amount of security, but there's no identity change involved."

"Identity change…? Is that a name change?"

"It's a full makeover. A complete transformation. We change everything. That's the reason our third plan is called 'Dropping Off The Grid.' It's our deluxe package, and the amount of protection depends on the individual and their situation—"

"I want the Dropping Off The Grid deal," she said, without hesitation.

"There's no turning back once you commit to that. You can never go home again. You can't phone old friends when you get lonely. No holidays with family—"

"Sounds perfect."

The waiter came back, and they watched him skillfully decanter the wine. "May I?" the waiter asked.

"Please," Jack said.

The waiter poured two glasses. "Enjoy!"

Jennifer raised hers and toasted, "To dropping off the grid."

She took the first sip. "Mmmm, delish" she moaned.

"Right?"

They both savored the French delight.

And then she asked bluntly, "So, what's your deal...? What are you running from?"

"Me?" Jack looked taken by surprise. "I just work here."

"C'mon," she pressed, "every expat's gotta be running from something."

"I'm not an expat."

"You have an English accent."

He shrugged. He wasn't going to discuss where he was from.

"Level with me," she whispered, trying to keep things light, "Was it a stalking girlfriend...or several?

He laughed.

"You no longer wanted to be a prisoner to the system, but still wanted the benefits of the system, so you had to find a way to beat the system—?"

"You're not even close," he told her. "I came to work here right after I finished school—" He paused. He really didn't like talking about himself. Or he couldn't. Jennifer realized he was making eye contact with one of men at the door in dark suits.

Jennifer had noticed several men of the same ilk in the room, and at her hotel. They reminded her of secret service people back home. *Are they watching him...us?*

"Do you like working here?" she asked.

"Sure."

"Helping people 'transform'?"

His piercing eyes saddened. He seemed pensive. "Did you ever hear the story about Jim Thompson?" he asked.

"Jim Thompson...the writer?"

"Jim Thompson the spy. Do you know what the OSS was?"

Of course Jennifer knew, but Eloise might not. "I think I've heard of it."

"Office of Strategic Services," he explained. "It was the predecessor to the CIA."

"Jim Thompson worked for them?"

"That's right. And after the war, he moved to Thailand, built a huge silk company, and made a fortune. Then one day, poof! He suddenly vanished. Friends knew the agency would never let him go willingly and they feared the worst—that he was killed on a secret assignment, or maybe by the OSS themselves. Neither was true. He had fallen in love with an aboriginal Semang woman and was living with her in a jungle village, happily ever after."

Jennifer sighed. "He escaped the OSS to live with the love of his life?"

"Exactly. He changed his name and lived his life in a way that made him happy."

"I love that story."

Jack beamed. "I love the idea of new beginnings and second chances."

"That's a very romantic notion." She took a sip of the red wine and felt her face go flush. "You like helping people that need a second chance."

Jack looked away. "Though the reality isn't always—"

"You mean the clientele here?"

He nodded, conflicted.

"They're not all dropping off the grid for aboriginal love?" she teased.

"No—" Jack sat up abstemiously. "We'll soon find out if you'll become one of them."

"A Flamingo?"

"A Flamingo."

"You're recommending me then?"

"I already did all that I can. Next step, you're going to meet my boss, Marshall Shore. He's the one you have to impress."

And convince. Jennifer thought of Roberta's claim that he was a ghost and she hoped that he couldn't see through her guise.

"Are you available tomorrow?"

"Yes. I'm ready. And available."

"Good."

"Anything I should know to prepare?"

"Just be yourself."

"I can do that." *Or I can be Eloise Concord.*

The band started playing "Wild World." Jennifer said, "I love Cat Stevens."

Jack hummed a bar and leaned in conspiratorially. "You mean the songwriter who changed his name to Yusuf Islam and disappeared?"

Jennifer grinned. "Is he a Flamingo?"

"If he was, I couldn't tell you," Jack's said with a smirk.

The bass was driving, the drums pounding. Jennifer got up and took Jack's hand. "Come on, I love Yusuf Islam." She boldly led him to the dance floor.

They moved well together, and all eyes were on the beautiful couple.

CHAPTER 18

JENNIFER HAD THOUGHT JACK'S office at Flamingo Properties had excessive security for a real estate company, but it was nothing compared to the Flamingo Enterprises' headquarters building where she was told to meet Marshall Shore. Roberta and Marcus had shown her the CAD renderings of the cold, corporate structure, so she already knew that it would be well protected, but when she saw it in person, she thought it made Fort Knox look like a yurt. As two armed security guards escorted her and Jack inside, she spied Wi-Fi cameras set with LED lights mounted throughout, door locks with motion sensors, built in alarms, intercoms, card access points, and very few windows looking out or in, like a prison; obviously it was a state-of-the-art fortress built to protect Flamingo affairs, holdings, and secrets; the epicenter of the omnipresent haven; command central.

She and Jack followed the guards down a dimly lit corridor, past rows of offices—all dark, stark, and oddly, seemingly unmanned. Jennifer slowed to get a better look inside one. She glanced hundreds of mail slots, each with a different corporation name, and they all had a Bank of the Caribbean deposit slot. Another room was packed with large plastic crates with Bank of the Caribbean logos. She wondered if these rooms were housing the shell companies with accounts in the Bank of the Caribbean, to hide Flamingos' offshore investments, or actual hard cash.

One of the security guards noticed Jennifer lagging. "Please keep moving," he snipped.

Jack waited for Jennifer to catch up and whispered, "Are you nervous?"

"A little. What if Marshall Shore doesn't like me?"

"Don't take this the wrong way," Jack said, "but you're impossible not to like."

She felt her face go flush and they continued down the hallway in silence.

They arrived at two large oak doors and were buzzed inside. The office was lush and cozy—more New York sophistication than tropical elegance—with dark oak floors, bookshelves that extended up to a sixteen-foot-high ceiling, and handsome maple furniture.

The security guards shut the door behind them and vanished. Jack crossed the room. "Good morning," he began, "I'd like to introduce Eloise Concord."

Marshall stood up from behind his bulky desk and smiled cordially. "Welcome, Ms. Concord. I'm Marshall Shore."

"Thank you, Mr. Shore. Really nice to meet you."

She turned to Dex who was sitting in a leather club chair, glaring, evaluating.

Jack said, "And our head of security, Dex Boonyai."

Jennifer smiled. "Hello, Mr. Boonyai."

Dex nodded. No smile. No intention of getting up.

Marshall gestured to the two chairs across from his desk. "Please, have a seat."

Jennifer felt his eyes upon her as she settled in, sizing her up, assessing, uncomfortably so. In turn, she tried to gauge and appraise.

So this guy started Flamingo…

It was amazing to her that he was able to stay invisible for so long, especially a man with such a formidable presence at first glance. She studied his face, wondering if she had seen him on any most wanted profiles over the years. She tried to imagine him clean-shaven with more pepper in his salt-and-pepper hair, before a nip and tuck and likely Rhinoplasty.

She also noticed how sparse his office was with very few personal items exposed—just like Jack's. In her experience, that was typical of unsettled executives with something to hide. She wondered if Flamingos had to take mobility a step further since they were all there to escape their past, always prepared to flee at a moment's notice. Maybe that was why Roberta had been so well aware of him, but never able to get to him.

Marshall glared back with a curious squint as he began, "Jack has filled us in on your desire to move here…and he's told you a little about us."

"Yes, he has."

"I'm familiar with Concord Hotels," he said. "You had an important position in your family business."

"Deputy Director."

Marshall looked impressed. "Were you involved in development?"

"I was involved in all aspects of the business, development and financial, but mostly management, marketing, and planning."

Marshall looked like his wheels were turning. "When did you leave the company?"

"Several months ago."

"And your father tried to change your mind?"

"He wasn't happy."

"Has he tried to contact you?"

"No."

"But you think he will…eventually?"

"My father frowns upon quitters," Jennifer said, trying to sound like an angry Wasp. "He will come for me, or I should say, he'll have someone come look for me."

Marshall looked satisfied.

Dex didn't, and asked her, "What about the rest of your family?"

"They won't come for me, no."

"That's not what I meant," Dex said. "You won't regret cutting off any other ties?"

She didn't hesitate. "No. Not at all."

All eyes were on her, waiting for her to explain.

"I was, as they say, the black sheep of the family," she said without a hint of remorse, "I won't be missed, and the feelings are mutual."

Dex got up from the chair and moved closer, leaning his hip up against the corner of Marshall's desk. "Sometimes people change their minds. After some time, old wounds heal, and they have second thoughts…"

Jennifer shot Dex a hard glare she hoped he would interpret correctly. *Back off, you probing wannabe dick.* "I won't change my mind," Jennifer assured him.

Dex pressed, "You're looking to change your identity—"

"Yes."

"Many of our clients have no choice when they come to us. They can't go back to who they were. They don't have a choice. But you're not on the lam, there's no bounty on your head, you're still young—"

Marshall added, "Not to mention your father is a prominent and influential man—"

"My father's an asshole," Jennifer snapped.

Everyone was taken back by her intensity and waited for her to elaborate.

She knew she had to get this right, and so she prepared for the most heart-wrenching response she could muster. "I understand what you're getting at, what your concerns might be, but let me reassure you, my feelings are not going to suddenly change. Growing up like a possession might sound like the complaint of a spoiled brat, but I swear on my life, as privileged as I was, no amount of money could replace the sociopathic manipulations and abuses I had to deal with growing up. I have no recourse. I never did. I'm not trying to make a point or rebel or change anyone.

I'm just trying to get away, to get my own life, to be my own person. I'm lucky that I have the means to do that. I deserve all of it for what I had to endure. I believe there are others like me here. That's my hope. But whether there's a place for me at Flamingo or not, I'm never going back. I can't. I won't. They're all dead to me..." She paused, taking a moment to process what was coming out of her own mouth. *Jennifer Morton does fucking Macbeth. Pull back the pathetic whining before the drama police come.*

When she looked up, though, she realized that she had hit all the right notes. Off her conviction, the room fell silent.

Jennifer took the break to search the room for more clues. On a mantel behind Marshall's desk were the only personal items she could find, a small cluster of framed photographs: Marshall at the Flamingo Casino opening, his arm around Jack; Marshall catching a marlin on his boat; and a slightly faded picture of Marshall holding a baby. Was he a dad, a granddad, an uncle? *If there's a child in his life, how bad could he be?*

Below the mantel was an enormous built-in cabinet that extended well beyond the length of his cumbrous desk, and she noticed a pink flamingo on one of the doors, just like the one behind Jack's desk.

Could this be where they keep the Flamingo files after they buy property and transform?

Jennifer already knew they didn't trust storing information in computers—and Jack's file cabinet only housed real estate applicants, those vying to become Flamingos. But they would have to keep records of their flock somewhere.

Marshall leaned forward and blocked her view, as if he knew she was trying to figure out what was inside the enormous safe behind his desk. "Everyone's secrets are safe here," he said, "because we have a system that works."

She nodded, as if that was a comfort to her.

"We have four golden rules," he continued. "Rule number one: One must never share their former identity with anyone. Two:

One must never inquire about any other Flamingo's past. Three: One must always be loyal to Flamingo—"

"You can never talk about where you came from," Dex interjected, "and you can never inquire about where any other Flamingos have been either."

"We never discuss our past lives," Marshall said. "It's all for the safety of our community. Our code of silence is our vow, to guarantee privacy. Our unbridled loyalty is our bloodline, the reason we've been so successful."

Jennifer imagined that Marshall had spouted that speech a thousand times and that his unbridled fervor never dwindled. He was all about it.

"Don't ask, don't tell," Jennifer said. "I get it. Like if a tree falls in the forest and no one really hears it fall."

Everyone laughed at her comparison.

"What's number four?" Jennifer asked.

Dex looked to Marshall.

Marshall looked like he was searching for an evasive answer.

Jennifer shrugged. "You said there are four golden rules; you only mentioned three."

Marshall smiled. "If you adhere to rules one, two, and three, you won't have to know about rule number four."

Was that a threat?

Dex took it as his cue to talk about his role. "To guarantee privacy," he explained, "we need to know everything about you. Every indiscretion. Every gaffe. Every enemy. Everything."

"For the protection of all Flamingos," Marshall added.

"Time to spill the beans," Dex said.

"This is the only time we'll ever ask," Marshall assured her.

"I haven't killed anybody," Jennifer said, flashing her drop-dead smile.

"We don't judge," Marshall said, dead serious, setting her up to divulge.

She turned to Jack, a bit flustered. "I think I told Jack everything."

"She hasn't killed anyone," Jack joked, to take the pressure off her and lighten the mood.

Dex didn't laugh.

"I guess I'm rather boring," Jennifer said. "Other than being a rebellious daughter, I have nothing to add."

"That's not boring, that's lucky." Marshall said as he stood up and reached across his desk. "It was truly a pleasure to meet you, Ms. Concord. Jack will see you out."

That was abrupt, she thought. *Did I say something offensive?*

She stood up and shook Marshall's hand. "The pleasure was all mine."

Jennifer hoped that she hadn't played it wrong. She wished she could add something, maybe offer up more family scandal or a better reason why her father was so evil, but Jack's nod and grin told her to walk away.

She and Jack followed the security guards back out into the long winding hallways. Neither spoke. But when Jack grabbed her hand and squeezed it, she knew he was trying to tell her that she had either done okay, that she would move on to the next phase of the process, or he was going to break Flamingo protocol about dating. Maybe both.

Hopefully both.

—

"Something about her…" Dex said to Marshall after the door shut behind Jack and Jennifer. "I don't know what it is, but something doesn't feel right—"

"I like her," Marshall cut him off. "We rein her in a little, she could be a real asset to Flamingo."

"If you say so," Dex scoffed.

"I want some time with her alone, though," Marshall said as he turned his attention to the World Cup scores on his phone. "Set something up."

—

JACK AND JENNIFER EXITED the Flamingo Enterprises building on the ocean side. It was another stunning day in paradise and Jennifer was beginning to thaw. They moved past the sun worshippers frolicking in the sapphire sea, surfers catching ample swells, joggers running along the beach to the beat of their iTunes, vacationers enjoying cocktails in beach huts as the salty warm breeze carried their problems away.

Jennifer took it all in. She liked being there. She liked being there with Jack. And she liked being there as Eloise Concord. She found it easier and easier to forget her former self, like a real Flamingo; she was starting to become her cover, and it wasn't as far as a stretch as she had expected, especially when she talked about her disdain for her father.

She turned inland and saw businessmen walking to their offices in Hawaiian shirts and cargo shorts, carrying briefcases only, not the weight of the world on their shoulders, and well-heeled retirees enjoying the fruits of their labors. She could understand the attraction of living in a place like this.

And then Jack told her, "I think you're in."

"Seriously?" she shrieked. "I thought I blew it."

"You were perfect."

"Then why did Marshall end the meeting so abruptly?"

"He always does that," Jack told her, "once he sees what he wants to see."

She sounded insecure, because she felt insecure. "What do you think he saw?"

"Hopefully the same thing I see," Jack said with a coy grin, "a ton of potential."

She laughed like a nervous schoolgirl and he squeezed her hand again.

—

FROM HIGH ABOVE, ON the Beach Club veranda, Dex Boonyai pulled out his Sharper Image pocket scope and focused in on Eloise Concord. He could understand why Marshall wanted her. She had good looks and deep pockets. But he was sure she was hiding something.

His job was to find out what.

He panned over to Jack and muttered under his breath, "Suck your mother." Something about Eloise Concord was troubling him. He hated when Marshall ignored his warnings. And he never liked Jack. He and Jack both were handpicked by Marshall; both put in a position to contend for stature and praise; both incredibly good at their jobs; and both well aware that Marshall would soon decide which of them would take over the Flamingo reigns. Dex believed he had an edge over Jack. He was loyal to a fault and he was sure that Jack's loyalty was conditional. He just needed a way to convince Marshall. And then he saw something that could do it: he tilted the scope down and saw Jack's hand over hers.

"Sweet Jesus!" he croaked, feeling hopeful. Neither Jack nor Dex were permitted to get involved with new Flamingos. Maybe this was the way to discredit his nemesis.

He turned the dial on his pocket scope and zoomed in on her face. Now he saw Eloise Concord as an applicant full of potential as well.

CHAPTER 19

JENNIFER SPENT THE NEXT few days following the new and improved Rupert Reynolds around town. She scoped out Flamingo Towers as he came and went, watched him tinker on his Swan from the Flamingo Harbor Café, and spied on his numerous romantic trysts. Like many expatriates who no longer had any ties or commitments for the first time in years, he enjoyed his newfound freedom took full advantage of every indulgence, and he took it to a new level. He partied into the night, slept late, and came and went as he pleased. He had figured out how to order his goddesses on the Internet; for a very reasonable fee, they came right to his door (or boat) whenever he had the urge, and they left as soon as he was done with them; no drama; catch and release.

He was euphoric. And it killed Jennifer that he was living like a rock star here after everything he did back home. She had to figure out a way to make him pay. If the Caymans didn't extradite, she needed to convince a Cayman authority with motive to go after him for a crime against a Cayman citizen or business. She had to catch Rupert Reynolds committing another serious crime, which she was sure he would eventually do. After all, zebras don't change their stripes, and lifelong swindlers on long holidays inevitably get bored.

She still needed to get inside Flamingo to get close enough to catch him. But she hadn't heard a word from Jack since the day of her meeting with Marshall Shore. There was nothing she could do but wait for Eloise Concord to get in.

In the meantime, she still had a job to do.

One evening, she spied Rupert Reynolds preparing his Swan for a late sail. The sun was setting blood orange, the winds were kicking at a delightful seven knots, and he had a lovely date popping a bottle of champagne in his cabin. It would be enough of a distraction for Jennifer to sneak inside his condo and see what the swindler had been up to.

She snuck into Flamingo Towers by blending in with a rowdy pack of twenty-somethings as they entered the lobby. They were definitely stoned, and the doorman might have been as well, not once looking up from whatever he was streaming on his devise as they all traipsed into the elevator.

When the doors opened on the top floor, Jennifer headed right toward Rupert's unit. The twenty-somethings turned left, where Justin Timberlake's "Say Something" was booming down the hall, and many more wild young things were spilling in and out of some billionaire's pied-à-terre.

Rupert's door had a conventional Schlage dead-bolt lock. Jennifer used a lever she kept on her keychain, she and moved swiftly. Easy as pie. But just as the door unlatched, she was startled by a sing-song voice, "Hey there, beautiful lady—"

She turned and saw a shirtless party boy approaching. "Sorry about the noise," he said as his eyes scanned her body approvingly, "we're throwing a little bash."

"That's okay—""

"I just saw you standing there and wanted to be neighborly. Wanna come over and do a line?" he asked, as if he were offering a cup of coffee.

For a second, she had thought she was getting busted by another CIA security guard, but this kid was...just a kid. "I'm good," she told him. "Have a good night."

He didn't take her cue. "Haven't seen you around here before, have I?"

"Probably not. I'm new."

"Hi, 'New.'" She didn't laugh at his joke, so he continued, "I'm Jason. Penthouse four-oh-three. It's my uncle's place, actually, but he's never around, so it's kinda like my place. My friends call it the local pharmacy…" He laughed and added, "I'm like your local pharmacist."

Bragging about being the in-house drug dealer, seriously?

What she couldn't know, and what Jason couldn't brag about, was that his uncle was a former Enron exec that cashed in $270 million in stock before the energy company collapsed and disappeared into obscurity, or that he couldn't return until the heat let up, which would be never. Jason had scored a killer pad for his drug store.

The pharmacist asked, "What's your name, pretty lady?"

"Reynolds," she lied, "Mrs. Rupert Reynolds. You may have seen my husband around. Big man. Angry eyes."

Her being married to a big man didn't seem to faze him. "If Mr. Angry Eyes isn't home, come on by. Promise to make it worth your while," he said, heading back down the hall.

"Thanks for the offer," she said, and then entered Rupert Reynold's lair. She locked the door behind her and moved swiftly from room to room, searching his closets, drawers, and bookshelves. His place was tastefully furnished. The drawers and closets were full. It seemed as if he had been there for years, except that every item was brand new. Jennifer wondered if Flamingo had staff decorators to put everything together like a production designer on a movie set, to make it look authentic when one person was transitioning into a new Flamingo identity. She couldn't find any remnants of the former Max Culpepper. No old photographs. No memorabilia. Nothing. Everything from his past had been wiped clean. The only thing he took with him during his transformation was his precious Swan.

She looked through his telescope, aimed it out the big bay windows, and saw *The Great Escape* moving out through the quay. While he was out at sea, she would have plenty of time to search his condo thoroughly.

She found his laptop and she checked his search history. Nothing but escort services, boating services, porn sites, restaurants, and news. He often checked the financial markets, but he wasn't active, didn't log into a single investment account.

She couldn't find anything to go on, no scheme he'd been planning, no clues that would show his patterns and behaviors. Nothing.

Just when she was about to head out, she saw his racing schedule beside his sailing trophies. All the races started from the Flamingo Harbor, every Sunday at ten. Rupert had participated in every one since he was settled. He would be out at sea for several hours on Sundays. That was something. A start. The more she knew about his whereabouts and patterns, the more likely she could devise a strategy.

But she still needed to find a crime.

Then she heard a horrifying scream. She ran to the door and looked out into the hallway. She heard it again. It was coming from the party down the hall. A woman's voice. Desperate. Horrified. A cry for help.

Jennifer sprinted down the hall. The door to the party in penthouse 403 was ajar with people shuffling in and out. She burst through the door like a pit bull.

Wasted scams and bikini-clad tramps were flailing about, tripping over themselves.

None of them noticed Jennifer. Nor did any of them react to the wailing cries, which continued from one of the bedrooms. As Jennifer headed down the hallway, two bodies crashed through a door. It was a scrappy bout. Two young men exchanging flailing punches. They were unskilled fighters, clearly inebriated, but deranged and violent. The thrashed aimlessly, both bruised and bloodied. One of the boys shoved the other's head into the wall, repeatedly. Jennifer pulled him off. He headbutted her. She fell back, stunned. He stalked toward her. His pupils were enlarged black holes. His nostrils turned red. Another young man came out into the hallway, jumped on Head Butter's back. They bounced off the corridor walls until they fell backward like chain-sawed trees, crashing to the floor, both laughing hysterically.

The horrifying screams continued. They were coming from the master bedroom. Jennifer got up and rushed inside. The shrieking girl was standing over another young man, who was lying on the ground. Blood was spraying from his hand like red champagne.

Jennifer knelt down and asked, "What happened?"

The bleeding boy shouted back, "I cut my fucking finger off!" He shoved his hand toward her face. His middle finger had been severed. He was holding a chef's knife in his other hand.

"Why?" Jennifer asked him as she tore a long strip off the bedsheet and began wrapping a tourniquet. "Why would you do that?!"

Severed Finger turned to Shrieking Girl and said, "'Cause she wanted me to."

Shrieking Girl said, "I was just kidding, you moron,"

They both broke into unstoppable laughter.

When Jennifer stood back up, she saw a nearly naked young woman lying on the bed, and she looked dead. Jennifer rushed over, tried to feel for a pulse, and shouted, "Call 911!"

No one responded. But the music stopped.

Jason entered the room, chill as a hippy on dankity dank.

"This girl needs help!" Jennifer shouted. "Call for an ambulance!"

"Everything's good," Jason said, cool as a cucumber. He reached into the nightstand drawer, pulled out a device of some kind, and hovered over Nearly Naked's sprawled form.

"What are you—"

Jason swiftly pulled the cap off of a syringe and stabbed the needle into the meaty part of her bare thigh.

Jennifer jumped up. "What the fuck are you doing to her!"

"It's Narcan," Jason said, completely unruffled. "She'll be fine."

Nearly Naked started to take shallow breaths.

"See?" Jason said as he turned and strutted back out to the living room.

Jennifer helped Nearly Naked to her feet. "Come on... Let's get you to the hospital."

"No!" She pulled away. "I don't wanna go."

"I'll go with you—"

"I took a Pill in Ibiza" started to play from the living room, and Nearly Naked screamed, "I love this fucking song!" She started to dance.

Severed Finger seemed to love the song, too, and he also started dancing, forgetting about his lost appendage.

Jennifer grabbed a sheet from the bed and tried to cover Nearly Naked. "You need to get out of here—"

The young woman pulled away again and moved to the music, spinning and threshing wildly, oblivious. Everyone followed. The party was back on.

"You have to listen to me," Jennifer persisted. "We need to get you to the hospital..." Jennifer turned to Severed Finger and said, "You too... You're losing too much blood."

They all just laughed like drunken buffoons.

A couple grinding on a love chair in the corner noticed. One of them moaned, "They can't hear you."

Jennifer stopped. "Why not, are they deaf?"

"No, silly," Grinding Girl said with a giggle. "It's the Devil's Breath."

"I don't know what that is," Jennifer admitted.

Grinding Boy groaned, "Burundanga!" as if that explained everything.

Jennifer started dialing the police when she heard a booming voice shout Jason's name. She went into the living room and saw four large Flamingo Tower security guards storm in. One of them, a native islander, was pulling Jason into the kitchen and lecturing him. He seemed angry.

Jennifer grabbed one of the others, as if she were the only sane adult in the room, and tried to explain that there was a much more serious situation, but he wouldn't listen.

She heard the native islander tell Jason that one of his neighbors complained about the noise, and since he had been warned about his parties spilling into the hallway, his guests would have to leave. Apparently disturbing other Flamingo Tower residents was more important than ensuring the safety of these kids, finding out how some of the boys got bloody faces, or dealing with possession of this perilous drug they were all on.

It took them a long time to herd these animals out. Jason got off easy and Jennifer's excessive sense of justice got the better of her, which is why she left the building with a large plastic bag of white powder that she took from Jason's closet. She knew that taking his entire supply of Devil's Breath would hurt him where it really counted. But she couldn't understand why Flamingo security guards were more concerned about him keeping a lower profile than dealing a drug that turns people into mind-numb merry-andrews. She assumed it was part of their motto—privacy is king—but like everything else that Jennifer would soon learn about Flamingo, there was more to the story…

CHAPTER 20

ANOTHER DAY PASSED. JENNIFER still hadn't heard from Jack Martin, so she took Eloise Concord on another shopping spree to fill the void.

"Welcome back, Ms. Concord," the daytime manager at Hotel Flamingo said to Jennifer as she drove up in her rented Vespa with bulging store bags strapped to the back. He whistled at two bellmen and shouted, "Take Ms. Concord's things to her room, and park her bike in a front spot."

Jennifer had been staying at Hotel Flamingo longer than the typical tourist, and the staff was treating her more like a princess than a guest overstaying her welcome. She hoped it was because they knew she was a Flamingo-in-process and were treating her accordingly. Flamingos were, after all, unspoken island royalty, and Eloise Concord was beginning to glimmer, her new island wardrobe even more awesome every time she returned. She didn't want anyone to think she was fronting, so she played it cool—polite but expectant—as if she were used to entitled treatment. She greased the manager two twenty-dollar bills and sashayed into the lobby, knowing all eyes were on her, guests and staff buying into her façade.

Jennifer had often wondered why people were so impressed with materialism and status. She avoided pursuing either because she was certain it didn't guarantee happiness. She had once heard that people who go without food or shelter are significantly happier when given food and shelter, but there is no rise in happiness if you give a million dollars to a billionaire. Avoiding money and fame clearly didn't guarantee happiness either. She was living proof of that, still single, still unstable, still seeking ever-evasive justice.

She felt a pang of self-doubt, but it went away when she spotted her Jersey pal, Alex the bartender. He had come through for her last time; she would seek his help again.

She hopped on a barstool and Alex headed right over. "Still drinking Scotch?"

"Only if you'll join me."

"Glenfiddich, right?"

Eloise Concord followed trends. "I hear the Japanese whiskeys are all the rage."

Alex brightened. "I have one you've got to try."

When Alex delivered a nice-sized pour, Jennifer leaned in so other guests couldn't overhear. "Remember when you said that you could help me out if I needed anything–"

"Name your poison," Alex replied conspiratorially.

She tapped her nose with her forefinger. "How hard is it to get something white and fluffy around here?"

Alex looked around to make sure his boss wasn't around. "It snows all year around," he said with a smile.

"What's the deal with Devil's Breath?" she asked.

Alex's smile faded. "You want Devil's Breath?"

"I don't know. What's it like?"

"It eliminates free will," he explained. "Wipes out any memory of what you did when you're on it—"

She thought of the buffoonery at Jason's party. "So you don't remember making an ass of yourself?"

"That's what I hear," he said. "I've never tried it but there are urban legends about what people have done. Crazy shit. Emptying out bank accounts without remembering. Walking the streets like zombies..."

A drug that wipes out memory, and bank accounts, seemed like something Flamingos would use when thoughts of their painful pasts became intolerable. Jennifer wondered if she could use it on Rupert Reynolds somehow, maybe another building block in her pursuit, and then, as if Alex was reading her mind, he leaned in closer and said, "I told you I can hook you up with whatever you fancy…but I can't get that stuff."

"Can't or won't?" she pressed, because Eloise Concord would want to try everything.

He looked as if he hated to disappoint her, "They're cracking down hard," he explained. "Cops catch you with it, they'll lock you up and throw away the key."

But Flamingo security guards seem to look the other way.

"So where are people getting it?" she asked.

"That's the thing. It's produced here on the islands and shipped all around the world—"

"Where…?" she pressed. "Which island produces it?"

"Don't know. But there's international pressure to cut the pipeline. You don't want to be made an example of."

She tried to look disappointed. "Thanks for the warning."

"Ms. Concord…" A voice from behind jolted them both.

A linen-suited concierge approached. If she found the thick stack of cash they had just passed to be suspicious, she didn't reveal a thing. Jennifer was getting a sense that Flamingo staff was trained to turn a blind eye to everything with a Flamingo logo on it, and it certainly appeared that Jennifer was about to get branded.

"This is for you, Ms. Concord." The concierge handed Jennifer an envelope with a pink wax Flamingo seal.

Alex moved away to give them privacy, as procedure dictated.

"Looks like a party invitation," Jennifer said.

"It's your tee time," the concierge said with a nod. "You may open it here."

"I didn't make any golf reservations."

"We do that for you."

Jennifer opened it and read the details. "I don't have my clubs or any golf clothes—"

"We'll take care of everything," the concierge assured her. "An appropriate set of clubs and all the accoutrements will be sent up to your room. Tee time is at nine so we'll have one of our staff meet you here in the lobby at eight to drive you to the course. Mr. Shore will meet you there."

Jennifer gleamed a polite smile. "Sounds like a plan."

The concierge headed back to her roost in the lobby.

Alex moseyed back toward Jennifer. "Golf with Mr. Shore," he said as he glanced her reservation with raised eyebrows. "South Brac? Impressive. That's the most exclusive golf course in the Caymans."

Jennifer said, "I don't really play golf—"

Alex laughed. "You do now."

CHAPTER 21

Marshall greeted Jennifer at the South Brac pro shop. She was wearing the golf attire he had sent to her room. It was skimpy, maybe a size too small, which may have been intentional.

"I knew that color would look good on you," he beamed.

"I like it…a lot," she played along. "You have good taste."

"Would you like to use the driving range to get comfortable with the clubs?" he asked.

"I'm good to go."

"Then let's do this."

Jennifer gasped when they arrived at the first tee. "It's stunning up here," Jennifer said as she gazed down upon the island's uniquely flat terrain and the spectacular scope of the azure Caribbean Sea.

"I never tire of it," Marshall told her. "This is my blue haven. Flamingo's true 'haven.'" He laughed at his own wit. "I bring potential Flamingos here, like you."

"I'm honored," she said, sensing he was getting serious about letting her in.

"But I don't talk business until the sixteenth hole," he added.

"Why's that?" she asked. "Does it take that long to know if you like them?"

"It takes that long to know if I trust them," he said, dead serious.

They played their game and enjoyed an easy flow of small talk. On the sixteenth hole Marshall said, "Jack mentioned that you're concerned about asset protection."

He was talking Flamingo business, she thought. *He trusts me.* "When I worked for Concord," she told him, "I put a lot of cash in offshore accounts—"

Marshall took his swing.

MarPing!

Jennifer held up her club and whistled, impressed. "Beautiful shot."

He smiled as his ball landed ten yards ahead of Jennifer's. He kissed his new $2,000 Majesty Prestigio and said, "You get what you pay for."

They both returned to the golf cart and Marshall continued. "So you probably know that there are many tax benefits and many advantages to offshore accounts."

"I also know that the government traces financial transactions," she said concernedly. "Especially large ones."

"Then how do you explain the twenty-one trillion dollars in offshore accounts, eighty percent of which is undeclared?"

"You tell me."

Marshall grinned with pride. "Most of our banks offer 'hold mail' options. They don't send statements or leave a trail."

"But how does the money get to them without being tracked?" Jennifer prodded, glad that she had hit the record button on her iPhone Voice Memo app.

"Best way to move money is to put it in the name of someone you can confide in."

Jennifer kept in character as Eloise Concord, girl on the run. "I'm trying to cut all ties, remember?"

"You can use one of our people."

Jennifer laughed as if he were responding to an inside joke. "I don't think so."

Off her incertitude, Marshall hopped out of the cart. "Some people aren't comfortable with that, and I completely understand."

"Of course you do."

He pulled his seven iron and stood by his ball, measuring the trajectory in his mind. "We can play corporate shell game just as easily."

Her face tensed. "Setting up a number of business entities that hold your assets and spend your money in their own name?"

"That's one way," Marshall said. "I have a few other methods as well—" But he didn't elaborate, just took his shot and yelped when his ball made it onto the green.

"Nice," Jennifer said as he approached her own ball. "How is the money invested?"

"Even more options there. Some islands offer citizenship to people who are willing to invest in their nations' futures and economies."

"A bribe?"

"An investment. Perfectly legal. Works like a government bond, but they pay eight to ten percent interest to the 'new you.'"

Jennifer repeated with reserve, "Perfectly legal?" Then she took her shot. It barely made it to the green, rolled back into the sand trap, and sunk. "Oh, damn!"

Marshall smiled, tossed her a wedge, "Should have told you, that's a bitch of a slope."

Jennifer could feel his eyes on her as she tiptoed onto the sand.

"Anyway, it's legal enough," he said. "Our banks are the safest in the world, and for our clients, the most flexible."

"You sound just like our lawyers back home, always looking for ways to maneuver around the system."

"Laws are malleable."

"So are people," Jennifer said with a knowing grin, "but you have to know them in order to bend them."

Marshall looked like he wanted to hug her. He couldn't have said it better himself. "You have a great mind for business, young lady. Many Flamingos have that in common. Do you think you can be of value to our community?"

"I don't pollute, and I have pretty good manners."

"Have you thought about how you will spend your time?"

"I'll find something once I settle. I'm not lazy."

"I could sure use someone like you in my real estate division. You already have experience in development and you're good with people...hard to say no to."

"Is that a job offer?" she joked.

He didn't laugh, seemed genuinely earnest, and said, "I have some ideas. Yeah."

Jennifer felt a surge of excitement. If she could work for Flamingo, she'd learn how they actually sheltered Max Culpepper, as well as their most insidious members.

And to prove that people are indeed malleable, she told Marshall, "I always wished I had a mentor, one that I liked, and respected."

Jennifer could tell that he liked his ego being stroked. She chopped down into the sand with her wedge. Her ball sprung up and out, plopped onto the green, rolled smoothly, and dropped into the hole.

They both cheered.

"Thousand bucks you can't do that again," Marshall joked.

"Toss it to me."

He did. Jennifer dropped the ball back into the sand trap, "A thousand bucks?"

"It was a figure of speech, but if you insist."

Jennifer took the shot and missed the hole by a few feet this time.

"Phew!" Marshall joked. "I was starting to think I was being hustled."

Jennifer held out her hand. "Double or nothing?"

Marshall tossed the ball back. "Seriously?"

Jennifer took another try. Missed again. Then said, "One more."

Marshall's smile faded. "Not a good bet."

"Come on," Jennifer teased.

"For you, it's not a good bet for you."

"We can both afford some good fun."

Marshall reluctantly retrieved the ball.

Jennifer took the shot and sank it. She jumped up and shouted.

He laughed. "You've got some moxie. You're going to do very well here."

She froze and looked stunned. "Does that mean I'm in?"

"Does that mean you're in?" Marshall repeated as he put his arm around her shoulder and looked out at the spectacular scope of the azure sea—his true, blue haven. Then he bellowed, "Welcome to paradise, young lady!"

—

WHEN JENNIFER RETURNED TO the hotel, word had already spread. She was celebrated with winks and pats on the back by an overly friendly staff. There was a chilled bottle of Moët & Chandon Dom Pérignon White Gold in her room. It didn't have a card. But it didn't need one. She knew it retailed for more than ten grand and that she was officially a Flamingo now. She went out to the terrace and popped the cork.

It tasted damn good.

She thought about how she would play her next steps—the possibility of working for Marshall Shore. She thought more about ways she could go after Rupert Reynolds from the inside, and ways she could set him up from the outside. She thought about a lot of things. But after the third glass of White Gold, she only thought of Jack Martin.

CHAPTER 22

JACK CALLED TO CONGRATULATE her in the morning. He was sweet but brief. He scheduled a time for them to start looking for her new home, which thrilled her more than he would know. He also made a joke about newly approved Flamingos splurging like drunken sailors once they knew their assets were safe. Since she had already shopped till she dropped at the local clothing stores, she decided to step it up a notch with a really obscene shopping spree that would turn heads Eloise Concord style. After all, Roberta had expected her to stay true to her cover and people would be watching. She returned her rented Vespa and bought a bright yellow Lamborghini Murcielago with gull-wing doors.

Her new life began with a roar.

The next day, she cruised around to familiarize herself with the different Flamingo neighborhoods. She fantasized about house hunting with Jack Martin, no doubt a slow process that demanded long drives up the coast to explore the island, and each other. Surely searching for the right home would require walks on the beach, spontaneous lunches, and romantic dinners. Her body ached, her mind raced, and her sexual thermometer soared. Their attraction was real, undeniable. Despite his full disclosure that he was forbidden to date new Flamingos, despite Roberta's charge that she had to resist temptations, and despite her own code of ethics that she would never get involved with anyone in an organization she was investigating, she was certain that some kind of an affair was inevitable. It had been a long time since she felt this excited about a guy. She had to wonder if it was because the guy she was pining for was unavailable, or if it had something to do with having a romantic relationship while she was impersonating someone else. After all, if Jack Martin were to reject her, he would really be rejecting Eloise Concord. Whatever it was, she couldn't stop thinking about that man. And just then, he appeared.

Literally.

She was driving down Shoreline Road and saw him in a Bank of Caribbean parking lot, getting out of his car. She pulled over on the side of the road, in front of a large truck. He was carrying what looked like a crumbled-up gym bag and headed inside. She didn't know what she expected to see but it was usually the most random run-ins that turned out the most serendipitous. So she waited. When he exited the bank, he was holding the gym bag like it was much heavier now, slung over his shoulder. Did he fill it up with cash? Is that how they bought and sold property? It seemed strange enough that she needed to see where he went next.

She followed him up into the hills, through a shoddy neighborhood peppered with corrugated metal shacks. Not the kind of neighborhood Flamingo had properties in. She kept a far distance behind, well aware that a yellow Lamborghini was not the kind of attention she wanted to draw just then.

He turned into a driveway leading up to a church, the Roman Catholic Mission Sui Luris. She parked farther down the street and watched him get out of his car. He carried the gym bag to the side of the building.

Jennifer got out of her car and strolled the sidewalk slowly, keeping him in her line of sight.

A nun came out of the side entrance. Jack handed her the bag. She wiped a tear and hugged him. They talked for another minute or so, and then Jack got back into his car.

Jennifer headed back to hers, her curiosity piqued.

Was Jack stealing from the rich to give to the poor; Grand Cayman's very own Robin Hood? Did he and the people that worked for Flamingo have as many secrets as the Flamingos they were protecting?

This was another reason to get closer to him, she justified.

Her phone rang, startling her back to reality. She glanced at her caller ID. It was Jack. She picked up, hoping he hadn't spotted her.

If he did, he didn't say so. "It's Jack," he pronounced with verve, "Jack Martin."

"I know," she said with a nervous giggle.

"Are you busy tonight?"

Here we go.

"I'm free as a Flamingo," she joked.

"Have you ever been to Batabano?"

"What's a Batabano?"

He laughed. "You'll love it. Pick you up at eight?"

"How about if I pick you up? I have a new car—"

"I heard," he said. "The Murcielago's are stunning. I've never been in one."

The news of her inconspicuous consumption had spread, as planned. "You will have the ride of your life," she told him, imagining his smile.

"Can't wait," he said. "I'll text you my address when we hang up. See you at eight."

He hung up, and her heart went aflutter. This man had that effect on her. And then she felt something else: a twinge of guilt for spying on him.

A first for her.

—

JENNIFER WENT BACK TO the hotel to prepare for the evening. After a three-mile jog on the beach at sunset, she took a nice, long shower, and then spent some time going through the constantly improving Eloise Concord wardrobe to find just the right amount of wrong. Most of the garments were hanging in the closet or folded in the drawer, especially the stuff she had bought since her arrival. As she rifled through her drawers she came across the saran-wrapped batch of white powder she had taken from Jason's Flamingo Towers party. Devil's Breath. Enough to turn a small village senseless. Her hotel room was not a very safe place for a drug that was so highly illegal and deadly. If Alex the bartender's warning was real—and she had no reason to think otherwise—the local police would be cracking down, especially if it was suspected to be produced locally and distributed internationally. She didn't need that kind of trouble, so she put it in an elegant purse from one of her shopping sprees and thought of how best to dispose of it. This gave her an idea: What if she framed Rupert Reynolds for a crime that he didn't commit?

She had always contended that she would expose the cheaters by any means necessary, but this would be taking it to a new level and the thought frightened her. She wondered if she could justify it, if it was going beyond her moral code.

Maybe.

But waiting for him to commit another crime on the scale of GCA might never happen. If she could set Rupert Reynolds up for something else, Max Culpepper would be screwed.

Does the end justify the means?

She didn't yet have the answer yet, but she decided to be ready if it came.

She continued to prepare for what she hoped was a real date with Jack Martin, fussed more than usual, and dressed in a true Eloise Concord showstopper. The off-shoulder lipstick-red dress looked even better than it had in the store. It was a stunner. She hoped that Jack would agree.

She felt anxious and wasn't sure if it was because of what she was thinking about doing to Rupert Reynolds, or what she was hoping to do with Jack Martin.

She headed out, dressed to kill, Devil's Breath in her bag; well prepared for both.

CHAPTER 23

THE BRIGHT YELLOW LAMBORGHINI rumbled into a marked-off space right in front of the open-air bars that served as the gateway to the Batabano festivities. Heads turned to notice the stunning couple that emerged.

Jennifer took in the carnival funfair. "It's a full-on Mardi Gras!" Jennifer observed.

Children paraded around George Town in a mass of color, enjoying face painting, mask decorating, and snow cones. The finest Caribbean musicians performed a kaleidoscope of song, dance, and pageantry with acrobats. Limbo dancers and masqueraders featured their arts and crafts.

"I'll bet New Orleans doesn't have that." Jack said as he pointed to the queen and king chasing a boisterous *Pancho* (prince) as he set fire to *Moma* (a big straw-filled doll).

"What are they doing?" Jennifer asked, amused by the scene.

"They're displaying our version of Easter, *Carne Levale*, giving up meat for lent."

"Which explains those shish-kabobs over there," she joked.

A *J'Ouvert* parade marched into the street. Muddied and painted masqueraders celebrating Caribbean culture and heritage surrounded a music truck and danced.

"Batabano is an annual event to promote business for local bars, restaurants, and shops," Jack explained. "It's a culmination of all the flavors and cultures of island life mixed with all historic and modern influences—a stimulus for all senses, often a collision of inherent conflicts."

Jack took Jennifer's hand and led her across the street where there was less tumult. They passed a young family, the mother and father both trying to wipe swaths of BBQ sauce from their little girl's face. Jennifer noticed that Jack was staring with a dispirited gaze. She assumed it provoked a memory.

"Are your parents still in England?" she asked.

"I'm not from England," he told her. "I grew up on this island, in the West Hills."

"But you have a British accent."

"I went to boarding school in Manchester. They pounded all the Haitian Creole out of me; it stuck."

"Haitian?"

"Half Haitian. My mother came from Port-au-Prince. My father is an Irish Paddy."

The boarding school explained his incongruent accent, but it didn't explain how a child from a shantytown was able to pay for such an expensive education. "A private school in Manchester must've been unusual for a kid from the West Hills," she prodded.

"My parents didn't pay for it…" He paused, seemingly reticent, and then he told her, "Marshall Shore did."

"That's…generous. Why—?"

He turned skittish and cut her off, "Rule number two, remember?"

She did. "Don't ask Flamingos about their past," she said. "But you're not a Flamingo, you just work there. Besides, you already know all about me."

"That's true, I suppose."

She put her hand in the crook of his arm and they walked in unison for a while. He looked like he wanted to tell her more, so she didn't press, waiting, and then he told her, "My mother had died, and my father was laid off when there was a building freeze.

We were dirt poor..." He paused, like that was all there was to say, or all he should say, but then continued, "I was working at the hotel, as a bellboy. I was lucky to have the job. Marshall thought I could be valuable to Flamingo if I got a proper education."

"He must have seen something special in you."

"That's exactly what he told my father." Jack looked away, conflicted. Maybe just sad. Then he repeated, "I was lucky."

Jennifer looked at him hard. "You were lucky if you want to devote your life to Marshall's dream, but something tells me that you have dreams of your own."

By the way he looked back at her, he did.

She couldn't hold back any longer. She put her hands on his shoulders.

He kissed her deeply. Right there. Right then.

It was even better than she had imagined it would be.

And it was just the beginning.

She whispered in his ear, "Let's go somewhere...."

He didn't object.

Or couldn't.

They took off together, to be alone.

She would soon learn, however, that Flamingos are free, but never completely alone.

—

ACROSS THE STREET, RUPERT Reynolds was enjoying the revelry with another lovely lady friend, this one Chilean. The carnival merriment was intoxicating and they both stopped to watch the attractive couple kissing at the crosswalk.

"To be young and in love," Rupert mused, noticing how Jennifer's skintight dress showed off her luscious form.

"She's gorgeous," the Chilean said, "but she's much too young for you, *mi amor*."

As she tried to pull him away, Rupert glimpsed their faces and all the blood drained from his face. He drew closer to get a better look, but a parade of costumed dancers pranced through, blocking his view. After they passed, Jennifer and Jack were no longer there.

"What's the matter?" the Chilean asked.

"I thought I saw someone I knew," Rupert told her, assuming his mind must have been playing tricks on him. How could it be possible that the IRS agent who went after Global Currency Arbitrage was standing in the middle of this wild Caribbean carnival kissing the man that sold him his Grand Cayman condo?

Ridiculous, he thought.

And it didn't matter if it was her, he concluded. The Caymans didn't extradite. The IRS had no jurisdiction. And Max Culpepper no longer existed.

But it did matter to Dex Boonyai, who was standing around the corner from the rum bar. He had followed the yellow Lamborghini to the fair hoping to get confirmation that Jack Martin and the newest Flamingo were getting involved.

Now he had proof. He called Marshall Shore right then and there.

Marshall was in the middle of a dinner party, but he answered. "What is it, Dex?"

"I'm at Batabano, and I just saw Jack with Eloise Concord—"

"He's showing her properties," Marshall cut him off, sounding annoyed.

"On his lips?" Dex snapped.

Marshall fell silent.

"We have rules in place for a reason," Dex added, just for effect, well aware that Marshall wrote the rules.

—

JACK LED JENNIFER INTO his home, an inspired visage with tasteful artwork framed by majestic ocean views. The decor was stunning and decidedly minimal, just like him, revealing little personal reflection.

Jennifer wasn't sure if the butterflies in her stomach came from the concern that she wasn't who she was pretending to be, or because she had never before wanted anyone this bad, and the attraction and desire risked her operation. This man who made her feel like time was suspended was clearly a conflict of interest, but she waved her code of ethics the moment she entered his bedroom.

His hands stimulated every tethered modality; his lips tasted of pure bliss. *This was inevitable*, she thought as she granted herself amnesty, putting aside any restraints, justifying that it couldn't be altogether wrong if it felt this right. She decided to truly let go, giving herself completely. Their bodies entangled between layers of silk sheets, enmeshed amongst warm, moist skin, moving to the rhythm of Jack's dated Dido album. Her starved emotional cavity merged with its counterpart; invariable emptiness was replaced with euphoric intensity; heightened, prolonged pleasure went beyond her imagination; their aftermath was in silence, intimate, and unlike anything before.

For them both, she was certain.

After a strawberry and champagne break, they washed, rinsed, and repeated, until they fell asleep, entwined like a snug fitting puzzle, finally put in place.

She dreamt that she was submerged under water, but this time, she wasn't alone.

And then morning came.

—

Soft light seeped in, illuminating Jennifer's new reality. They locked eyes, neither one spoke of the indescribable,

Since she had grown cynical—or what she considered to be practical—about love, true love, kismet, or fate, she wanted to do what she was best at, sweeping the night under the proverbial rug, at least until she could separate, retreat, and try to remember why she did this. She had used sex in the past as a weapon; never to get closer.

And did she really know anything more about Jack now, other than he could make her feel a way she never had?

All she knew was that this was something different than she had ever experienced. Potentially painful.

She dressed with her back to him. Jack put on his robe and retreated into the kitchen.

Over cappuccinos, he was first to break silence. "No one..." his voice cracked. He took a sip of water. She could tell that he too was shaken. "No one can know about this."

Normally, that would have been music to Jennifer's love-'em-and-leave-'em ears. Instead, she said, "Don't worry, I don't want to cramp your style."

Did that really just come out of my mouth?

"It's not my style that I'm worried about," he said.

"I get it. You could lose your job," she scoffed and started for the door. "Let's never do this again."

Jack released a nervous laugh. "That's not what I meant."

She turned back. "What did you mean?"

"That we need to keep this to ourselves, that's all."

"That's all?" There was a tone in her voice she couldn't help. She felt vulnerable and wanted to crawl away and reassess. She continued to the door.

Jack cut her off. "You don't have to leave," he said.

"I do actually." She kissed him tenderly to reassure him that she was not angry or disappointed. "There's something I have to take care of," she said.

"On a Sunday morning—?"

"I'm a very industrious girl." She revealed her wondrous smile. "Call me later?"

He smiled back wistfully. "Of course."

She walked away and could feel him standing at the door watching her.

She knew that she would be counting the minutes until she saw him again.

CHAPTER 24

THE YELLOW LAMBORGHINI ROARED down Bowden Town Road, past the aftermath of the carnival. There was not a soul in sight; no sign any fête or foul had taken place.

Except the scent of Jack permeating Jennifer's brain. Never before had she gotten romantically involved with someone she was investigating. She thought about the men she fended off over the years. At a stoplight, she removed her four-inch Jimmy Choos, tossed them on the passenger seat, and looked down at her now rumpled, but stunning off-shoulder lipstick-red dress. It was far cry from the conservative Liz Claiborne business suits she usually wore. There was a fine line between getting close and getting intimate. She clearly did the latter this time.

Will I regret it?

The light turned green and she moved on, switching gears and downshifting her thoughts to Rupert Reynolds. Could she go through with the other previously unthinkable act she was considering? Could she give herself permission to set up a criminal for a crime he did not commit so he would be punished for the ones that he did?

If she could forgo her moral code once more, she was sure her plan would work, but it would have to happen now. The timing was right. It was Sunday, when most islanders slept late, enjoyed long brunches, followed by golf and tennis, beach clubs and boats, and more importantly it was the day when Rupert Reynolds would be

racing with the Flamingo Sailing Club. Spectacular sailing weather
was expected, with clear skies and respectable winds. Rupert
Reynolds would be heading out to his Swan at ten. This was her
window and she would have to move quickly.

———

SHE PARKED THE LAMBORGHINI on a quiet side street near the
Flamingo Marina. She retrieved the stash of Devil's Breath she had
hidden in a concealed compartment inside the purse, and headed
down to slip fifty-eight.

The harbor appeared to be clear. Not a soul in sight. Rupert
Reynolds' Swan looked peaceful swaying in the gentle harbor
swells. Jennifer crawled inside the cabin, made a tear in the saran
wrap that covered the Devil's Breath, and doused the powder over
some windbreakers and lifejackets. Then she placed the stash into
a storage nook behind a pile of gear. She set a tracking device onto
the fiberglass wall and began to climb out of *The Great Escape*, but
froze when she heard the harbor gate slam. When she peeked out
and saw Agents Shannon and Perretta storming down the pier,
heading toward the Swan. Just like last time. *Were there motion
sensors on Rupert Reynold's boat*, she wondered as she tucked back
inside the cabin, hoping they had some other purpose for being
there so early on a Sunday.

Luckily, they did.

She heard their footsteps continue past her down the dock.
She peeked out again, when they were far enough away, and
saw them approach a fifty-five-foot double engine cruiser, a Sea
Ray Sundancer. Painted on its rear were black dice and the name
Lucky. The agents didn't board the yacht, but just stood beside it
and waited.

A few minutes later, a forty-foot black Cigarette Firefox with
a long nose and menacingly loud engine approached. Four well-
dressed Colombian businessmen hopped out with armed sentries
behind them revealing their muscle.

Jennifer snuck off of the Swan and stalked behind the next boat to get a better look.

Agent Perretta handed one of the Colombians a leather briefcase. The businessman opened it and nodded, seemingly satisfied. Jennifer could make out even rows of green. Had to be cash. A Colombian shut the case. Everyone was noticeably tense.

Two other Colombians went back inside the Firefox and reappeared with a spherical receptacle with bright red words printed on the bottom.

Jennifer snaked along the dock to get closer. She pointed her phone and snapped a picture. She blew up the image so that she could read the label: "PROPERTY OF PETROLEOS DE VENEZUELA."

One of the Colombians opened the container. Cold, frosted air escaped and revealed an organized cluster of miniature test tubes.

Everyone seemed pleased and nodded approvingly.

The Colombians took their money, filed back onto their vessel, and pushed off.

Agents Shannon and Perretta lifted the heavy receptacle up to *Lucky*. Two men emerged from the cruiser and helped the agents bring the receptacle on deck. These men were casually dressed, both in their fifties. One had a thick mane of white hair, gold chains around his neck, and he was wearing a designer sweat suit. The other was of the same ilk, but less tawdry, and bald.

Jennifer knew what a drug deal looked like; this certainly fit the bill. She wondered if this was the reason Perretta and Shannon had harassed her the first time she climbed on Rupert Reynolds' Swan. They wouldn't be the first federal agents to take kickbacks.

Jennifer snuck away from the docks, unseen, convinced that the CIA agents were double-dipping.

—

JACK JOINED MARSHALL AT a large private table under a shaded canopy and watched the salient array of colorful sails kicking off the Sunday morning race. A waiter poured French press coffees.

Marshall waited until the server left before he began. "Where were you last night?"

"At the carnival," Jack told him, knowing that the island had few secrets, and getting caught in a lie was much worse than an off-limits romantic tryst. Jack looked out at the sailboats and tried to change the subject. "Perfect day for a race."

They both watched for a while. The top deck of Flamingo Beach Club gave them an ideal vantage point. It also gave them privacy. It was only available for Flamingo Enterprises principals. No cameras were allowed. Tourists down on the beach could only see a large deck covered in purple Bougainvillea and a sign: Members Only.

"You know why you can't get involved with potential Flamingos?" Marshall said.

"I always assumed it was so you would get first dibs on the pretty ladies," Jack joked.

Marshall didn't laugh. "It's because it could cloud your judgment. New Flamingos often bring surprises we don't foresee—"

Jack sobered. "I understand."

Marshall stated his unmitigated credo, "If you stay loyal to Flamingo, Flamingo will always be loyal to you."

Jack had heard Marshall say it a million times, to every new Flamingo, Flamingo employee, and every time Flamingos flocked together. It was used as a metaphor, a value, and a threat. This time it was the latter, Jack was certain. Marshall had molded him to be an important part of the future of Flamingo and often made sure that he understood that protecting Flamingos was a privilege and a lifetime commitment. Jack had been entrusted with the secrets of changing money, asset protection, and identity change. His role as a screener, and the foremost gatekeeper, came with great responsibility. As such, Marshall had laid out some policies to eliminate distracting temptations. One of them was dating. Flamingos in positions of power were discouraged from dating other Flamingos; dating potential Flamingos, as well as the newly minted, was absolutely verboten. People changing their identities often had many landmines. Marshall knew it took time to diffuse them all. Jack hadn't questioned the policy before. It had never been an issue. His gateway clients were always much older and loaded with umbrageous baggage. When he met Jennifer, however, he couldn't resist.

"I realize you're disappointed," Marshall said. "She's beautiful, charming, bright—"

"And too young for you," Jack said, surprising himself that he did so.

Marshall let that one slide. A girl like Jennifer was as rare as a blue diamond. "I see real possibilities in her," Marshall said.

So did Jack.

"She has an impressive business background. She can be a real asset to Flamingo."

"I get it," Jack assured him.

"Then I have your word?" Marshall said with a hard look. "We don't have to ever have this conversation again?"

"No."

"Good. How far along are you on her transformation—?"

"I'm using a small law firm in Bodden Town for her new passport and birth certificate," Jack said to show that he hadn't been sleeping at the wheel. "They're fast and discreet. Her assets will be routed to a Bank of Caribbean branch on Saint Maarten and she'll be good to go."

"What's her name going to be?"

"I haven't gotten that far—"

"Olivia Pelican," Marshall blurted, as if he'd been waiting for the opportunity to name her himself. "I want her to be Olivia Pelican."

Jack restrained himself from laughing out loud. "Do you have a thing for birds or something?"

Marshall finally smiled. "Flamingos and Pelicans are kindred spirits, likeminded creatures. When you get to my age and stature in life, you want to leave a legacy."

Marshall had mentioned it many times before, usually as a carrot, since he treated Jack and Dex like competing heirs.

"Most people have children," Jack remarked out of spite.

"If you haven't noticed," Marshall laughed, "I don't do things like most people."

Jack's chest tightened as he forced a polite laugh. "I've noticed."

CHAPTER 25

High noon

T HE BRILLIANT WINTER SUN glimmered off the yellow Lamborghini as it raced along West Bay Road, from George Town to the borders of West Bay, past multimillion-dollar villas stretching the length of the white-pink sandy beach. Jennifer dialed Roberta Coscarello's home number, assuming she'd find her new boss still lounging in slippers, relaxing in her Tribeca apartment with the *Sunday Times*.

Roberta answered on the first ring, but she wasn't lounging, or relaxed. Matter of fact, she was livid. "What the hell! Where are you?" she shouted, wiping sweat off her forehead with a kitchen towel from the jog up to the High-Line she had just taken to calm herself.

"Driving up the coast," Jennifer said. "Why?"

Roberta paced. "I have been worried sick, praying that you hadn't gone AWOL or been found out."

"What? Why—?"

"Why?" Roberta repeated. "I gave you an undocumented identity and access to a fortune. I took a giant leap of faith, probably the most careless, stupid risk I've ever taken. I left you three messages—"

"I've been busy," Jennifer interjected.

"Clearly. But you're there to nail Max Culpepper, not Jack Martin!"

Whoa!

Now Jennifer was livid. "Are you having me followed?"

"Dammit, Morton, I thought you were better than this! I have a good mind to pull you—"

"Don't worry," Jennifer told her, "the deed is done."

"Excuse me?"

"It's over, the job," Jennifer told her, "Rupert Reynolds is going to prison."

After a long pause, Roberta said, "I'm listening."

"Rupert Reynolds was in a sailboat race this morning to Cozumel and back..." Jennifer checked her watch. "Going on an unidentified tip, Mexico's Drug Enforcement Agency found his boat stocked with a shitload of illegal substances."

"You're fucking kidding me?" Roberta said. "You planted drugs on his boat?"

"Really bad ones," Jennifer said, prepared for Roberta to explode.

Roberta made a loud squeal, but it wasn't an angry one. She was pleased. Elated. "Tell me everything," she told Jennifer, "and don't spare any details."

—

AS THE PACK OF psychedelic sails approached the Cozumel Port, preparing to come about, a tough, leathery officer looked out from a border security boat through binoculars and shouted out to his men. "*La roja vela. Vamenos!*"

The Mexican Blue Jackets started up a fleet of six *pangas*—confiscated marijuana smuggler dinghies they used for stealth operations and ambushes. They torpedoed toward the Swan with the red sail, leaving Rupert Reynolds no chance to flee or abort. The other Flamingo sailors were ordered to keep moving, which they gladly did, racing back toward the Caymans even faster than they came, their reigning champion now permanently disqualified.

The Blue Jackets boarded the Swan and waved their guns, shouting orders in Spanish. One of the officers cuffed Señor

Reynolds, knowing he would have cause very soon. The others searched the vessel. Sure enough, one of them brought up the saran-wrapped bag Jennifer had planted, cut it open, sampled the powder, and shouted, *"Aliento del Diablo!"*

"That's not mine," the former Max Culpepper pleaded.

"That's what they always say," the officer that cuffed him said.

The others laughed as they took him away.

———

"I can't believe you got a financial fugitive on drug possession," Roberta said.

When Jennifer heard those words, she couldn't believe it herself. She snickered, "When they couldn't get Al Capone on murder, they nailed him on tax evasion."

"That's true."

"Ironic, right?"

"Right."

"No one will know what happened to Rupert Reynolds. He can't admit that he's really Max Culpepper in Mexico. They would double his sentence…" Jennifer paused. She heard a clicking noise. "Are you still there?"

Roberta sounded concerned, "I'm checking to confirm the arrest. Hold on…"

———

As Rupert Reynolds was led out of the Cozumel Marina in handcuffs, a helicopter descended from above, causing everyone to cover their eyes. The whirlybird forced fierce winds as it landed. Three men emerged and pulled the Mexican authorities aside. They had words. The top Mexican Bluejacket made a phone call. When he hung up, Rupert Reynolds was uncuffed and escorted onto the helicopter with the three men.

———

"A LOVELY SWAN CALLED *The Getaway* was confiscated by Mexican DEA," Roberta quipped. "Drugs were found in the cabin."

"Told ya...you had nothing to worry about. Maybe you'll loosen the leash next time." Remembering that she had nothing and no one to go home to, Jennifer figured she should be angling for another assignment, "You want someone that'll do what it takes to get results, I'm your girl."

"There was no arrest!" Roberta blurted. "The Mexican Bluejackets found the sailboat with some drugs, but there was no one onboard. No Max Culpepper. No Rupert Reynolds. No one."

Jennifer was stunned. "You think he jumped and swam to shore—?"

"No, I think Flamingo protects their people and Rupert Reynolds is now on his way to some other island, using another name, and will never be seen again. Thank you for your service, Jennifer. You will be compensated accordingly."

Jennifer's belly ached. Roberta was using past tense. And it hit Jennifer in the same way as when Simon Brisco said: *"Been nice working with you, kid."*

And she responded the same way: "I'll find him!"

Roberta sighed.

Jennifer sighed, too. Her job was finished. Max Culpepper got away. Again. She would have to return to her lonely, jobless life as Jennifer Morton.

And she would never see Jack Martin again.

She glanced at her reflection in the rearview mirror, her faux blonde hair flowing in the draft of a hundred-thousand-dollar sports car. Roberta had been clear: *"Everything must be accounted for and returned. Including you."*

Finally, Roberta spoke: "How?"

Jennifer brightened. Roberta was open to the idea. "I don't know how I'll find him," Jennifer said, "but I won't rest until I do. You've never had anyone inside Flamingo. This place is everything you thought it was. Maybe worse. Give me a chance—"

Roberta cut her off. Her voice was raspy. She uttered one name, "Marshall Shore."

"Excuse me?"

"If you figure out a way to take him down, Flamingo Enterprises would crumble. That's the only way you'll get to Max Culpepper now."

"Then that's how I'll do it."

"You'll need a better strategy, though," Roberta said. "You won't get him on drug possession, I promise you that. He has people on his payroll throughout the Caribbean and beyond, airtight security. Flamingo owns property everywhere. They probably own the banks—"

"And businesses," Jennifer interrupted, "which is why I'll be able to figure out a way to get to him. He wants me to work for him. I'm going to get to see how the entire thing works."

Roberta was quiet.

Jennifer tried harder, "You and I know too well, every business has cracks; a place like this has to have gaping holes. I'll find them."

Roberta said, "Then get to it."

Jennifer's heart raced again. "Just one request..." Jennifer paused. She didn't want to offend Roberta, but she didn't want any limitations, especially when it came to Jack. "Let me do it my way," she said, "without monitoring where I sleep, and with whom."

Roberta sighed, her voice cracked, "Sleeping with the enemy is never a good idea."

"You sound like you speak from experience."

Roberta fell quiet again. Jennifer realized she might have struck a nerve and she didn't want to push her luck. "I'm sorry, I didn't mean to—"

"Go to it," Roberta said. "You're unleashed."

"You won't regret this."

"I hope not. You get compromised, you come home. You get caught..."

"We never met. I know the deal," Jennifer assured her.

After they hung up, Jennifer floored the pedal, opening up the angry engine, her inner monster released, a fiery smile on her face.

—

JENNIFER SLEPT DEEPLY THAT evening; her entire body reset. She had a vivid dream. Not one of her reoccurring nightmares where she was trapped underwater, but it was a dream that she had had before, several times, in various incarnations throughout her life. Her childhood therapist had been big on dream analysis and got Jennifer in the habit of writing down the ones that shook her up.

She sat up, grabbed a pad of paper, and wrote:

The chiffonier from my childhood room was strapped onto my back—a hefty solid oak dresser that was once my father's, left behind, just like me. I took it with me to my grungy apartment in the city and anguished to refinish it—sanding and buffing and oiling—hoping it would come out differently. But it never did. It always returned to its original form, reminding me that it would never be the way I wanted. Just like my father. Just like his secrets, hidden in the chest of drawers, forever lost. Others were coming for it, for the hidden secrets, chasing me into the stairwell, to the top of the building, gaining on me, armed and angry. I looked down at the dizzying drop, timorous, woozy, the weight of the chiffonier unbearable. The only way out was to surrender or jump. I tried to scream, but I was unable to speak, my voice hollow and empty. No one could hear me.

No one ever could—

Jennifer put her pencil down and rubbed her throbbing head. The dream was a motherload, full of vivid images and blatant trope. She always had these bountiful ones when she stopped focusing on a target, an inevitable loss of purpose blended with the satisfaction of her triumph. This time, there was no triumph. She still hadn't completed the assignment. She had to recharge, recompose, realign; she was going to get one more chance. She was going to get Culpepper by bringing down Marshall Shore and his Flamingo racket. Only then would her anxieties and night-mares drop like an anchor in the sea, she decided.

Jack called to say that her transformation was nearly completed, and that he was actively looking for properties to show her. He kept it professional, didn't ask to see her socially and their conversation was short.

She didn't give it much credence. After all she would have more time with him now since her gig wasn't over, and another chance to figure out what their undeniable connection meant.

Marshall Shore called, too. He said that he would like her to come to his office and get her started, but he didn't say what he wanted her to get started doing. And she didn't care. She was invited into her new target's den.

She felt unusually tranquil and went through her new morning ritual: five sets of pushups, five sets of sit ups, a little yoga, a brisk shower, and a light breakfast out on the terrace, where she looked out at the view that she would never tire of: pink Flamingos flocking to a pristine golf course, surfers catching ample swells, joggers running along the beach to and fro.

Just another day at the office.

She went inside to get dressed, a wardrobe decision from Eloise's well-endowed suitcase, and took a long gaze in the mirror.

Jennifer was gone. Eloise was gone, too. Just like that.

She smiled at her reflection and said, "Hello, Olivia Pelican. Welcome to paradise."

CHAPTER 26

O VER THE YEARS, I'VE developed a foolproof system for maintaining privacy," Marshall explained as he walked Jennifer through the dark empty corridors of Flamingo Enterprises, "and I've broken it down into three stages."

Her new target was spelling it all out for her and she was giddy, recording every word on her phone.

He continued, "Phase one, 'misinformation.' We destroy all the known data, everything that binds a Flamingo to their past. Phase two, 'disinformation.' We create fake trails. Phase three, 'reformation.' Getting them to their new place without leaving clues. I'm going to teach you everything. I've built a business like no other and I want it to thrive when I'm gone. I want to teach a select group of young people—like you—Flamingos with business savvy. The ones I can trust. A legacy, if you will."

"I'm flattered...and fascinated."

They turned down another hallway and Jennifer saw the large plastic crates with Bank of the Caribbean logos again. Every office they passed was filled with these crates, stacked high, and this building had nearly one hundred offices. Was this where they stored the information for shell companies and their untraceable bank accounts? She wanted to ask if they were just for Flamingos or if this was how tax evaders hid their trillions offshore—the salacious cheats that CNN's Kelly Keefer was after. But she didn't want to be blatant, so she simply prodded, hoping he would spill the beans, eventually.

"I know how difficult the hotel business is," she said, "I can't imagine adding all the complexities of protecting expatriates."

Marshall brightened. "That's just a fraction of what we do."

"You have other businesses?"

"We're involved in many things and they're all intertwined to facilitate each other."

"I'm not sure I follow."

"We own property, so we have legitimacy, for example. We own banks, for control."

She nodded toward the room with all the bank boxes. "You own the Bank of Caribbean?"

"We have a stake, nothing traceable."

"Enough to give you flexibility?"

"Flexibility is important," he admitted. "We also house thousands of corporate and government entities." He grinned. "And we do all that with very few employees, very little overhead, very low risk. And no taxes."

"Impressive," Jennifer said as she pointed inside one of the vacant offices with floor to ceiling mail slots, all with different company names. "Are those all fictitious corporations then?"

"They exist. Most just need Cayman addresses for tax purposes or banking services, just to move money. We take management fees. That's our bread and butter. Everything else is gravy."

"What's everything else?"

"Flamingos, of course."

"People with old money and new names?" Jennifer asked off of Marshall's smirk.

"How are they profitable?"

"Human nature is profitable," Marshall professed. "People who have money always want more, right?"

"Right," Jennifer absently agreed.

"Flamingos are people with means and talents. I don't let them wither away in the sun and get bored. Bored people are boring, and people without purpose just get old."

"That's why you asked me to come work for you."

"We all benefit. We all get richer. Like the locals say, 'Everything is *irie mon.*'"

"Everybody's happy."

"It's the way you feel when you have no worries. That's how we want Flamingos to feel all the time… I assess people that come here and make sure they reach their potential."

Jennifer followed Marshall into his office. He sat at his desk, turned around to face the enormous cabinets, and opened one of the doors. She could see that there was a safe inside, just like the smaller one in Jack's office. She felt emboldened and asked, "Is that where you keep all of our files?"

He pulled a bottle of fifteen-year-old Solera that was hidden around the side and admired the label. "What files?"

"When I first inquired about buying property," she said concernedly, "I had to fill out an extensive application with all my personal details. Jack put it in a folder. I'm hoping you keep that information in a safe place—"

"We call those New Deals," Marshall told her, "and you have nothing to worry about. Jack keeps them locked up while he vets new applicants. At the end of every quarter, Dex transfers them to me, where they remain…forever." Marshall smiled as he took out two glasses. "I'm told you have a palette for fine Scotch. This is a wonderful single malt."

"It's not even noon."

"No, it's not, but today is special." He poured two fingers, neat, and handed her a glass. "To your first day working for Flamingo."

Jennifer took a sip and puckered her lips. "Delish."

"My one indulgence."

"Man after my own heart," she teased.

He laughed.

She felt giddy. And pointedly asked, "What will I be doing here exactly?"

"You're going to find new Flamingos."

"Isn't that what Jack does?"

"Jack's a screener. You'll be a recruiter. You will be working closely with me," he said with an inflection that possibly hinted at other intentions.

Then she saw the framed pictures behind his desk. She had first noticed them when Jack took her to meet Marshall. She wished she could get a good look and learn more about him. He was the most protected of all Flamingos. Everyone was aware of his importance, but there was nothing documenting his position. Jennifer wondered if it was because he was the biggest crook of all, bigger than Culpeper. She felt another surge of excitement, more certain that she would find the cracks and big gaping holes. She flashed her infectious smile, clinked his glass, and said, "Everything is *irie mon!*"

—

WHEN JENNIFER GOT BACK to the hotel, there were no voice messages. Jack hadn't called as she had hoped. So she went for a sunset run, showered, dressed, and then went down to the outside taproom, a four-top portico overlooking the beach, where she had a bird's-eye view of a wedding. The bride was a striking femme fatale. The groom looked like a distinguished statesman hoping for one more play at the plate with a woman close to his daughter's age.

Jennifer took a seat, ordered a drink, and then things got interesting.

The Justice of the Peace was addressing the couple before a small gathering of hotel guests, "And Monique, do you take Sheldon as your lawful wedded husband, to love him and cherish him until death—?" The Justice of the Peace stopped in midsentence when he realized that the bride looked horror struck. "Is something the matter, Monique?"

Sheldon chimed in, "Are you okay, honey?"

Monique was flustered, staring at a man rushing away on the beach, tripping on the sand, clearly panicked.

Her voice cracked, "I'm sorry…"

The groom reminded her, trying to get her to look away from the intruder, pulling her aside to recompose. "Do you know that man?"

"Yes."

"Who is he?"

"My husband."

"Your husband? I thought he was dead!"

Monique was visibly shaking. "So did I."

Jennifer was watching this little fiasco with regard. Flamingo couldn't guarantee privacy in such a public place. No one could be completely protected. Everyone had a past that had the possibility of catching up with them, no matter what precautions were taken—even for those on the Dropping off the Grid plan, their deluxe package—there would always be risks, potential peril, unexpected ignominy.

She thought of her father's words of wisdom: *"There is only one way to truly disappear."*

Which brought her back to Max Culpepper.

Roberta was most likely right about him getting sent off to another island, some remote place where he would no longer be able to order South American super models every night. That was punishment all on its own for a guy that wanted to get laid like a rock star, not lay on a hammock all day. But he still needed a punishment worthy of his crimes, she decided. She would find the cracks, the vulnerabilities, like she had done with every crooked establishment she audited.

And then she heard a voice from behind: "You have a message, Mrs. Pelican."

When Jennifer turned, the concierge was standingbefore her. Yesterday, this man had addressed her as Eloise Concord. Today, Oivia Pelican. Nothing phased anyone here. No worries. Everything is *irie mon.*

The concierge handed her an envelope with a Flamingo seal. Jennifer opened it, assuming she had to play another round of golf with Marshall, maybe another tour of his offices. She hoped so. The closer she got to him, the better chance she would have to find his weaknesses.

This invitation was for a party at his house on Saturday night. Formal attire was requested. Attendance was mandatory.

CHAPTER 27

Flamenco music boomed throughout Marshall Shore's estate as the guests arrived. Valets greeted the black-tied and sequined guests, helping them out of their Teslas, Rolls, and limos, while escorts led them up a white Hibiscus pathway to the enormous villa.

Jennifer emerged from her yellow Lamborghini in a stunning Versace dress that she picked out two hours earlier from the overpriced hotel shop's Dorchester collection. Awestruck eyes were upon her as she entered the fray, but it was she that was most in awe. This gathering proved that the Flamingo population was even bigger than she had imagined. She felt like an FBI agent invited to a mob family wedding and imagined swiping DNA samples from the wine glasses, but that wasn't her assignment.

She was there for Marshall Shore.

She remembered Roberta's words: *"If you figure out a way to take him down, Flamingo Enterprises would crumble."*

She entered his French chateau ballroom. It was from another time and place, and it was roaring, electrified. An eight-piece Spanish Mariachi ensemble was playing their hearts out. Twin Cantaores sang in tandem while they pounded on cajón drums. Flamenco dancers performed a classical routine downstage, their bright red and blue skirts fanning in succession, harmonious, festive.

The lead Flamenco dancer spun off from the rest, grabbed Marshall Shore, and they spun onto the center of the dance floor, demanding attention, commanding the room. The guests backed off to give them space, clapping in unison.

A bespectacled and bejeweled lady, gaga from the gaiety, whispered to Jennifer without taking her eyes off the couple. "Wonderful, aren't they?"

"Yes. Wonderful," Jennifer agreed.

The song and dance finished boldly. The crowd cheered. Marshall waited for the obligatory praise to settle down and then took the microphone from one of the singers. "Thank you. Thank you all for coming," his throaty voice sounding even more omnipresent than usual.

Jennifer searched the room, wondering if Jack was going to be there.

The residual applause subsided until you could hear a pin drop. Marshall began, "Tonight we are here to welcome the new Flamingos among us. You know who you are!"

There was more applause and polite laughs for his rye reference to Flamingo privacy.

Jennifer watched the exclusive assembly and thought about Marshall's commitment to them, how his entire value is based on their perceived security.

Jack snuck up from behind and wrapped his arm around her waist. Her heart beat heavy. Her face went flush. She may have even gasped.

He had that effect on her.

Marshall looked over in their direction. They both stiffened, like school children caught talking in class.

"Flamingos are loyal birds," Marshall continued, "and very social creatures. They live in large colonies to best avoid predators, maximizing food intake, and use nesting sites more efficiently…"

The crowd hung on to his every word, searching for any hidden meaning that could affect their wealth, as if he were their Federal Reserve Chairman and his words had the power to make their stocks go up or down.

"...When resources are scarce, or one of them gets trapped, they reorganize, and sometimes they flock to different islands..."

Jennifer couldn't hold back a laugh and whispered in Jack's ear. "Is he some kind of zoologist or something? What's with the fucking animal metaphors?"

Jack smiled. "I know, right?"

Their eyes met. She ached to be with him again. He squeezed her hand.

He feels it, too.

The crowd parted as Marshall moved through, slow and methodical. "One of our newest Flamingos was almost arrested in Cozumel. We will find out how this happened and do everything in our power to prevent such a thing from happening again... If any of you have any information, I expect you to contact Dex Boonyai or myself immediately."

None of the guests made eye contact; the idea of being arrested was horrifying; they were all just as vulnerable; the idea of not cooperating with Flamingo, was unthinkable.

"Needless to say," Marshall said with admonition, "we are on high alert, and should we have to move any of you, we appreciate your flexibility and understanding."

There was some rustling and moaning in the crowd.

"The price we pay for freedom never comes cheap, but know this..."

You could hear a pin drop.

"As long as you're loyal to Flamingo..."

The crowd joined him in unison: "...Flamingo will always be loyal to you!"

Marshall charged. "Flamingo is the safest place in the world!"

They applauded.

"Protection is guaranteed!"

They applauded louder.

Marshall beamed. "So tonight...let's celebrate that! Let's party... Flamingo style!"

The musicians cranked up again.

Jennifer led Jack to the ballroom floor, and just as they started to dance, she noticed the two men she had seen at the pier with a yacht named *Lucky,* Anthony Marino and Grant Hall. They cleaned up nicely wearing elegant Tom Ford suits like the Wall Street royalty she used to love auditing. They were strolling through the room, greeting people like they were hosting an Italian wedding. They seemed to know everybody, and everyone knew them.

"Who are those guys?" Jennifer asked Jack

Jack shrugged. "Flamingos."

"I saw them at the harbor the other day," she whispered. "I'm pretty sure they're running drugs."

Jack laughed. "I don't think so. They do boat tours around the islands."

"Right. Like Jim Morrison and the Crystal Ship Tour," she joked. "Did they work for Pablo Escobar before they came here?"

Jack laughed harder. "I could tell you, but then I'd have to kill you."

"Right," she mused. "Is that Flamingo rule number four?"

Jack's smile faded fast. He said, "Some people would rather risk the consequences of getting noticed than live a life of seclusion."

Jennifer let that sink in as she watched the men work the crowd. Masters of their universe, their taut and tucked girlfriends following behind like ornamented cabooses.

Jennifer tried to discreetly take a snapshot, so Marcus could run a search.

She was startled by a voice from behind, "Mind if an old man cuts in?"

She turned. Marshall was standing there. His hand reached out. And he spun her away.

Jennifer looked back at Jack, but Marshall whisked her across the floor before she could say anything. Marshall had moves, aggressive moves. He looked at her like a lion savoring red meat and he growled, "You look ravishing this evening."

"Thanks." She felt awkward and responded with, "Your home is beautiful."

"I'm glad you like it," he said. "I'd like you to join me here tomorrow night."

Jennifer searched for an excuse.

"For dinner."

He wasn't asking.

"Eight o'clock. Arrive a little before."

"Oh... I..."

"We'll be entertaining potential Flamingos. A husband and wife...from Austria. She loves everything equestrian. He loves money. They could be a real asset to Flamingo. As my recruiter, you'll have to be charming and debonair, which won't be a stretch."

Jennifer feigned a smile. "I don't have a thing to wear—"

"For the love of God, wear that!" He glanced down. "It's nothing short of spectacular."

She looked away and saw Jack watching from the sidelines.

—

THERE WAS A TAP on Jack's shoulder. He turned to see Dex standing behind him with a taunting grin. "They make a lovely couple, don't they?"

"Bugger off," Jack snapped back.

"Word of advice," Dex said leaning up to Jack's ear. "Behave foolishly and you'll end up right back where you came from, or worse."

"Mind your own business, Dex."

"Everything is my business," Dex reminded him. "Like the file for Flamingo number six-five-eight."

"What about it?"

"Where is it?"

Jack was annoyed. He turned to face Dex with a sneer. "What are you talking about?"

Dex whispered his ear, "Max Culpepper...I came by your office to collect the New Deals...his file wasn't in the cabinet."

Jack's mind raced, trying to remember the last time he saw Culpepper's file. It had been a while since Jack sold him the condo in the Towers. Had he taken his file out for any reason? He couldn't think of any and told Dex, "It should be there—"

"It's not."

"I always keep my cabinet locked—"

"I'll give you a day to find it."

Flamingo's motto was, "Ownership has its privileges and privacy is king," which translated to their ultimate promise: "Protection is guaranteed." Jack couldn't imagine how Marshall would react if Jack's carelessness was the reason a new Flamingo nearly got arrested and had to be repositioned, retransformed, and reborn.

But Dex obviously could, because he walked away grinning.

CHAPTER 28

J ENNIFER WOKE UP THE next morning thinking about why Jack had left the party without saying goodbye. She hoped it didn't have to do with Marshall. When she started Operation Marshall Shore, she had hoped that Marshall's interest in her was purely for Flamingo business. Now she was getting a strong vibe that he had other intentions. Keeping him at bay would not be easy. He was persistent. And he wasn't the type to take rejection lightly. The thought made her uneasy. Not only was he old enough to be her father, but just like her old man, he was the embodiment of everything she despised. He was king of the empire for liars, scammers, schemers, and cheaters and her excessive tenacity and sense of justice stirred.

She had her breakfast out on the terrace and a text lit up her phone. It was from Jack: "I have a condo I want you to see today. Are you available at eleven?"

Her heart beat fast and her thumbs plucked even faster. "Yes!"

He sent her the address and said he'd see her there.

She spent a long time getting ready, choosing an outfit that would knock him out, while thinking of ways to let him know that she only had eyes for him.

She arrived at eleven sharp and double checked the address. She was standing in front of Flamingo Towers, by the harbor, and as soon as she checked in with reception, she realized that the unit she was about to see was Rupert Reynold's penthouse, which she already knew intimately.

She was escorted up and delivered to a realtor waiting in the hallway, a middle-aged woman with too much jewelry, makeup, and verve. She introduced herself as Lonna Lux.

Nice name, Jennifer thought. *Had to be a Flamingo redo.*

"Come inside," Lonna said, "this place is fabulous."

Jennifer entered and brightened, seemingly impressed. "Lovely view."

"Isn't it?"

She looked down at the entrance to the building. "Jack must be running late."

"He had an emergency at the office," Lonna Lux explained, "but he wanted you to see this unit before anyone else. The Towers rarely have anything available and the owner is offering a long-term lease."

"How long?"

Lonna Lux shrugged, and Jennifer knew it was because she had no idea if Culpepper would ever return. "Jack thought this would be a nice option for you while you get to know the island. When you're ready to purchase a property, you can always get out of this lease."

Jennifer asked, "Mind if I take a look around?"

"Go right ahead."

Jennifer scoped everything out, pretending to be interested, noticing that they hadn't removed any of the Rupert Reynold's personal items. She headed for his telescope and aimed the viewfinder at slip 58. Now empty. No more Swan. His pride and joy was now likely the property of the acting head of Mexico's Drug Enforcement Agency, in exchange for letting the Flamingo fly away.

Jennifer could smell Lonna Lux approaching from behind, her excessive use of *J'adore Eau de Parfum* reeking.

"You like boats?" Lonna Lux asked her.

"I'm thinking about getting one," Jennifer told her. "Does this condo come with a slot?"

"For a little extra, sure."

Jennifer moved the scope farther up the pier and sharpened the image. Anthony Marino and Grant Hall were moving about their yacht *Lucky*. CIA agents, Shannon and Perretta approached—just like last time—positioning themselves on the bow like bullyrag bodyguards. No way they were doing boat tours like Jack had told her. Marshall had told her that Flamingo was involved in several businesses. Could this be one of them? She thought of Roberta's charge about Marshall Shore, *"He has cops on payroll, airtight security…"*

Was the CIA his security?

Jennifer headed for the door and said, "I'll take the condo."

"Wonderful. I'll let Jack know and we'll draw up the papers. I just need for you to fill out this one sheet—"

When Lonna Lux turned, Jennifer was already gone.

—

JENNIFER HAD A CLEAR view of *Lucky* from behind the boathouse. She saw Grant Hall, Anthony Marino, and agents Shannon and Perretta preparing for another clandestine deal. She took a series of photos with her phone, sent them to Marcus back in New York, and asked him to track the boat and find out anything he could on these suspects. She didn't mention that Shannon and Perretta were CIA operatives, because she didn't want him to shut her down.

Jennifer bought a newspaper, took a seat, and waited for him to respond. Her mind drifted to thoughts of Jack Martin, her favorite new pastime.

—

JACK WAS BESIDE HIMSELF, thinking about the party last night. Marshall was all over Eloise, now Olivia Pelican, staking his claim on the dance floor for all to see.

To make matters worse, Max Culpepper's New Deal file was missing, and Dex would love nothing more than to pin the blame of Rupert Reynold's unprecedented slip up on Jack. It made no sense that Mexican officials would select Rupert Reynolds' Swan from twenty-five sails and just happen to find a package of hallucinogenic drugs considered to be one of the scariest in the world. Jack wondered if Dex had arranged the arrest to scare everyone and taken the missing file so Jack would take the fall. Dex had it in for him, always wanting to prove to Marshall that he was a most loyal Flamingo, so he would be chosen to take over the reins.

Jack decided that such a conspiracy was too farfetched; Dex was jealous, but not that clever. Still, Jack felt angry, frustrated, and alone in his thoughts. There was no one at Flamingo he could talk to.

So he got into his car and took a drive to his childhood home in the West Hills, to the past he left long ago, where he was no longer welcomed.

—

JACK'S BIG BROTHER SEAN was taken by surprise when he saw Jack standing at the front door. "What are you doing here?"

"I need to talk," Jack explained.

"Papa's home and he's in a foul mood."

"So, what else is new? Let's sit on the porch."

They were separated when Jack was fifteen years old, but still dependent on each other for every major decision. They often met for drinks in town, because their father forbid Jack to visit ever since he stopped sending money. Even though Jack had only stopped sending money because his brother refused to take it. Sean was too proud, now making a decent wage himself, and Jack respected his wishes.

The brothers sat out on the porch, on peeling Adirondack chairs. The familiar scent of eucalyptus and the cacophony banana leaves flapping in the wind comforted Jack. Sean was only a year older than Jack, but now looked ten years older. Working under the tropical sun during a decade-long building boom will do that.

Jack told Sean about his predicament, all about the missing Max Culpepper file, what the consequences would be if he was blamed, and then he went into detail about the new girl that Marshall Shore had prohibited him from getting involve with.

"You haven't talked that way about a girl in a long time," Sean said.

"I haven't felt this way about a girl in a long time—maybe ever—and it was over before it could begin."

"Marshall Shore gave you a life of luxury and privilege. You always knew there would be a price to pay for that."

Sean understood the depth of Jack's predicament.

Jack felt ill. Had he sold his soul and burnt every bridge? He couldn't go back to life in the West Hills. And no one in town would hire him if he left Marshall Shore on bad terms.

He had always considered himself to be the lucky one. He got the education, the fancy job, and the upward mobility that came with it. But his brother was right. It came with a price.

Sean reminded Jack, "Mr. Shore was always clear about your obligations—"

"What is he doing in my house?" A familiar voice growled from inside the house.

Jack's father appeared in the doorway. He was withered and weathered beyond his sixty-five years, and as wretched as ever. He slammed his fist on the door to show his disgust, as if the boys didn't know.

"Just give us a few minutes, Papa," Sean said. "We're finishing up."

The old man took a swig from a fifth of Jamaican rum and looked Jack up and down with disgust. He wiped his mouth with his sleeve and said, "You're in some kind of trouble?"

Jack didn't deny it.

"I suppose you could afford to fix it, Mr. Fancy Pants," he said as he spotted the Land Rover parked in front. "Did Mr. Flamingo buy you that gas guzzler, too?"

"I bought it myself," Jack said. "I have a job, remember?"

His father grunted, "You don't know what real work is," and headed back inside.

The brothers were numb to such outbursts. A lifetime of harsh disappointments can destroy a man, and their father had had more than his share of those. He had moved their family to the island just after the boys were born, for work opportunities and a better life, but nothing panned out. He worked construction gigs on and off—more off than on. Things took a turn for the worse when his wife died of leukemia when the boys were six. The old man started drinking heavily, overwhelmed by bereavement and the task of raising two sons on his own. Then he fell ill with tuberculosis. Sean stayed home to take care of him, while Jack got a job as a bellhop at Hotel Flamingo, working every day after school until midnight, and impressing the hell out of Marshall Shore.

It was the time that Marshall first became obsessed his own legacy. He didn't have a son, and he saw so much potential in young Jack, who was open, eager to learn, and clearly bright. Marshall worked him to the bone, introduced him Flamingo culture, and sent him off to boarding school in London "to smooth out the rough edges." Jack loved it and excelled in their business program. He wanted to stay in London and pursue a career in finance, but that wasn't remotely an option. By then it was clear: he was obligated to Marshall.

Forever.

Upon his return, Jack was groomed to be the head screener, entrusted with all the confidential operations, transformation tactics, and security measures, as well as Marshall's process for misinformation, disinformation, and reformation—to keep Flamingos safe.

It was around this time that Marshall also took interest in a loyal young soldier on his security team—Dex Boonyai—and groomed him to keep Flamingo safe in a more traditional sense, with muscle and heat.

Marshall hand-picked two surrogate sons that could possibly carry on his empire; two boys he had pulled out of impoverished homes, who would always be in his debt. They would have better lives because of him, but those lives would never be their own. Marshall never asked if that was something they wanted.

Nor did he care.

Over the years, he had pitted Jack and Dex against each other. It was implied that whomever proved to be the most worthy would fill his shoes when he stepped down; it was healthy competition, without the healthy part. Jack knew it was coming to a head. Marshall was getting up in years. And Dex was stepping up his game.

Jack spent another hour talking over it all with his brother, covering the broad strokes of their inversed lives. When Jack got up to leave, he looked around the decrepit shack his brother had stayed in all these years, and he felt a familiar pang of guilt. "I'm sorry for leaving you with all this," Jack said. "I don't expect you to ever forgive me for taking Marshall Shore's offer, but I love you, my brother, more than you know—"

Sean put his hand on Jack's shoulder and said, "I would have done the same."

Sean had never told Jack that before.

Jack drove back down the hill realizing that those words had real power, what he had always hoped to hear. It released him from the guilt that he had carried since the day he left and gave him the strength he needed to head back to Flamingo with a clear head.

He was just a boy when he made the decision to follow Marshall out of the impoverished West Hills and he had accepted the consequences. When he met Eloise Concord, something changed. He wanted to be with her. He wanted his own life. He no longer wanted to be indebted to anyone.

He now had to choose between his loyalty to Flamingo and the betrayal in his heart.

CHAPTER 29

Rupert Reynolds woke up with a stiff back, on a stiff bed, and even though he had closed the windows at night, he still awakened to dozens of new mosquito bites. He sat up and tried to remember how many days he'd been holed up in this timeworn, stucco room attached to a Carthusian monastery in the remote, hurricane battered interior of Granada. Flamingo security had promised that he would only have to stay until they determined he was safe again, but they couldn't say how long that would be. He knew he was much better off than the overcrowded, violent, and disease infested Islas Marías federal prison he would have been locked up in if they hadn't whisked him away from his arrest in Cozumel, but this was not what he had in mind when he opted for Plan B. If the former Max Culpepper hadn't taken the rapacious risk and fled before his sentencing, he probably would be in a maximum-security country club with his cohorts. He wouldn't get to ride his Swan or have any erotic South American romps, but he would only have had to be there for a few years, and when he got out, he and his wife could have taken the few million he stashed away and enjoyed a comfortable retirement. Instead, he was hiding out in some far-flung rainforest, alone, lonely, and itchy.

"You have a visitor," a monk called out to him.

When he peeked out and saw Dex Boonyai at the door, he felt hopeful. "I can be ready in a jiffy."

"I'm not here to move you just yet."

"How much longer—?"

Dex huffed. "It'll take as long as it takes."

Rupert's stomach sank. They had promised him a relocation to one of their most sought-after properties. They had guaranteed his new identity would be foolproof and his assets would be transferred and secured. They had even told him that they would purchase him a brand-new Swan, on the house. But he couldn't get a straight answer about how long he would be holed up in this isolated hideaway.

Dex came inside and opened the windows. The light filled the small room.

Rupert felt uneasy. "If you're not ready to move me, why are you here?"

"I'm trying to find out how you were pegged...so that it never happens again." Dex sat down on the corner of the unmade bed and asked, "Any idea who set you up?"

"You want to know if I have any idea?" Rupert fumed. "Isn't that your job?"

Dex stared back, waiting for an answer.

Rupert had had plenty of time to think about this and every time his mind drifted back to the night he thought he saw the IRS agent who testified against him in court. He looked out the window and watched the monks head back into the ancient chapel, and then told Dex, "The night before I was arrested, I was at a carnival, and I saw someone—"

"At Batabano?"

"Yeah. It was crazy and crowded. But I saw the kid that did my condominium deal."

Dex brightened. "Jack Martin?"

"Yeah. Jack Martin... And he was with a young woman."

Dex stood up again. He seemed excited, maybe just anxious.

Rupert wondered if Dex would think he was crazy when he told him who he thought the young woman was. "This will sound ludicruous—"

"No it won't," Dex interrupted. "I was there. I think I know what you're going to say. Tell me who you think you saw."

"I think it was the IRS agent that screwed me," Max spewed. "Her name is Jennifer Morton. She looked different than she did in the courtroom. She had long brown hair then, now she's blonde—"

Dex shook his head, looking doubtful.

"You don't believe me?" Rupert asked.

"The girl he was with is a new Flamingo," Dex told him, "just a spoiled little rich girl from Boston. Not any Jennifer Morton."

Rupert folded his arms and leaned back. "You sure?"

"I'm sure. I know her. She went through the same vetting as everyone else."

This infuriated Culpepper and he hissed, "Then you vetted a former IRS agent who came here looking for me...! It won't look good to other Flamingos that pay your ungodly fees when they learn that you let in a mole."

Rupert noticed that Dex didn't look offended by the accusation. In fact, he was grinning. But Rupert didn't know that Jack Martin would be blamed if Eloise Concord wasn't who they thought she was, or that Dex was looking for reasons to bury Jack Martin.

Dex asked, "Why would an IRS agent come after you here? She has no jurisdiction—"

"So she could set me up and plant drugs on my boat!" When the words came out of Rupert's mouth, it seemed to make perfect sense. And Dex looked like he was contemplating the possibility. Rupert pressed, convincing himself and Dex further, "It had to be her. That shit wasn't mine."

Dex nodded.

Culpepper leaned closer and said, "If she came for me, she's come for others."

"If you're right about this..." Dex didn't finish the sentence and headed for the door.

Rupert watched him storm away, his hope returning. If Dex could take care of Jennifer Morton quickly, then he could get on with his life, lavish lifestyle, and the promise of Plan B.

CHAPTER 30

Jennifer's FaceTime flashed, and she accepted the call.

Marcus appeared. "I think I found something."

Jennifer straightened. "Tell me."

"The boat *Lucky* is registered to both Anthony Marino and Grant Hall."

"I already knew that—"

"But it can't be. Know why? Anthony Marino is a man that worked for the mob in Vegas back in 1994 and went into witness protection after he testified against a man named Grant Hall. Anthony Marino is living in Calabasas, California, now. According to my source, he's still there. Grant Hall is the man that owned the Palace Casino back then and is now living in an Arizona penitentiary—"

"They're using false identities, like everyone at Flamingo," Jennifer said. "We need to find another way—"

"So I ran a face recognition scan," Marcus cut her off, "and I got a real match."

Jennifer felt a rush. Her digital detective was sharp. "And?"

"Your Anthony Marino is actually Tony Romano, known at Lehman Brothers as Tony-the-Tiger. Grant Hall is really Daniel Mann. They were the bozos that started the collateralized debt obligations department at Lehman Brothers. They cashed out and fled just before the subprime mortgage bubble burst. They're wanted for nine counts of pandering and fraud."

"And now they're doing deals with CIA operatives?"

"What are you talking about?"

Jennifer lowed her voice, "There were two other men in the photos I sent you. I know one of them is Special Agent Kirk Shannon...he showed me his CIA badge when I met him."

"I can't get you intel on the CIA." Marcus said.

"Something about national security—"

"Exactly."

She paused and then said, "You could see my dilemma, Marcus. I have two CIA operatives running some kind of racquet with those Lehman Brother scammers...and we both know that Federal agents wouldn't work with anyone wanted on federal crimes, unless..."

"Unless what?"

"You know what I'm getting at," Jennifer said, insinuating.

"If they're double-dipping or on the take," Marcus said, "I wouldn't know."

"I don't like being restricted."

"And I don't like to be manipulated."

"Sometimes we have to bend a few rules to break a few scumbags."

Marcus snickered. "Sounds like bumper sticker."

Jennifer took another approach. "Marshall Shore has enlisted Flamingos to run illegitimate businesses. I've observed exchanging of money for some big receptacle with test tubes inside, labeled *Petroleos de Venezuela*, which means property of Venezuela oil—"

"That's not illegitimate," Marcus snapped.

"I don't think they're dealing in oil—"

"They're not. But you're wasting your time. You have to trust me."

She could see that she was wearing him down and she pressed, "I need to know what I'm dealing with."

Marcus sighed. "The US helped Chávez turn Venezuela into a big oil producer," Marcus explained. "They thrived for a while, but after Maduro took over, years of corruption and economic mismanagement took its toll. They had to slash oil prices, profits tanked, and inflation went through the roof. Now we're helping them stabilize—"

"How?"

"By switching to a commodity more profitable than oil."

"What's more profitable than oil?"

"Beef." Marcus said, "They're cloning Argentinean cows."

Jennifer didn't see that coming. "What? Why?"

"Because it's perfectly marbled, tender and tasty, best in the world. Oil companies have the production and distribution means, so they helped them turn their infrastructure and it's been successful."

"Why is it a secret?"

"The cloning is still pending FDA and international health approvals. The CIA helps keep it quiet until they can move forward, monitoring the facilities That's all—"

"That's absurd."

"Sounds crazy, I know. But it has nothing to do with your objective. You need to focus on your actual assignment."

"Are you sure about that? Why would they involve Flamingos, especially Flamingos wanted for federal crimes? Why wouldn't they transport those receptacles directly to Venezuela? Why involve middle men?"

Marcus's voice sounded raspy, "That's all I know, I promise."

"There's probably nothing more to know then..." There was no reason to press him, Jennifer decided. Either he didn't know what was going on, or he was ardently loyal. She couldn't blame him for either. She would find out the truth herself. "Thanks for your help."

"I'm here if you need me..." And his face evaporated from her screen.

—

THE FORTY-FOOT BLACK CIGARETTE Firefox pulled up in front of *Lucky*. Jennifer stalked down the dock to get a better look. Just like last time, well-dressed Colombian businessmen hopped out and were greeted by agents Perretta and Shannon. Shannon handed one of the businessmen a briefcase. He acknowledged the rows of cash inside. Another businessman set a spherical receptacle at the agent's feet. The container's label read: PROPERTY OF PETROLEOS DE VENEZUELA. After the Colombians pushed off, the agents lifted it up to Grant Hall. Anthony Marino fired up the engine. *Lucky* revved. Agents Perretta and Shannon headed back down the pier, got in their car, and drove off.

Jennifer considered Marcus's advice. The agents did only seem to be offering security. But she wasn't satisfied. Jack had told her that these old Flamingos were taking people on boat tours. Clearly that was not what they were up to. And whatever it was, it did not look legitimate. Maybe Marcus or Jack didn't know what was really going on. Marcus's explanation still sounded incredulous. Commodities were commodities but switching from oil refineries into butcher shops seemed ridiculous. Jennifer couldn't let it slide. She needed to find out what these former Lehman Brother fraudsters were up to.

Just before the yacht pushed off, she crept down the dock and leapt, grabbing onto the rail. She pulled herself up and over and snuck inside. As the boat moved through the no-wave zone, she climbed into the galley and located the large receptacle strapped to the fiberglass side. She tried to yank the latch, to get a look inside, but it was locked. It was a fairly simple combination padlock, one that she could easily crack if she could listen for the subtle ticks of the dial, but *Lucky's* deafening baritone hum made it impossible. She looked around to find something solid to break it open when the cabin door opened. She tucked into a closet and hid behind a pile life jackets just as Grant came down looking for his Dramamine. He searched the medicine cabinet, then a first aid kit, and soon got frustrated.

"It's not here!" he shouted up to the deck. "Are you sure we have some?"

Anthony hollered back, "Check the closet!"

Jennifer knew there was only one closet he could be referring to and she had nowhere to go.

The cabinet door handle turned. Jennifer froze, preparing to be exposed, when the boat hit a choppy wave, knocking Grant off balance, and bumping his head. Slow to get up, he shouted, "Slow down for Chrissakes!"

The boat eased, Grant opened the cabinet door. Instead of finding pills for nausea on the shelf, he got a fist in the nose.

Crack!

Blood squirted. He fell back on the floor, knocked out cold.

Jennifer leaned over him and saw that his nose was crooked. "It's an improvement," she mumbled as she yanked it back in place. Grant groaned, but his eyes didn't open, and then fell back unconscious. She laid a broom over his face, as if it were the culprit that had sprung out from the closet to knock him out.

"Did you find it?" Perretta shouted from above.

Jennifer looked up through the cabin and saw Anthony's shadow. She had two options: hide in the toilet or leave through the hatch. She chose the latter, seconds before Anthony came down the steps.

"For the love of God!" Anthony hissed when he saw Grant on the floor."

Jennifer traversed along the side of the boat, arm over arm, until she reached the stern. There was a flat board over the double engines. She hopped onto it and braced herself to the mounted metal ladder.

Anthony helped Grant up to the deck. Grant's eyes opened, and he moaned, "What happened?"

"You tell me, klutz,"

He had no idea.

"Still up for this?"

"I'm fine." Grant got up and untied the lines.

Minutes later, the engine revved higher. The boat reached cruising speed.

Jennifer tucked in and prepared for a long ride as the yacht powered into the endless, sapphire void.

CHAPTER 31

Dex Boonyai ordered the on-duty hotel manager to open Olivia Pelican's room, but he didn't explain why.

The manager waited in the hallway while Dex went inside with his security deputy, Jan Maitland, a husky Jamaican and distant cousin. He was a high-ranking Shotokan master, a difficult and deadly style of karate, and he was a highly skilled bloodhound and deputy. Dex trusted him implicitly.

The bed had already been made and there was no sign of her.

"Let's turn this place over." Dex started for the bathroom and told Jan, "Check every drawer, every pocket, every corner."

In just seconds, Jan pointed to the nightstand drawer by the bed and asked, "Is dis significant?"

Dex thought his cousin was referring to the Gideon's Bible. "Not a good time for jokes."

"No joke, cousin," Jan said, holding up a folder with a pink flamingo on its cover.

Blood drained from Dex's face. He rushed over and snapped the folder from Jan's hand. A smile emerged as he flipped through dozens of pages about Max Culpepper's transformation into Rupert Reynolds.

Jan said, "Nu matta how boar hog hide under sheep wool, her grunt betray her."

It was a Jamaican saying: the true self always prevails.

Dex smirked at his cousin and shouted back at the hotel manager. "Notify your staff... Soon as Olivia Pelican returns to the hotel, I need to know."

The manager nodded obediently. "Yes, sir."

Dex turned to Jan. "She drives a yellow Lamborghini. Shouldn't be hard to find. I don't want to spend all day looking for this bitch."

—

JENNIFER'S EARS RANG AS the twin engines revved lower. *Lucky* was slowing down. She peeked out the opening between the fiberglass ledge and chrome rails. She saw the horizon and approaching coastline, pristine and green, full mangroves and lagoons, home to more pink flamingoes, and pelicans, too.

Anthony Marino steered the cruiser into Morrocoy Harbor. Day laborers waved him into a prearranged slip. Grant Hall threw out the rope, and then doled out cash, like he was greasing door-men at nightclub.

Jennifer tucked back down as Grant descended back into the cabin. He had a bandage covering his nose, which was now black and blue, and likely why he sounded angrier. "Why the hell didn't we put this thing on wheels?" he complained as he unlatched and released the hefty container with the Petroleos De Venezuela label. "Can't we pay one of these wetbacks to take this to the car?"

"Wetbacks are Mexican," Anthony said with a snicker. "These guys are Venezuelan."

"You're so politically correct."

"If you're going to be racist, at least get your slurs right."

"What's up your ass?" Grant grunted as they lifted their heavy parcel together and set it on the dock. "I'm the one that broke my nose."

"It's not broken."

"Feels like it is."

Anthony laughed. "Do you serve cheese with all that whine?"

They stumbled down the dock with their bulky cargo.

When their banter faded away, Jennifer climbed off the boat. Her legs tingled from the long ride. She followed them into the parking lot and watched them secure the receptacle into the back of a Jeep.

Jennifer searched the lot for a car that would be easy to start up. She tried four cars before she found an '86 vt500 with a tool pack exposed. Typically, it would take her at least five full minutes to hot wire a motorbike, but these older, simpler models were much easier. She took off the back plate of the ignition, turned the plastic piece underneath, and the engine turned right over, just as Anthony and Grant exited the harbor parking lot.

She followed the Jeep onto Highway 10 and kept a good distance. After twenty minutes or so, they turned onto La Pica, a one-lane road that zigzagged through hilly landscape and into farming territory.

She glimpsed a sign: *Maturin, Venezuela. Population 401,384.*

After a few more twisting country roads, they arrived at a sprawling complex—too industrial to be used for farming, and too secluded to be open to the public.

Jennifer immediately recognized the *Petroleos de Venez* logo on the front gate. Oil had been the State's national treasure, and if Marcus's intel had validity this refinery was now being used to clone cows, repurposed into Argentinean beef factories.

Even if the CIA was helping them subsidize sinking oil profits with another industry that could make use of existing infrastructures, why were these Flamingos involved?

Then Jennifer stepped on a jagged piece of plastic. She looked down and noticed there was an American flag embedded. There were several more parts sprawled on the ground, and when she found the propeller, she knew exactly what it was: a US predator drone. They were used for surveillance in foreign countries. Marcus had told her that the US was monitoring the conversion from oil to cow production at this refinery, but if the drone was down, there were no eyes in the sky, which meant no one was watching any more. Jennifer had to wonder, what was the CIA really doing with these oil companies that they didn't want to be discovered?

A half dozen weathered roughnecks on horseback emerged from the corrugated metal buildings and giant tanks and trotted down a dirt path to meet the Jeep. Alejandro Macondo, a strong, imposing kingpin, dismounted his horse and greeted Anthony and Grant. Grant headed to the back to unlatch the receptacle.

Jennifer tucked behind a large oak tree by the road, too far away to hear what they were saying, but close enough to see the exchange.

Anthony opened the combination lock on the receptacle so that Macondo could examine the rows of test tubes inside. Macondo then grabbed a case from one of his ranchers. Grant opened it to reveal neat stacks of bolívares, Venezuelan cash.

The deal went down quickly. The Flamingos got back in their Jeep and drove away. Macondo and his men galloped back to the buildings.

Jennifer waited a good ten minutes before she moved farther onto the property.

First, she checked the tanks on the outside. They were inactive. She continued into the production buildings. They were definitely no longer producing oil. Marcus's absurd assumption had been correct, and it was shocking to see.

This refinery had been transformed into a slaughterhouse.

Jennifer watched as cattle were moved from the fields into overcrowded warehouses. The cows were chained in single file rows and led through a small door. When they arrived on the other side, steel supports broke apart and the floor dropped away. One by one the cattle fell onto a conveyor belt where a ranger shot them with a stunner, injecting metal bolts into their brains. Chains attached to the rear legs lifted them onto a trolley where they were bled and taken through a series of stations to gut, clean, and cut.

The stench was unbearable. Jennifer covered her mouth with her sleeve as she moved on to the next building.

This was another converted warehouse, but it had been transformed into a laboratory. Jennifer watched as the roughnecks she saw during the deal delivered the spherical container onto a stainless-steel table, while men and women in lab coats buzzed about removing the contents inside.

Jennifer found the locker room. There were lab coats on hangers and stacks of hair caps and face masks. She put them on and checked her reflection in the mirror to make sure her blonde hair and face were completely covered.

She ambled through the lab, her eyes scanning the various stations and chemists at work. She spotted the container with the Petroleos De Venezuela label on a table. The receptacle had been emptied and test tubes had been placed on racks next to it. They were all stamped. She moved closer and read, *"Embriones de vaca."* Jennifer had taken enough high school Spanish to translate "cow embryos."

But she also had also taken enough high school biology to know that there were no embryos in those test tubes. They were filled with seeds.

Something else was going on in this lab.

A loud noise made Jennifer step back and look up. Technicians were moving across rafters above, a catwalk thirty feet high that led to several small stations. Jennifer climbed a fire ladder and followed through a web of rooms, where chemists were mixing formula in large vats, steam rising to a murky cloud on the ceiling.

Jennifer tucked behind a water heater as some of the workers passed by, then grabbed the last one by the neck, a slight man with silver hair. He flailed, gasping for air, and she pulled him into a utility closet.

"Stay calm and you won't get hurt," Jennifer hissed. He seemed to understand English because he immediately stopped struggling. "What are you working on here?"

The frightened man stared back blankly.

Jennifer tried again, *"Que pasa en su lab?"*

Still no answer. Not even a blink.

"Tell me—!"

The man panicked, pulled away with everything he could muster, broke from Jennifer's grasp, and burst out of the closet. He was disoriented and scared. He slipped off the catwalk and then fell all the way down to the floorboards below.

Thunk!

Other workers rushed to his aid.

Amidst the chaos, Jennifer spotted an exit at the end of the ramp. She snuck away, but when she pushed through, Macondo's roughnecks were there to greet her. She was outnumbered six to one.

Señor Macondo came around the corner. He was angry. He shouted something that Jennifer's high school Spanish couldn't track. But she had an idea what Macondo had ordered when one of the men came at her with a blunt object.

And then everything went dark.

CHAPTER 32

Macondo's men had bound and dragged Jennifer into a temperature-phased-anaerobic-digestio (TPAD), a facility where unsalable waste was dumped into an extreme-heat oven and converted to fertilizer. Former oil workers shoveled sludge into the mouth of the reactor and raging blue flames immediately turned the substance into fatty liquid, Jennifer's likely destiny.

Macondo entered the room. Jennifer went into survival mode and blurted the first excuse she could think of, "I'm an American journalist. I work for a magazine. I'm doing a story about Venezuelan oil refineries."

Macondo laughed, "You mean cow factories?"

Was that common knowledge?

Jennifer continued, hoping to engage the kingpin enough to stall. "I was just following a lead, to find out if it were true—"

"I think you are full of cow manure." Macondo laughed. "You are no reporter."

This was not going well. "You're right," Jennifer admitted. "And it probably wouldn't matter if I were."

Macondo drew closer. "Do you know what we do to trespassers?"

"No, but it can't be good."

One of the men in a lab coat brought in the receptacle and placed it in a pile of things to be incinerated. There was a sticker on the bottom of a tree with beautiful white and yellow blossoms drooping ever so innocuously from slender branches. Jennifer couldn't take her eyes off it, and then realized why.

It was a Borrachero tree.

After Alex the bartender had told her that authorities were cracking down on Devil's Breath, she had skimmed a federal briefing about the War on Drugs and learned that the seeds, flowers, and pollen of Borrachero trees were used to process Scopolamine, also known as "Devil's Breath," or *"Burundanga,"* the world's scariest drug. It possesses hallucinogenic chemical substances used to turn people into mindless zombies in which they lose both their memory and free will, and can easily be convinced to empty their bank accounts, hand over the keys to their homes and cars and lives.

Macondo waved his hand, signaling his men.

Jennifer backpedaled until she hit the wall.

Macondo held out a small petri dish and blew the yellow powder at Jennifer's face. Jennifer coughed and winced wildly, then fell back, frantically wafting the dust away from her face.

The kingpin and his men howled.

Jennifer looked away. The viscous flames reflected in her watering eyes. She could feel the men approaching. Time stood still. Then she sprang up, delivered a powerful front kick that nailed Macondo in his knee, forcing him on his ass, and onto a sharp pitchfork.

The ranchers laughed.

Macondo didn't like to be the butt of a joke. "Kill her!" he shouted. *"Matarla!"*

As his men attacked, a flurry of violent images flashed in Jennifer's brain. Possibly she hadn't been successful in wafting away the Devil's Breath and it was taking effect. Possibly it was a long, anticipated build-up of violent anger. Probably both.

She exploded, busting the tie around her wrist, punching the first thug in the nuts, and meeting the next with an uppercut to the gut.

The fallen writhed in pain allowing Jennifer enough time to release the ties on her feet, grab the pitchfork, and swing for the bleachers, connecting solidly, one after the other, until all of her assailants were sprawled on the ground, unconscious.

Macondo was the only one to rise back on his feet. "Why do I have to do everything myself?" he asked before making a raging dive, which Jennifer deflected, using the momentum to slam him into the wall.

She cranked the pitchfork like a baseball bat and swung hard. She answered his question with a question, "Is it because you want it done right?"

Señor Macondo smiled back at Jennifer before he fell unconscious.

—

SEVERAL MORE WORKERS CAME out from the main building to see what the ruckus was about. When they saw Jennifer stumbling out of the TPAD building, they chased after her.

As she ran, Jennifer spotted a pickup truck parked by the road leading onto the grounds. More workers appeared as she scrambled inside. The keys were in the ignition. She cranked the engine and drove away like a bat out of hell.

She glanced the trounced ranchers in her rearview mirror as she made it onto the highway. On the drive back to Morrocoy Harbor, she worried that Anthony Marino and Grant Hall had already taken off. She didn't have enough cash to buy a plane ticket. And she didn't have her passport. She had good reason to worry.

—

JENNIFER DROVE THE STOLEN pickup truck into the Morrocoy Harbor parking lot and saw that the slip *Lucky* had docked in was now empty. The Flamingos were long gone. It would be dark in just a few hours. Macondo's security tapes would be delivered to the authorities when they regrouped. Every airport and port would be teeming with police and security officers. She would have to figure out a way to get back to the Caymans.

She looked around the pier. Most boats were heading in for the night or were already tied and tarped. Some were occupied, setting up for moonlit dinners, but they weren't going anywhere. Then Jennifer noticed some local fishermen unloading their wares behind the lighthouse. She walked over to get a better look and saw a rickety fishing boat drifting in, steered by a fisherman with an unruly white beard.

Old man and the fucking sea.

Jennifer waved to get his attention. *"Hola Señor!"*

The old sailor drifted closer.

Jennifer fanned out all the cash she had. "How much for your boat?"

The old sailor didn't seem to understand so Jennifer once again tapped vague memory of high school Spanish, *"¿Cuánto de…for your boat…barco…su barco?"*

The old man scoffed, and answered in perfect English, "My boat is not for sale."

Jennifer tried another tact. "I'll pay you to take me." She fanned the money again. "You can have all of this. You can buy another boat…or a better boat, whatever you want." Which was probably a stretch, but worth a try.

The sailor looked up at the sky. "It's going to be dark soon."

She pulled out the keys to Macondo's pickup. "You can also have the truck parked over there. See it? The blue one."

The old man's eyes widened, and he said, "Welcome aboard."

She tossed him the keys and he made room for her.

Jennifer hopped on and took a seat while the old man rearranged his ice buckets, ropes, and leftovers from lunch.

She noticed that there was a checkpoint at the main harbor exit where all boats were expected to pass through and asked, "Is there any other way to get out of here?"

"That's the only *legal* exit on from this harbor," the old man said, accentuating the word "legal," as if he knew Jennifer was running from something.

"I left my passport at home."

The old sailor pulled out a flip phone and dialed. "I'll see what I can do."

"Who are you calling?"

The old man spoke into the phone, "*Necesito un pase, mi amigo.*" Then he held the mouthpiece and told Jennifer, "Local fishermen are sometimes allowed through a narrow channel, so we don't have to wait, mostly for the coast guard's convenience."

Jennifer smiled. "Perfect. Great. Thank you. I love you—"

"*Yo también te amo,*" the sailor said with a grin.

He had a sense of humor. He was kind. And Jennifer knew she was lucky.

Damn lucky.

Once they made it to the open sea, the shoddy boat rocked amok in the heavy swells, and the old man finally asked, "You didn't tell me where you want to go. I can get you to Costa Rica in less than an hour."

Jennifer told him, "Grand Cayman."

"Grand Cayman?"

"I know it's far," she said, a desperate tone in her voice. "I have to risk it. I have to get back—"

He tossed her a life jacket and warned her, "Hold on tight. It's going to be a bumpy ride."

Lucky as hell!

CHAPTER 33

THE FLAMINGO SECURITY TEAM widened their search for Olivia Pelican from Grand Cayman to Cayman Brac and Little Cayman—covering over one hundred square miles. Jan Maitland requested help from local police departments and Dex sought surveillance assistance from the local CIA branch whose drones had located her yellow Lamborghini in the Flamingo Harbor parking lot earlier in the day.

But still no sign of her, and Dex feared that she had fled the Caymans for good.

Dex had also confided in his CIA contacts—Agents Perretta and Shannon—about Rupert Reynold's claim that she was a former IRS agent by the name of Jennifer Morton. He still hadn't heard back from them with confirmation. As he was heading back to Flamingo headquarters to fill Marshall in on everything, Agent Shannon called and said, "Can you come in now?"

"I don't have time," Dex said. "I just need to know, is she or isn't she—?"

"It's more complicated than that," Shannon said. "We need to talk...in private."

Dex was tired, frustrated, and in no mood for guessing games. "Just verify—"

"We'll explain when you get here." Shannon hung up.

Dex knew they wouldn't need to talk in person unless there was highly confidential information, and he needed to get his facts straight before he continued his pursuit. He made a U-turn and headed back toward the financial district.

—

THE OLD MAN DROPPED Jennifer off at the lighthouse just adjacent to Flamingo Harbor. It was a short walk to the parking lot where she had left her yellow Lamborghini. She got inside and took off, unaware that the CIA satellite would be tracking the car, or that her cover had been unveiled. If she had, she might have stayed in Venezuela and taken her chances with Macondo's henchmen, or had the old man and the sea drop her in Costa Rica instead.

But she hadn't.

She had come back to Grand Cayman to find a way to expose Marshall Shore. If Devil's Breath was causing international fury and she could prove that Flamingo was spearheading the production of the deadly drug, then there had to be recourse. Roberta had warned her that Marshall Shore was immune, but Jennifer was determined to find a way, and she was feeling empowered as Olivia Pelican, back on land, racing back in her yellow Lamborghini so she could be on time for her dinner date with the puppet master himself.

She glanced her Rolex. It was 7:30. She had promised Marshall Shore that she would accompany him at his estate at eight to entertain potential Flamingos. She had a half hour to get back to her hotel room, change into her dress, and head out. She reached for her phone to let him know she would be a little late. She started to dial, taking her eyes of the dark island road for just a second, and when she glanced up, she saw a silhouetted form emerge in the middle of the street holding up a hand. She slammed on the brakes and skid, stopping only a few feet from the last person on earth she expected to see.

Roberta Coscarello.

"What the hell!" She wondered if the Devil's Breath blown in her face was causing her eyes to deceive her. She leaned out the window.

It wasn't.

Roberta approached the passenger side. Jennifer released the latch and the gull-wing door flipped up. Roberta climbed inside. She was seething. "Drive!" she ordered.

Jennifer pressed a button so the hydraulic door shut and peeled out.

Roberta strapped on her seat belt, ran her hand along the lush interior, and shook her head. "Nice wheels. Very discreet."

Jennifer was too tired to defend why she had spent Eloise Concord's money the way she had. "What are you doing here?" Jennifer asked. "I almost ran you over—?"

"Saving your ass," Roberta said. "You've been compromised."

Jennifer's heart sank, remembering Roberta's deal, *"If you get compromised, you come home."*

"I'm so close," Jennifer said. "I'm on my way to Marshall Shore's home right now."

"No, you're not. They know who you are."

How? Jennifer's mind raced. She asked Roberta, "How did you find me?"

"There's a tracking device in the watch I gave you," Roberta told her matter-of-factly.

Jennifer looked at the rose gold Sky Dweller Rolex Eloise Concord never went anywhere without.

"For your protection, not mine," Roberta added.

"Yeah, right," Jennifer said, like a defeated chess master admiring her opponent's move.

"Turn left at North Sound Road and we're going to go all the way to the end."

Jennifer knew that was the way to the airport. She was going home.

They drove in silence for a bit and then Roberta asked, "Why did you go to Venezuela?"

"My best shot at bringing down Marshall Shore is—"

"Was."

"Was to prove that he's running illegal businesses. I followed two Flamingos—wanted fugitives—to Maturin. They were delivering a package to a petroleum refinery. The CIA agents I told you about were setting up the deal—"

"I warned you to stay away from them!" Roberta shouted.

"There is more going on there than you think!" Jennifer shouted back.

"I don't care what they're doing," Roberta cut her off. "The CIA has always used businesses and bribes to fight communism or socialism or any 'ism' that isn't an American 'ism.' So this time they are cloning cows... That's not why I sent you here!"

Jennifer was livid. "I don't give a fuck that they're making organic hamburgers in test tubes to fight for their 'isms,' but I'm not going to look the other way while they're producing the world's supply of Devil's Breath!"

Roberta shrugged. "I don't know what that is."

"Either did I," Jennifer told her. "It's a chemical made from the Colombian Borrachero tree. It eliminates free will. And it's deadly. Kids are all over the world are dying from this shit—"

"If that's true..." Roberta looked conflicted, even pained. "There's nothing we can do about it."

—

DEX FOLLOWED PERRETTA AND Shannon past a half-dozen agents scanning security monitors from cameras hidden all over the island.

"Still no sign of her," Perretta said, "but we'll keep looking."

Dex grunted, "That's what you're paid to do."

The agents ignored his dig and headed inside a room in the back. Shannon shut the door. They took a seat at a round table.

Perretta asked Dex, "Does Marshall Shore know why you're looking for her?"

"He doesn't know anything yet because I still don't know..." He paused, noticing the agents looking at each other skeptically, and he added, "Are you going to tell me—?"

"Mr. Shore will need to know immediately," Perretta said with a disparaged look. "What we're about to tell you will be disturbing—"

Dex said, "What could be more disturbing than learning that we let in an IRS agent?"

"Former IRS agent," Shannon corrected him.

"So it's confirmed?"

Perretta told Dex, "She audited Global Currency Arbitrage and testified against Max Culpepper, just as he told you."

"She was fired after he fled," Shannon added.

It took Dex a moment to process. "She came here for him, but she didn't come as an undercover agent—?"

"The IRS doesn't plant illegal drugs on people they can't get to," Shannon said.

"Only you guys do things like that," Dex cracked.

Shannon was about to snap back, but Perretta, the calmer of the two, cut him off, "We're trying to help you."

Dex knew there was no point in antagonizing them, but he was angry. He took a deep breath, let it all sink in, and said, "She came here on her own to set up Culpepper."

"Culpepper got away, and she got fired," Shannon said. "Revenge knows no bounds."

"She went to all the trouble to become a Flamingo, change her identity…" Dex paused and then asked, "How did she know—?"

Perretta flipped the light switch off, turned a desktop computer on, and said, "That's the really disturbing part."

CHAPTER 34

Jennifer sighed, "What am I missing here?"

Roberta looked out her window. "I've made two major errors in my career. Both of them involved your father. Maybe if I tell you, you won't make the same mistakes."

Jennifer gripped the steering wheel tight and focused on the road. She felt Roberta's eyes on her, monitoring her reactions. She tried not to show any. "I'm listening."

"My assignment was to go after a bank in the Bahamas that we suspected your father was using as a tax shelter. I helped set up a sting called Operation Haven. The press called it 'The Briefcase Affair.'"

Jennifer remembered the *60 Minutes* clip that showed an operative posing as a prostitute to distract a bank vice president while other agents broke inside his briefcase. "That was you?"

"I had a lot to prove in those days," Roberta said defensively. "I was angry, like you are now—"

"I get why you did it," Jennifer cut her off. "The bank records you stole exposed the people that were hiding money offshore to avoid paying taxes—celebrities, major American business leaders, heads of organized crime. I would have done the same."

"I know you would have. That's why I'm telling you this. What I did completely backfired."

"It backfired," Jennifer said, "because you confessed to the court how you got the evidence. That's what I don't understand. If you had just kept your mouth shut—"

"They knew that evidence could only have been acquired illegally," Roberta explained. "There was no point lying."

"So you made a deal?"

Roberta nodded. "I promised to admit everything on the stand and the courts agreed to let the evidence hold. It was all worked out. We were going to set an example of these people, send a message."

"But the courts rejected your evidence—"

"That's right. They did."

Jennifer had read everything she could find about this case over the years. She even memorized the verdict: "The Court finds that the fourth amendment standing limitation permits the IRS to purposefully conduct an unconstitutional search and seizure of one individual to obtain evidence against third parties…"

Roberta shook her head as if she still couldn't believe it. "It should have been a major coup for the IRS, but instead it was a bust. All those people got off. Including your father. Other banks like Nassau Bank & Trust sprouted all over the world. Operation Haven was a complete failure."

"What happened?" Jennifer asked. "Why didn't the court uphold their end of the deal?"

"The CIA forced the Justice Department to reverse their decision."

"Why?"

"When our evidence was presented, it exposed something else."

"Something about the CIA?"

"Now you're getting the picture," Roberta said, her voice getting raspier. "The Agency was using the same bank in the Bahamas to launder money, so they had the court reverse their decision, hoping that no one would find out. But it was too late. The evidence had been presented. The Nassau Bank & Trust statements were available to the press. Every account was tracked and traced. And the CIA was exposed."

"Why was the CIA laundering money in the Bahamas?"

"Covert military operations, like selling weapons to support right-wing Nicaraguan guerrillas. This was during Reagan's second term. Senior officials secretly facilitated the sale of arms to Iran. Money from the weapon sales was used to fund anti-Communist rebels in Nicaragua."

"You mean...the Iran-Contra Affair—?"

"Otherwise known as Congregate and Irangate. The IRS exposed the entire mess. We didn't do it intentionally, but when one hand of the government doesn't know what the other is doing, bad things happen. That's why I went to work for FinCEN. We monitor every government bureau to minimize overlap. We share everyone's information to solve financial crimes...but we don't discuss CIA business. And that's why I told you to stay away. They get no regulation because of national security. I wasn't making that up. I knew they were cloning cows, but I didn't know anything about Devil's Breath."

"If they don't have any regulation or oversight, then maybe the production of Devil's Breath isn't coming from the CIA. Maybe it's just a few sleazy agents."

Roberta nodded. "Maybe."

Jennifer said, "You said there you made two major mistakes. What's the second?"

"Getting too close to my next target," Roberta said, wistful.

"Who was your next target?"

"Your father."

Here it comes. Jennifer knew Roberta had hadn't told her everything.

"The IRS dropped Operation Haven," Roberta explained, "but they didn't drop the investigation of Michael Morton. Your father had been all over the media, boasting about how his constitutional rights were ignored, how the IRS was getting away with illegal searches, the injustice of all. The IRS doesn't respond well to slander, or any kind of publicity really."

Jennifer knew too well, *"Agents should be felt and feared, never seen or heard."*

"I was assigned to audit him personally," Roberta. "I was supposed to get enough dirt to send him away...and I got too close."

Jennifer felt her body stiffen.

"Your father didn't die in a boating accident." Roberta told her.

Jennifer had always thought as much, now she was finally going to learn the truth.

—

DEX SHIFTED IN HIS seat. He felt anxious. His mind raced: *Did Jack Martin know who she was? He slept with the enemy, after all. Did he give her Culpepper's file?*

He had a moment of thrill.

I'll finally bury him.

But the moment was short-lived.

"Do you know who Marshall Shore was before he came here?" Perretta asked.

"No," Dex admitted. He knew that Marshall had a relationship with the CIA that predated his move to the Caymans, and with these two agents before Dex became head of security.

"Do you know what his name was?"

"No." Marshall had shared every file with Dex, every transformation, except his own. Dex needed to know everything about everyone, so he could keep them safe. But Marshall had his own set of protections. He was the first Flamingo—F1—and Dex knew why the files started at F2. Marshall Shore never made a file on himself.

Shannon stood back up, unable to conceal his fervor, and he told Dex: "Marshall Shore was a tax attorney by the name of Michael Morton." He paused to see the reaction on Dex's face.

Dex's stomach sank.

Shannon said: "And Michael Morton had a daughter."

Perretta clicked a JPEG file on the computer.

Dex's eyes bulged as Jennifer's IRS badge photo appeared on the screen.

"She came here using the identity of Eloise Concord," Perretta explained, "before Flamingo transformed her into Olivia Pelican. But this is Jennifer Morton."

Shannon grunted. "Marshall's little girl.

Dex took a harder look. Jennifer seemed to be staring back almost mockingly.

Perretta added, "He hasn't seen her since she was five years old."

Dex blurted, "Crap!"

"That about sums it up," Shannon said.

An operator shouted from the hallway, "We found her!"

Perretta, Shannon, and Dex followed a young woman back to the bank of monitors. She pointed to one image of the empty parking space at Flamingo Harbor, and another of a yellow blur. "There she goes," the agent told them.

Dex hit speed dial. When his cousin Jan answered, he shouted, "She's heading north on Central."

"I get mi dojo and take care of yuh problem," Jan said, sounding giddy.

"No!" Dex shouted back. His cousin's dojo took care of targets the old-fashioned way, and those targets never walked again; some never took another breath. Dex told his cousin, "I need to bring her in…and I need her healthy. You get me?"

"Why?" Jan asked, sounding disappointed.

Dex wanted to say it was because if Marshall Shore found out that they killed his daughter, he might kill them all. But instead he shouted back like a petulant parent, "Because I said so."

—

"I KNEW THAT THEY never found his body, or his boat," Jennifer said. "But it never made any sense that my father fled after he and all his clients got off."

"He didn't run to avoid going to jail," Roberta said.

"Why then?"

Roberta took a deep breath. This was clearly hard for her to discuss.

"Why did he run?" Jennifer pressed.

"He was a very clever tax avoidance strategist," Roberta explained. "He used every loophole, bent every rule, pushed the limits like no one had ever seen before. It took us several months to build a case against him that would hold..."

"And?"

"And then I threw it all away. I cleared him... Turn left! Now!"

Jennifer made a screeching turn.

Roberta looked back. A black Mustang skidded and made the same turn they had just made. "We're being followed," Roberta said. "Step on it."

Jennifer accelerated.

"We have to get off the island, immediately. I have a plane waiting...just get to the airport."

Jennifer looked up through the moon roof and saw a helicopter circling above and a spotlight shining down on them. "Getting to the airport might be a problem."

CHAPTER 35

THERE WERE NOW THREE sets of headlights behind them, supped up muscle cars that could give any overpriced sports car a run for its money. Roberta had a panicked look on her face. "This is why it wasn't a great idea to buy a bright yellow Lamborghini."

"This is why it was." Jennifer said as she downshifted hard, floored the gas, and took off like a bat out of hell, proving what a true performance vehicle could do.

The V12 screamed and the yellow blur ripped through town, causing their tags confusion, zigzagging through parking lots, alleyways, even along a train track—sending her assailants into a tizzy.

But Jennifer still couldn't shake them.

Roberta pointed to the bridge extending over the causeway. "The highway's just on the other side of the bridge and the airport's two exits away from there. We still might have a chance. Our guys will be armed."

"So will theirs," Jennifer countered. She accelerated, and the yellow bullet pushed 120 in less than ten seconds.

From the cliffs above, a scope focused down on the bright yellow blur, tracking them as they approached the bridge.

Jennifer noticed that Roberta's fingers were gripping her seat hard. She was holding onto something else, too. "Why did you clear my father?" Jennifer shouted.

"I didn't want him to go to jail," Roberta admitted.

"Why?"

Roberta wiped a tear. "I was pregnant with his child."

"What?" Jennifer was completely flummoxed. "You and my father—?"

"He didn't only abandon you," Roberta said.

Jennifer remembered what Roberta had told her when she had asked her to go after Marshall Shore: *"Sleeping with the enemy is never a good idea."* Jennifer was incredulous. "So he was your second biggest mistake."

"Yes—"

They hit a bump just before the bridge that sent them airborne. The car landed, zigzagged, and skidded. Jennifer got control of the car, but her mind raced away. She had so many questions. She knew her father wasn't happy at home when she was a little girl. Her mother wasn't an easy woman. Jennifer couldn't blame her father for having an affair, but she did blame him for the way he left, and for abandoning her. Her father was her only anchor to sanity. And then he disappeared. She knew in her gut that he hadn't died in a boating accident. She knew in her heart that he had betrayed her. And she wasted her entire adult life avenging the injustice.

Roberta had good reason to blame him, too, Jennifer decided. If he had run away when he learned that she was pregnant, then she and her child had suffered just as much, or more.

"That's why you sent me here, isn't it?" Jennifer shouted over the deafening roar of the V12 pushed to its limit.

Roberta nodded.

"My father is here, on this island, isn't he?"

"Yes."

"He's a Flamingo."

Roberta nodded. "The very first Flamingo."

Jennifer knew exactly what she meant. Marshall Shore was her father. Marshall Shore was Michael Morton, the founder of Flamingo. He built Flamingo Enterprises, an impenetrable safe haven to harbor the largest network of financial fugitives in the world. "You sent me here for him, didn't you?"

"Yes."

"This operation was never about Max Culpepper. You just wanted me to get inside Flamingo. It was always Operation Marshall Shore."

"It was both."

Jennifer's voice was raspy, "You knew damn well I'd find a way to get even, for the both of us."

There were tears running down Roberta's cheeks. "I'm sorry, yes, I'm so—"

"Don't be, I'm glad you did," Jennifer told her, newly empowered. "I'll get you out of here. But I'm not leaving. I'm going to finish the job."

Before Roberta could object, Jennifer ran over something, blowing out the front right tire, causing an immediate tailspin, yellow haziness spinning out of control.

Jennifer countered, but the Lamborghini skidded into the rail, flipped up and over, and then dropped into the dark waters, leaving nothing but a diminishing ripple.

And a deafening silence.

—

ROBERTA'S EYES MET JENNIFER'S as they descended; she was barely conscious. She wanted to explain why she couldn't have told her sooner.

Jennifer held her hand and stared back, assuring her that she already knew why.

Roberta's eyes started to glaze over, and her memories flashed, like a final entry in her diary:

He was everything I was against. Unprincipled. Deceptive. Appalling. And then I got closer, too close.

He was handsome. Devilishly handsome. And charming. He could persuade anyone. Even me.

I pursued him with a vengeance, with intention. Me, persistent, aggressive. He, always a step or two ahead, clever. Like a fox.

At some point, it turned.

I was beguiled, then helpless. I gave myself to him. I let it happen. Against all my principles and better judgement, I let him in. And I was never the same. What I did could never be hidden. He left, left me wondering, and then aching. The life growing inside me would always remind me. He never returned. I never forgot. And then I found you.

Roberta's eyes rolled back, and she let go.

—

UP ON THE BRIDGE, the black Mustang spun off, nearly meeting the same fate as the Lamborghini, but instead dangled from its chassis. Dex climbed out and looked over the rail.

The other two muscle cars stopped right behind. Jan got out of one, and a local security guard from his dojo emerged from the other. They looked down at the abating air bubbles on the surface of the flow.

"There goes the hottest car on the island," the security guard moaned.

Jan Maitland agreed, "Ova and out,"

Dex pulled up in the next car and shouted at his cousin, "Call the rescue units!"

Dex took a running start.

Jan shouted, "Weh yaah guh—?"

Dex jumped over the railing and dove into the dark water.

—

ROBERTA FINALLY LOOKED PEACEFUL, her prosaic gaze confirming that she had left this world. Jennifer touched her cheek to say goodbye, and then squeezed out through the window and swam into the blackness.

CHAPTER 36

MARSHALL SHOWED HIS GUESTS to the door, hoping that he had convinced them that they could safely secure a few hundred million Euros in Flamingo property before their Caribbean vacation ended.

"Thank you for lovely evening," said the much younger wife with a thick Austrian tongue. "So sorry your lady friend could not join."

So was Marshall. He had texted and called her twice and still hadn't heard a word. "You'll meet her on your next visit, I'm sure," Marshall said with his gallant smile.

The husband shook Marshall's hand and assured him with a wink, "I'll be in touch soon."

Marshall watched from the doorway as one of his chauffeurs drove them away and his two tuxedoed waiters cleared the remnants of the elegant bouillabaisse dinner, and one untouched place setting.

As soon as the guest's town car drove off, Dex appeared from around the corner. "We need to talk," Dex said as he headed into the front room, his damp hair and soggy clothes still dripping from his dive off of the bridge.

"Come right on in," Marshall said sarcastically, glancing down his driveway to make sure the Austrians were far enough away not to notice Dex's intrusion.

Dex went inside and waited for Marshall to close the door.

"What is this about?" Marshall asked.

"Eloise Concord...Olivia Pelican."

Marshall felt a pang in his belly and knew it wasn't the shellfish digesting. She didn't show up for dinner, didn't even call, and Dex had never stormed in like that before.

"I told you that there was something odd about this girl," Dex began. "I warned you when Jack wanted to let her in—"

"We all let her in," Marshall snapped.

"Jack is our first line of defense," Dex snapped back. "His job is to vet potential Flamingos, not fall in love with them..." Dex ripped open the Velcro pocket on his windbreaker and reached for something inside. "He's supposed to start the New Deal files, keep them locked up, and guard them with his life until I transfer—"

"Slow down," Marshall said, thrown by Dex's unusually edgy and skittish rant. "Just tell me what's going on."

Dex took a step closer, concealing an item behind his back. "When I went to collect the New Deals in Jack's office, there was one missing. He claimed he didn't know what happened to it." Dex revealed the New Deal file like he was presenting evidence in court. "Flamingo six-five-eight...formerly known as Max Culpepper."

"Obviously you found it," Marshall said.

"In her hotel room!"

Marshall was used to Dex looking for something to hang on Jack. Maybe what he had perceived as healthy competition had finally gone too far. "Are you're implying that Jack gave it to her—?"

"How else would she get this?"

"He wouldn't do that," Marshall objected, "he has too much to lose."

"You would think," Dex said. "You would also think he should have known that the trust fund baby he brought to us actually worked for the IRS—"

"What did you just say?"

Dex handed Marshall Jennifer's IRS mugshot.

Marshall stared at the photo, into Jennifer's steely gaze, and he felt pure rage. He pounded his fist on the sofa. An IRS agent had duped them.

"Take a closer look and tell me if she looks familiar," Dex said.

Marshall prepared himself. "Who is she?" he muttered.

"Jennifer Morton."

Marshall went aphonic. He couldn't move.

"Jennifer Morton," Dex repeated. "Your daughter."

Marshall's pupils enlarged and his nose flared, like a raging bull. His worst nightmare had manifested.

—

JACK MARTIN LEFT HIS apartment, got into his Land Rover, and headed out to his favorite bar to grab a few beers. He needed to unwind.

Once he turned onto the main road, he heard a thump. He was sure that it had come from the back of his car. When he turned, he heard a familiar voice. "It's me."

"What the hell—!" he yelled, almost losing control of the car.

Jennifer sat up in the back seat. "They're coming for me."

"Who is?"

"I couldn't tell you this before… I'm not Eloise Concord. My name is Jennifer Morton. I used to work for the IRS. I was the lead agent who went after Max Culpepper and his fund, Global Currency Arbitrage. I came here for him—"

"If they find you, they will kill you."

She thought of Roberta's last gaze.

Jack shook his head. "They will kill me, too, if I don't turn you in."

"You're not going to turn me in."

Their eyes met in the rearview mirror and then he pulled over onto the shoulder of the road. "You have to run, and run fast. I can't be seen with you."

She didn't move.

"Did you hear what I said—?"

She leaned up to the front seat. He could see that her hair and clothes were soaked. He could also see that her eyes sparkled. He wanted her as much as the first time he laid eyes on her. "Come with me," she said pleadingly.

"Are you crazy?"

"I'm not leaving without you," she said, steadfast.

He wanted nothing more just then but to run away with her. If it were only that simple. "I'm letting you go," he said. "Just say thank you and leave. You have no idea what these people are capable of."

"I think I do," she said. "And you don't belong here."

He felt like he didn't belong anywhere. "Marshall won't let me leave. I know too much."

"He built this place for people like himself, scum that will do anything for money. You're not like that. You hate yourself for helping those people hide—"

"You don't know anything about me—"

"What I do know, I like. Very much. And I want to know a lot more."

The feeling was mutual, but he couldn't let her know.

"You will die here," she said. "If not now, because of me, then later, when helping these cheaters and liars eats you up inside—"

"Some of them...some of the people that I protect do deserve a second chance." This had been his longstanding justification. When it left his lips now, it sounded ridiculous.

"Most don't," she said, confirming his new belief.

Jack reached in the back and opened the door. "I won't tell anyone that I saw you. That's the best I can do."

She tried once more. "Please, come with me—"

"I can't," he said, cutting her off. "I can never leave. I have to be loyal to Flamingo."

She looked stunned as she got out. She paused before shutting the door and told him, "I followed you to the Roman Catholic

Mission and saw you give that nun a bag of money. I get it. You think by playing Robin Hood, by stealing Flamingo's dirty money to give to the poor, you'll be forgiven—?"

"You didn't see what you thought you saw. I'm no Robin Hood."

"What then?"

"Goodbye, Jennifer Morton." He was resolute. There was no changing his mind.

She shut the door and he drove away.

Regretful.

—

WHEN THE EMERGENCY CREW had arrived, Jan Maitland reported that his cousin had jumped in, seen a yellow Lamborghini sink to the bottom, but had been unable to confirm any bodies, dead or alive.

The crew blocked off the bridge, sent divers down, and netted the entire area.

Large floodlights beamed down on the water as a towing vehicle hauled the Lamborghini up and over the rail. Roberta's body was removed, covered, lifted into an ambulance, and taken to the morgue.

CHAPTER 37

Dᴇx ᴀɴxɪᴏᴜsʟʏ ᴀɴsᴡᴇʀᴇᴅ ᴀ call from his cousin. "What did they find, Jan?"

"Di passenger. Dead." Jan told him.

"They searched the entire area?"

"Nuttin else dung there."

Dex hung up and told Marshall, "She got away, but she won't be able to get off the island."

Marshall felt more uneasy. He wouldn't have to make a decision if his daughter were already dead. "We're going to have to lock down immediately."

"Of course," Dex agreed, sounding eager.

Marshall recalled the conversation he had with her on the golf course:

"I don't talk business until the sixteenth hole."

"By the sixteenth hole you know if you like them?"

"By the sixteenth hole I know if I trust them."

He had misread her game, bigtime. "We've never had a Flamingo break rule number four," Marshall said, feeling like a president with his finger on the button, deciding, processing a new reality. His daughter had snuck into Flamingo like a Trojan horse and Jack had opened the gates for her. Marshall thought about the potential he saw in her, in them both, and he felt physically ill.

"I understand your ambivalence," Dex pressed. "You thought you could trust Jack and she's your daughter. Blood is blood. But they broke the fourth rule... If we don't clean up this mess, you could lose everything you worked so hard for... Think of all your Flamingos, the promises you made—"

"You have my authorization," Marshall cut him off. "But do me one favor. Bury them on the sixteenth hole on the Big Bluffs, near the cluster of trees."

Dex nodded his head, as if he knew why. "So you can visit—?"

"So that no one will ever find their bodies," Marshall said. "It's my land. Digging is prohibited without probable cause. And probable cause is never granted."

Marshall headed upstairs to prepare for the lockdown, and his escape.

—

JENNIFER WALKED ALONG THE breakwater, contemplating everything that had happened that day. She nearly got killed in Venezuela. Her Lamborghini flew off a bridge into the bay. She watched Roberta die. Jack let her go. And now she was being hunted with no way off the island. The distant sirens reminded her how exposed she was. She needed to find a safe haven, at least for the night. And then she remembered that Rupert Reynolds' penthouse was vacant.

She hid in a dark lot across the street from Flamingo Towers and waited. People came in and out of the front door. Sometimes the lax guard walked away to do something. But there were cameras in the lobby and every Flamingo building would be on high alert.

Then an opportunity presented himself. "You buyin', pretty lady?" a young man said.

She turned around. He was wearing a hat and a long coat, but she knew who it was instantly: Jason. "Maybe," she said. "Are you holding?"

"Whatcha looking for?"

"Devil's Breath. Can't get enough."

"I'm your guy."

"The local pharmacist."

He took a step back. "You a cop?"

"No, I'm not a cop."

"Have we done business before?"

He didn't remember her. And she doubted he would remember this either. She delivered a snap kick between his legs, and when he lunged forward, she threw a temple punch to the right side of his head. Whatever brain he had left jiggled in his skull and he blacked out immediately.

She put on his long coat, tucked her hair inside his hat, and took his keys from his pocket. He only had three keys. One was for his Jag. One had P403 embedded, his uncle's unit, which meant the third key would likely work on the front door of Flamingo Towers.

It did.

She went to the top floor, picked Rupert Reynolds' Penthouse door lock again, and took a badly needed reprieve. She took a long steamy shower, changed into silk pajamas, and refueled with a meal of roasted almonds, dried fruit, and microwaved chicken potpie. She washed it all down with a glass of Merlot from a vintage bottle, and then took a Cabaña from Rupert's well-stocked humidor.

She had never smoked a cigar before, but she lit up just to see what the billionaire crook saw in such indulgences. The first puff made her immediately nauseous, so she went out to the terrace and looked out at the moonlit sea. She was now on the run, all alone, and choking on expensive smoke, just like the former Max Culpepper, and she didn't like it one bit. She could see the beefed-up security at the marina below. She had no idea how she was going to get away. She thought of Jack's warning: *"If they find you, they'll kill you."*

Then she remembered that she still had one ally.

Marcus answered on the first ring. "I've been waiting for your call," he said.

Jennifer's voice was raspy, "Roberta's dead."

He sounded tired, too, and sad, "I know."

"She told me there was a plane waiting—"

"The plane couldn't wait," Marcus told her. "The island is swarming with police and Flamingo security. There's nothing we can do right now. You're safe in Rupert Reynolds' place until morning. I'm working on your exit strategy."

Jennifer glanced the Rolex that Roberta had conned her into wearing by telling her that Eloise Concord never went anywhere without it. She was glad that Marcus was tracking her now and remembered what Roberta had said: *"For your protection."*

Marcus said, "I'll do everything I can to get you back."

"No one is going to help us," Jennifer warned him. "Roberta can't vouch for us. And I didn't make a lot of friends at the IRS."

"I know," Marcus said.

Jennifer gulped the Merlot. "Your employer's dead. Your job is over. You're not getting paid. Why haven't you packed up and gone home?" She already knew why.

And he confirmed it. "I am home," he told her.

Jennifer closed his eyes and remembered the cozy Tribeca apartment where she met Marcus and Roberta. It was not your typical surveillance building. The doors to the bedrooms and other living spaces were all closed. The name on the buzzer in the lobby was "Tenant in B12."

"Your last name is Coscarello, isn't it?" Jennifer finally asked.

"Yes."

"Roberta was your mother."

"Yes," Marcus confessed, his voice cracking, "Roberta was my mother."

"I'm so sorry—"

"Thanks."

"Do you know…" Jennifer paused, realizing that he had to know, or he should know, "Marshall Shore is your father, too."

"Yes."

"Roberta told me just before," Jennifer said, "but I didn't know that you were her son and…" She took another sip of Merlot. "You're my brother."

"Half-brother."

"Half-brother," she repeated, liking how it sounded to have a kindred spirit, someone who could relate and understand. She felt a little less alone just then.

"I wanted you to get our father more than anyone," Marcus said.

Jennifer dunked the Cuban cigar in her wine and watched the smoke snake upward. "I'm sorry, Marcus. I really am. Roberta seemed like a great lady."

"She was. Now get some rest. You'll need it. We'll figure this out tomorrow."

After they hung up, Jennifer crawled under Vera Wang eight-hundred thread count sheets, allowed herself to pass out in to a deep and desperately needed slumber, and dreamt that she was trapped in dark waters at the bottom of the sea, desperate to feel safe again.

CHAPTER 38

GALE FORCE WINDS DROWNED out the sounds of Dex and his cousin breaking into Jack's apartment.

Jan struggled with the lock.

Dex fidgeted impatiently. "Can you open the fucking thing, or not?"

"Mi wi get dis." Jan jimmied the Schlage lock with intensity, twisting a torsion wrench into the keyhole. "Breathe easy," he told Dex.

The pin-pusher clicked. The lock opened. Jan turned back to see if his cousin was impressed, but Dex was already moving past him with his next order, "Cover me!"

Jack's apartment was extremely dark and quiet.

"Maybe him nuh here." Jan whispered.

"His SUV was in his space, still warm," Dex reminded him. "Let's split up. I'll check the bedroom. You go through the kitchen."

Dex disappeared down the long hallway.

Jan moved through the kitchen that opened into the living room. He looked out toward the balcony. The curtains were fluttering. The sliding glass door was ajar. Jan stalked quietly toward them, a ninja in the night, hovering inside the shadows, ready to attack. He leaned into the wall, just beside the flapping curtains, listening for a sign of Jack out on the terrace, any movement or sound that would reveal him. The wind and rain were making it futile, so he gripped his gun and swung onto the balcony.

It was empty.

Jan looked over the railing to make sure Jack's Land Rover was still in his parking space, and that he hadn't slipped past them when they arrived.

It was. He had to be in the apartment.

Just as Jan headed back inside, Jack sprung out from behind a brass Buddha sculpture and charged into Jan's midsection, full force. Jan was a highly skilled martial artist who knew how to use momentum to respond to a surprise attack. Unfortunately, this one didn't give him the opportunity to put his years of training to use. He was so close to the ledge when Jack struck that his body flipped right over the wrought iron railing. He grasped and flailed, but Jack, and gravity, got the best of him. He fell six stories and hit the parking lot pavement facedown.

Thud!

Dex was at the back end of Jack's serpentine-shaped closet and hadn't heard a thing. He continued to stalk through the bedrooms and bathrooms, slowly, cautiously, checking under the beds, inside every cabinet, around every corner.

He found nothing. No sign of Jack.

He headed back down the long, dark hallway. When he got to the kitchen, he saw no sign of Jan either. "Cuz!" he hissed. "Where the hell are you?"

Then he saw the fluttering curtains that had lured Jan toward the balcony. He didn't want to shout, so he moved toward them, close enough to slide open the glass door and peek through.

The balcony was empty.

He stepped out onto the balcony and looked up at the sky. The rain was coming down in sheets. He looked down at the parking spaces in front to make sure Jack hadn't slipped away. He saw Jack's Land Rover, still there. He also saw his cousin sprawled on the pavement, just beside it.

Dex went ballistic and charged back inside, moving from room to room, no longer trying to be quiet, "Show yourself...there's no place for you to run."

There was no response. No sounds. No movement.

Dex fired his Glock 19 three times into the darkest corner of the room.

The bullets rang out and reverberated.

Then there was stillness, only the pulsation of the rain echoing off the Terra Cotta tile roof.

"So this is how it's going to be," Dex shouted, unnerved, firing into the kitchen between each statement. "I always knew what you were about…"

Boom!

"That it would come to this…"

Boom!

"I should have done something about it long ago…"

Boom!

"I'm coming for you!" Dex fired as he moved down the hallway, spraying bullets as he went. In the bedroom, he fired at the bed, under the bed, into the closets, and through the bathroom shower curtain.

He stormed back down the hallway trying to guess how many shots he had just wasted. He had a thirty-round mag. It had to be close to done. When he got to the living room, he looked around and noticed that something was different. Then he realized, there was a stream of light spilling from the terrace now, illuminating him. It hadn't been there before. He felt vulnerable.

And for good reason.

Just as he tried to step away, a gunshot blasted, and it had not come from Dex's gun.

A warm sensation moved from his shoulder down his spine. He grabbed his arm where the blood was oozing. He couldn't tell if a bullet grazed his shoulder or went inside. Either way, he was still alive, and he wanted to keep it that way. He moved to the corner of the room, squatted behind a chair, and glanced the front door. It was his only way out of there, unless he wanted to leave the way his cousin had. To get to the door, he would have to run through the open, lit living room—exposed—and he didn't want to take another bullet. He needed a distraction, so he reached for a pillow on the chair he was hiding behind and tossed it across the room.

A bullet exploded through the pillow before it hit the ground.

"Damn!" Dex grabbed a tray on the end table and threw it at the wall across the room. When it hit and rang out, he made his move toward the front door.

The kitchen light went on and Jack stepped out into the foyer, blocking Dex, aiming a Beretta he had always kept under his mattress but never used. "Drop your gun," Jack said, his voice calm, steady, and clear.

Dex lifted his arm instead, his hand shaking, and squeezed the trigger. Nothing came out. No bullets left.

"Maybe now you'll listen," Jack said. "Walk out to the balcony."

Dex scrambled back. "You don't want to do this, Jack."

"You're right. I don't."

"Let's talk this through," Dex pleaded, holding his wound with his blood-drenched hand. "I'm sure we can come to an agreement."

"That's rich," Jack said. "You came here to kill me and now you want to negotiate."

"I came here for Eloise Concord...Olivia Pelican," Dex cried out in a panic. "She's not who she said she was. She's come to Flamingo...for Marshall—"

"What made you think she would be here?"

"I'm just doing my job!"

"Just doing your job, Dex? Really? Maybe you thought this would convince Marshall that I wasn't loyal, an opportunity to prove that only you deserve the keys to the kingdom?"

Dex searched for something, anything, but he had nothing that could convince Jack otherwise. The blood was running down his shirt and he was beginning to feel woozy.

"You should have trusted me," Jack said. "We both came from similar places. We both used Flamingo to get out, to have better lives. We could have supported each other. Instead, you made me your enemy."

"Yeah, right." Dex stopped backing up at the glass door leading out to the balcony.

Jack approached him. "Keep going. Outside."

"Fuck off." Dex spit at Jack.

Jack slapped him across the face with the butt of his Beretta.

Dex's head bounced off the glass door, hard. He saw a white flash and his knees buckled. When he hit the floor, he felt a sharp sensation flooding his right side. Jack shoved Dex with his foot, out to the balcony. Dex reeled wildly and screamed.

When the pain subsided, he realized he had passed out from the pain. The glass door was now closed. He got up to open it. It was locked. He could no longer see Jack inside. "Where the hell are you?" he called out.

There was no response. Then he heard an engine start.

"No!" Dex shouted weakly, turning toward the balcony railing. When he looked down, he saw the Land Rover backing up past his cousin's corpse and driving away.

"You should have killed me," Dex shouted out into the unrelenting storm. "You should have killed me when you had the chance!"

CHAPTER 39

Crack of the sparrow

Jennifer awakened in the opulent condo feeling like a different person. The glass of vintage Merlot combined with utter exhaustion had caused her body to crash for a solid eight hours. But she immediately remembered that she was back to her true identity—Jennifer Morton—and everyone at Flamingo Enterprises was searching for her.

She went out to the terrace. The sun was just coming over the horizon, glowing amber over the harbor. The air was a fragrant mix of flowers and salty sea. She thought it was ironic that she had come to this place looking for a financial fugitive in the most guarded haven in the world, and now she was in his home, wearing his pajamas, and on the run, forced to think like an escape artist.

She texted Marcus to see if he had an plan yet. He replied right away, "Working on it." That didn't sound too promising and she was starved. She had finished everything that was edible in Rupert Reynolds' cupboard the night before and it wasn't nearly enough sustenance for the day she was about to face. She knew the Harbor Café just outside her building would be open for the early rising fisherman, and she hoped that one of those trawlers or trollers would be her ride off the island.

She selected fresh clothes that were gender neutral enough to pass off as hers, including Rupert's captain's cap and dark shades. The forecast predicted more rain, so she grabbed an L. L. Bean poncho to make her even more unrecognizable, and then headed out.

—

THERE WERE A HANDFUL of customers at the café. None looked like fisherman. She decided to order some food and wait to see if any showed up. She sat at a corner table, kept her cell phone next to her silverware so she would see if Marcus came up with something. She tilted her sunglasses up to read the menu and heard a man's voice behind her, "I'm sure it's her—"

Jennifer turned and recognized the man and the woman he was with immediately. They were the couple she witnessed getting married in the Flamingo Hotel courtyard. They smiled at her. Jennifer readjusted her dark glasses to cover her eyes completely.

An overly singsong early shifter approached. "What can I get you, honey?"

Jennifer handed her the menu without looking up. "Breakfast burrito, please. To go."

Above the counter, a TV was tuned to the morning news, a repeat of the previous evening's news. An American reporter was talking about another former White House aide who was threatening to leak new voice recordings that would shock the free world. The Twittering president responded with outrage and a 280-character rant that ended with the words: "very sad." A pundit came on beaming about the bravery of people coming forward, and another pundit countered by denouncing the aide as treasonous and a threat to national security. They went back and forth debating transparency, Edward Snowden's NSA leaks, Julian Assange's Wikileaks takedowns, and the snowballing convictions that came from the Special Counsel's investigation. She spun around.

It was the newly married couple, and they smiled at her again. "Sorry to disturb you," the man said, "I'm Sheldon Strom...and this is Monique."

"Nice to meet you both."

"People don't want the NSA or CIA or IRS to invade our privacy," Sheldon said, looking up at the TV, "but they don't want another Nine Eleven either. Am I right?"

"You can't have it both ways," Jennifer agreed, hoping a political connection could lead to a friendship, ideally one with a boat leaving the island. Sheldon was paying his check and Monique was gathering an overstuffed boat tote. Jennifer asked, "Are you guys sailing this morning?"

Sheldon said, "We are, actually."

"You know, I would love to get out there. It's a gorgeous day—"

"Then again, there has to be some kind of regulation," Sheldon continued, still fixated on the news. "If the government has free rein, they can abuse their power, like Orwell predicted."

Monique chimed in, "I don't want those people listening to my conversations."

"They don't make policy, they just enforce it," Jennifer said, her old stock answer, but for the first time not drinking the Kool-Aid, and backing off, "I can see both sides, actually. It's complicated."

"You have a real dilemma, don't you?" Sheldon said with a wink. "If you're going to protect us, you need to be free to get the job done."

Jennifer thought it to be an odd comment—the delivery too provoking—and then Sheldon stood up to leave and lowered his voice. "I know who you are. I saw you on TV."

"You must be mistaking me for someone else."

Nope. He was certain. "On CNN...when you busted Max Culpepper."

Jennifer had been identified twice while undercover, Simon Brisco's warning echoed in her mind: *"Agents should be felt and feared, never seen or heard."*

"You have a good memory," She said as the waitress delivered her breakfast. Jennifer handed the waitress a twenty and got up to leave. "Keep the change."

Sheldon came closer, Monique in tow. "I remember everything from that day," Sheldon said, "I had a lot of my own money invested in Global Currency Arbitrage. Lost it all. Damn shame Culpepper got away..." he lowered his voice, "Damn shame they let you go."

"I'm still going to find him," Jennifer said conspiratorially.

Sheldon looked as if he was going to hug her, "That's why you're here, isn't it, to find him?"

"I'll tell you all about it if you take me on your boat and get me off this island."

Monique gave Sheldon a concerned look. Sheldon picked up on Jennifer's urgency. "We chartered a boat with another couple, to Little Cayman, Cayman Brac, and back. We can drop you off maybe—"

"That would be amazing," Jennifer said, already heading for the door. Little Cayman and Cayman Brac were separate islands and likely not to have much Flamingo presence as they did on Grand Cayman.

The singsong waitress waved goodbye. "Come again real soon."

Jennifer followed Sheldon and Monique down the docks, devouring the breakfast burrito, her blood sugar lifting, feeling somewhat normal again.

They arrived at a Jeanneau forty-five-foot stunner. Another middle-aged couple emerged from the cabin. Sheldon started to make the introductions when someone shouted across the pier. Everyone turned. There were two men charging toward them from the parking lot. It was Agents Shannon and Perretta.

Jennifer felt like a trapped animal.

Sheldon stayed calm. "Go back through the café," he told her, "next to the men's room, there's a back exit."

Jennifer took off.

CHAPTER 40

J ENNIFER SPRINTED ACROSS THE four lanes of West Bay Road,
weaving through traffic.

The gun-wielding CIA agents followed after, causing skids
and spinouts. Perretta waved his credentials. Shannon shouted,
"Federal agents…! Get the hell out of our way!"

A Prius slammed into a street sign to avoid her, metal scraping
metal, distracting a young man in an SUV, who plowed over
a park bench on the sidewalk and crashed into a brick building,
followed by a Mini Cooper running over a curb, breaking through
a storefront window.

Shannon ran past the carnage, shouting back to his partner.
"Let's get a move on, Grandpa."

Jennifer ran along the shoulder until she reached Peninsula
Avenue, an even busier thoroughfare that crossed into growing
rush hour traffic. None of the cars slowed for her to cross, but she
had no choice.

She darted across, head down. Cars slammed on their brakes
and skidded.

More collisions. More pandemonium.

An elderly lady in an old Mercedes hit a lamppost and a UPS
truck smashed into her rear end. Two tourists in rentals collided,
forming a blockade and stalling the agents.

But only briefly.

Perretta followed Shannon through an underground pass that led to the cluster of shops.

Galleria Plaza was a three-story strip mall peddling discounted jewelry, Duty Free liquor, designer sunglasses, and island clothing. The stores were just opening for the day. Perretta stopped to take a breather at the main entrance, nearly coughing up a lung from his pack-a-day habit, when he spotted Jennifer climbing the outside staircase to the top floor. "She's up...up...up there!"

Shannon took off for the stairs. Perretta went for elevator.

The third floor was mostly clothing shops. The agents weaved through, searching frantically.

Shannon spotted Jennifer entering a dress boutique and charged toward the store.

Patrons screamed and ducked out of the way. Clothing flew off the rack. Literally.

Jennifer reversed her course and headed down a hallway leading into a food court. She saw Perretta coming from the other end toward her, and she reversed again. There was a clear path to the exit. She went for it.

Shannon took her by surprise, attempting a diving tackle.

She spun out of the way, stiff-arming past him. The elevators were up ahead. One of them was just closing. "Hold it!" Jennifer shouted.

A kid inside grinned back as he pushed on the close button.

Jennifer dove like she was sliding into third base. The elevator doors bounced off her body. The kid ran out. Jennifer pushed on the close button as the agents raced toward her. The doors seemed to take their sweet time, the agents getting closer and closer and closer.

But no cigar.

Jennifer flashed her infamous grin just as the doors shut in Shannon's face.

Shannon slammed his gun against the door and sputtered every profanity he knew.

Perrette yelled back, "The stairs!"

The agents scrambled down the stairwell, Perretta trailing a flight behind Shannon. By the time they made it to the first floor, Jennifer had already burst into the alley.

They chased her back onto Peninsula Avenue. It was busier now with a lot more foot traffic. Perretta was panting and wheezing too hard to speak. Shannon wasn't doing much better. He gasped, "Where…where'd she go?"

"Think we lost her," Perretta said.

"That's helpful, genius."

———

MARCUS HAD BEEN FOLLOWING the tracking device inside Jennifer's rose gold Sky Dweller Rolex all morning as he looked for a way for Jennifer to get off the island. He knew by the fast and frantic movements on his 3D map that Jennifer was running, most likely being chased. She had to be in trouble and he had to get her out of there.

He finally found a viable solution at a nearby dive shop. He registered her for a scuba trip that was heading out soon. He promised the divemaster a huge tip if he waited until she arrived. Now Marcus had to find a way to get Jennifer to pick up her phone and get over there. He started to write her a text—

But it was too late.

Before he could hit send, he saw a sniper on the rooftop of the building next door. The gunman had a clear shot through the kitchen window.

Marcus knew in that moment that he was done for. He thought of his mother. Roberta persuaded him to steer away from fieldwork. She wanted a safer life for him, and since he loved computers, he took her advice. But it didn't make a difference. He was going to die on duty before his career even started. He loved his mother. He knew she didn't have it easy as a single, working parent. A wave of memories flashed in his mind. He remembered when she put the *Cucina Bella* sign up on the wall when they moved in; how she loved to cook her grandmother's heavy Italian recipes for him, but never ate them herself; how she wanted a better life for him, despite his desire to go into her field. He recalled how she had hoped that Operation Morton would settle her score and set her free. She had assured him that it would be her last job, and that she would retire from FinCEN once it was completed. He closed his eyes, hoping that he would see her soon, and then the bullet came for him.

The sniper only needed one shot, between the eyes. Marcus didn't feel a thing.

A few minutes later, operatives stormed the Tribeca apartment. They were moonlighting CIA agents that Perretta and Shannon had paid off once they ID'd Roberta's corpse, to make sure she wasn't working alone.

The first agent inside the apartment pushed Marcus aside and took over the map tracking the Rolex GPS movements. "She's heading up Peninsula Avenue," he told the two others as they entered, "and she's moving at a good clip." They all crowed around Marcus's monitor and watched the orange dot run up the map. "Advise them to move their fat asses."

One of the men called Perretta to inform him, but it was too late.

—

THE REASON THE ORANGE dot was moving so quickly was because Jennifer had boarded a bus. When she found a seat, she dialed Marcus to see if he had a way off the island yet.

One of the operatives answered Marcus's phone.

"Marcus?"

Silence.

They got Marcus!

Jennifer hung up quickly and felt sadness and remorse for the brother she never got the chance to know.

Jennifer knew that whoever got Marcus was tracking her, as long as she had the Rolex with her. She once again recalled Roberta's claim: *"For your protection..."*

Jennifer removed the Rolex and looked at the engraving. "Love Dad."

Ironic, I know.

The gift that keeps on giving. Maybe she could use it to lead her pursuers astray, so she could get away.

There was an old native man sitting in the next seat over, his clothes tattered and his hands leathery from a lifetime of hard labor. Jennifer got up and handed the old man the watch. "Please, sir, take this."

The old man pushed it back. "Too much."

"It's free," Jennifer insisted. "A gift."

The old man smiled at his good fortune. Jennifer gave him the Rolex and got off at the next stop, desperate for an exit strategy, and completely on her own.

CHAPTER 41

J ENNIFER STROLLED THROUGH THE morning farmers' market—four long blocks of artisan vendors and their customers—looking for a place to take refuge. Hopefully then she could find a truck driver that would transport her to the other side of the island where Flamingo would be less likely to look for her.

She spotted a cybercafé, went inside, but no truck drivers. She booked a corner cubby and spent some time searching the Web for transport options leaving Grand Cayman. She concluded that Marcus was right. Every port would be swarming with police.

And then her cell phone rang. It was a blocked call. Jack's phone was always blocked, so she took a chance and picked up, "Hello?"

"We have to get off the island," Jack said.

She had never heard a "we" sound better.

"What changed your mind?" she asked, "I thought you'd always be loyal to Flamingo?"

"That's when I thought that Flamingo would always be loyal to me."

He was a good man. Maybe a great one. "I've been looking for a way off the island," she said, "but everything's guarded."

"The only way is by boat."

"I just came from the harbor and the CIA was all over me."

After a beat, Jack said, "We need a private harbor. Marshall docks his Aquariva Super behind his gardens."

"What's an Aquariva Super?"

"The most expensive speedboat you've ever seen. The inlet behind his estate leads right out to the ocean. If we can sneak onto his property, I think we can get to it."

"If I recall, his property has a brick wall around it."

"But it's not that high. We can meet by the boat once it turns dark."

Jennifer felt a sense of hope. "Jack..." she paused to think it through a moment more. "You have a file cabinet in your office with information on Flamingo transformations...New Deals."

"How do you know—?"

"When I met you, the door was unlatched, and I took Max Culpepper's file."

Jack sighed. "That nearly got me killed."

"That wasn't my intent."

"I know."

"Flamingo would fall to pieces if those New Deals were exposed..." she said.

Jack agreed, "The innocent would want out. The guilty would have to run."

"Marshall told me that Dex collects them at the end of every quarter and brings them to him... Are there any copies—?"

"Never. No paper trails. And no information is ever input into a computer. Marshall was always afraid of getting hacked or robbed. Only one file per Flamingo exists."

"Best way to avoid a data leak is to avoid anything digital," Jennifer said. "Which means we have to get into the safe behind his desk."

"I don't know the combination," Jack said. "No one does."

"It's not an easy lock to crack," Jennifer told him, "but I may be able to get it open if I pick up a few tools..." She had seen a garage on her way to the cybercafé and the mechanics probably left some tools lying around. But getting into the Flamingo Enterprises headquarters would be nearly impossible, it was like a fortress. She could shut down the Wi-Fi cameras and motion sensors if she could get inside, but that was a big if. She sighed, "The security system for the building is a bigger problem...way beyond my scope."

"I have that code," Jack said, without hesitation.

Jennifer brightened. She was in her zone. "Can you get the guards' schedules?"

"There are no guards after dark. They're only there to protect Marshall and he's likely off the island by now. I'll text the alarm and key codes to you when we hang up. But I need one from you... They gave you a passcode when Eloise Concord's trusts were transferred under your new name. Only you have access."

He wants access to all that money?

"If we make it out, we're going to have to live on something."

"I know but—"

"If we don't transfer it now, you'll never be able to get to it again. Flamingo will track you the second you withdraw any. This is our only window."

He had thought this through thoroughly, which made Jennifer feel uneasy.

"I know a thing or two about asset protection," he reminded her. "We need to move the money into an account that they can't trace. I can get the lawyer that set up the account to do it for us, but I'll need the passcode."

"You want to move all my money into another account?"

"Eloise Concord's money," he reminded her.

She remembered Roberta saying that everything had to be returned, including her. But Roberta was dead. And Jennifer may never return home. If she made it off the island alive, she may be on the run forever. She may need to build her own safe haven. Hopefully with Jack. But what if he were playing her right now? She hated the thought. She had asked him to have faith in her. Now he was asking her to have faith in him.

"I'm asking you to trust me," he said. "Do you think you can do that?"

It would be another first for her.

—

THE OPERATIVES HOVERING OVER Marcus's monitors were under strict orders to stay glued to the static orange light on the tracking map and report each stop to the Cayman CIA office.

"She hasn't moved for almost a half hour," one of them observed. "I think she's settled for now."

Another operative stepped over Marcus's corpse to grab his phone. "I'll call it in."

The operator that picked up in the Cayman outpost relayed the address to agents Shannon and Perretta, who in turn gathered their posse and head for West Hills.

—

JACK HAD CALLED THE Bodden Town lawyer and told him to keep his office open until he arrived. The local attorney was happy to abide, as Jack expected. Flamingo deals paid well, always in cash, and never left a paper trail.

"You look a little haggard," the Bodden Town attorney told Jack. "Everything okay?"

Jack didn't tell the lawyer that he was almost killed the night before. He just handed him a slip of paper with the passcode Jennifer had entrusted him with. "Her new name has been compromised. I need to reroute all her money. Everything. Immediately."

"It will take at least a week."

"That's okay. We won't need the money immediately, just secured, and untraceable."

The attorney looked up over his bifocals. "We?"

"I'm escorting her off the island," Jack said. "I'll also need access."

"This is the second person compromised this month, is something going on?"

"Potentially," Jack said. "I don't want to put it in the Bank of the Caribbean, or any of our subsidiaries."

This lawyer had moved Rupert Reynolds' money, too, but Jack hadn't escorted him away, and they had put his money in a blind trust, in a Bank of the Caribbean account, per their standard.

The lawyer didn't press the issue though, "Do you have a place in mind?" he asked.

"You've probably never heard of it." Jack pointed to the routing number, also on the slip of paper, and said, "Bank of Barbuda."

"Barbuda…" the lawyer said as he started the paper work. "Isn't that one of those islands that's completely undeveloped."

Jack felt a surge of excitement, and hope. "Exactly."

—

CIA AGENTS SHANNON AND Perretta drove up narrow, unpaved roads, accompanied by two other vehicles, one with the Flamingo security logo, another with the Cayman Police's. They passed dozens of scattered cardboard and corrugated metal shacks before they arrived at 7568 Porta Janita, the West Hills address that the operatives in the Tribeca apartment had sent in. It had a sorry hovel with a '79 Impala retired on cinder blocks out front, like a trophy.

The agents and their search party parked their cars up the road and took positions surrounding the property. It was only seven o'clock, but the storm clouds had turned dusk into an early night, and since there were no streetlights in these hills, it was even more difficult to see.

Shannon signaled his men to cover him from behind the rusty Impala, where they would have a clear shot.

The kitchen light inside the house gave them a clear view of the family moving about. They seemed jovial and completely unaware that they were about to have visitors.

Until there was pounding on the door.

The old man considered himself lucky to have shared a bus with Jennifer earlier that day and receive her gift. Now he frowned. He took a gander at the Rolex, knowing his good fortune was about to change.

Shannon and his entourage filed inside without saying a word. The family watched on, horrified.

Perretta stayed by the door.

The old man's wife couldn't tolerate the invasion and didn't want them to turn over the place. It was clear what these men had come for, so she pulled the Rolex off her husband's wrist handed it to Perretta. "I told him it was stolen."

Perretta looked at the watch, remembering the one detail that made him believe that Jennifer was a potential Flamingo when he first saw her snooping around Rupert Reynolds's Swan.

Shannon emerged from the bedroom. "She's not here!"

Perretta said, "She duped us."

"What are you talking about?"

Perretta showed his partner the Rolex and slammed it against the wall. "This is her watch." Perretta peeled the shattered glass away and pulled a miniature tracker board. "She sent us on a wild goose chase."

"She's still trapped on the island," Shannon reminded him. "Every exit is secured."

"It's a big island."

"Sure is." Shannon agreed, and then waved at the other men, "We have a lot of ground to cover."

Perretta tossed the Rolex back to the old man—or what was left of it—as if leaving the scraps there apologized for the intrusion.

After they left, the old man mumbled under his breath, "Anything too good to be true usually is," and tossed the watch in the trash.

—

THE HEADHUNTING CARAVAN SPED away down West Hills Road, nearly running over some wandering goats and swerving past wayward vehicles vying to get out of the rain.

Five minutes after they left, a Land Rover, driven by one of their two primary targets, charged up to the highest point of the shantytown hills, and turned down a potholed, eroded road that led back to his childhood home.

Jack's brother answered the door. "Papa is going to have a fit. After you were here he—"

And just like the last visit, the old man emerged with a growl, "What are you doing here again?"

"I just came to say goodbye," Jack explained. "I'm going away."

"You've always been away," his father barked back.

"Where are you going?" Sean asked.

"I don't know yet... But you were right all along, Papa. Marshall Shore is a bad guy. I should have listened."

The old man softened. "I knew this day would come."

"How long will you be gone for?" Sean asked.

When Jack didn't answer, Sean said, "Forever is a long time."

Tears came to their father first. "Come inside and have a good meal before you go."

On the drive up, Jack had debated whether he should go back one final time. Now he was glad that he had.

Sean had already made jerk chicken and banana bread, and they all enjoyed a family meal together, like they hadn't done in so many years. For an hour or so, they told stories and laughed.

Then Jack received a text from Jennifer: "I'm inside Flamingo." Jack pushed himself away from the table and prepared for his final farewell, "Time for me to go."

CHAPTER 42

J ENNIFER USED THE CODES Jack had given her to get into Marshall's office and stepped back. A hydraulic mechanism was released, the door disengaged, and the red light turned green. Normally Jennifer would need weeks of prep to break into a security system like Flamingo had in their corporate headquarters. Having the password almost made her feel guilty.

Almost.

Her hunt to capture evidence by any means necessary had never been so desperate.

Or personal.

She entered Marshall's forbidden den and went directly to the cabinet behind Marshall's desk. As expected, the lock had a standard plunger, which she came prepared to crack. She felt a rush, imagining hundreds of files loaded with incriminating evidence on the biggest financial fugitives in the world, all in one place. Her head was spinning. She would need something large enough to transport them.

She searched the closets and found several very large Burberry briefcases. Marshall obviously liked the style because there was an entire row of them, each with a designated space. She noticed that there was empty space at the end of the row, indicating that a few briefcases were missing, but she would only need two judging by the size of the cabinet. So she headed back and went to work on

the lock, her mind wandering back to the conversation she had
with Marshall when he had shown her around his offices:

*"We put talented people to work. They get richer, we get richer.
Everybody's happy. The locals say, 'Everything is irie mon,'—the way
you feel when you have no worries. That's how we want Flamingos to
feel all the time..."*

"Everything is *irie mon*," Jennifer said out loud as she
manipulated the driver and bottom pins to shear line. The lock
broke free.

Easy as pie.

But when she looked inside, her stomach sank.

The drawers were empty.

She searched the office for other possible hiding places:
bookshelves, closets, desk, cabinet drawers.

No files. No New Deals. All gone.

She noticed another box under the desk. It was locked, but
as it was just a store-bought container it took her only seconds to
open. Inside were a dozen or so movie DVDs, old favorites like *The
Godfather, Casablanca*, and *It's a Wonderful Life*. Jennifer wondered
why Marshall would keep these locked up. Then she found two
worn videotapes at the bottom of the box without labels, only
black marker scribbled on the side: "Personal and Confidential."

The chiffonier cabinet had every kind of player connected to
a built-in plasma TV, including an old VHS player. She inserted the
first tape and hit play.

It was news report. The graphic read, *"Irangate."*

A New York news reporter made an introduction: "A few
months ago, the president told us that he did not trade arms
for hostages. Today, he told the nation otherwise, that he had
allowed his personal concern for the hostages spill into the
geopolitical strategy to reach out for Iran, and that he had made
unforeseeable mistakes..."

The video cut to Ronald Reagan's broadcast to the American
people from the Oval Office: "As personally distasteful I find secret

bank accounts and diverted funds, well, the Navy would say, 'this happened on my watch.' I did not know we were trading arms for hostages. Both the sale of weapons to Iran and the funding of the Contras violates administration policy…"

Jennifer pulled the videotape out. Roberta's explanation about the IRS exposing the CIA and the Iran-contra scandal was confirmed. But the next video revealed something more.

The images reflected in her eyes: the birth of a baby, her first-year milestones, first family holidays. The child was *her*. The grainy video played snippets of her early days with her mother and father in the few happy times they shared. It was surreal watching the imagery she had never seen but always knew must exist somewhere other than her imagination. There was her missing piece, her dad, just the way she so distantly had remembered him over the years.

She looked up at the photographs behind Marshall's desk. The last two times she had been in that office, she hadn't been able to get a good look at them. Now she was close enough to make out the faded picture where he was holding a baby.

Jennifer's feet wouldn't move.

Seeing these images of her past had even more impact than when Roberta told her why her father had abandoned her. She wanted to tear down his kingdom even more than before. Punish him for his abandonment. But it was nearly dark outside, almost time to meet Jack, and she didn't have the evidence they had hoped for. She put everything back in its place, headed out, and texted Jack: "The files are gone!"

She was nearly to the exit when she came to the office that had been stacked with plastic crates with Bank of The Caribbean logos. All the boxes were now gone, cleared out.

As she left the building, she heard thunder and looked up at the sky. Tropical lightning lit up the sky like the Fourth of July, the squally tempest at the ready to unload her fury.

Jennifer's phone rang. Blocked call. She answered.

It was Jack. "What do you mean the files are gone?"

"The pink flamingo cabinet was empty," Jennifer said. "Could they be somewhere else?"

"Not that I know of."

"There were several large Burberry briefcases in a closet, it looked like a few of them were missing—"

"Shit!"

"And when I was leaving, I noticed that one of the offices that used to be packed with those plastic Bank of Caribbean containers was empty now—"

"Those are called 'Gift Baskets,'" Jack told her. "They're full of cash, in every denomination, enough to live off for at least a few years."

"Do you think all the Flamingos are being moved to safer havens already?"

"This place was built to disperse quickly without leaving a trail," Jack said.

Her heart sank. The king of fleeing, got away again, and he took all the Flamingos with him.

She felt cool drops coming down on her and looked up at the hovering dark Cirrus clouds. "Maybe this storm will slow them down."

"Yeah, maybe." He didn't sound too convinced.

"Would Marshall leave by plane or boat?"

"All depends," Jack said. "Why?"

"What if he already left and took his Super Aquariva?"

"It's an Aquariva Super," Jack corrected, as if it made a difference. "I'm hoping he hasn't taken it because it's the only way off the island I can think of. Let's stick to the plan."

Jennifer agreed. "I'm on my way."

—

JENNIFER MADE HER WAY to Marshall's estate, but Jack had another stop to make. He had an insurance policy that no one knew about, so he headed to the Roman Catholic Mission Sui Luris to cash it in.

As he drove down the hill, he thought about his role as a screener and the promise he had made to every Flamingo: Protection is guaranteed. He knew if push came to shove, Marshall would leave them all in the dust. Jack wanted to make sure that the Flamingos that deserved a second chance, the ones that helped him justify his work, didn't get sold out.

Sister Caterina Gabriel came out of the back entrance carrying the stuffed Balenciaga bag Jack had dropped off several days ago. They hugged briefly, old friends from early childhood.

"I was tempted to look inside," Sister Gabriel confessed. "This mysterious bag made me curious."

"But you didn't," Jack said as he took the bag. "That's why I trusted it with you."

"I didn't just break the law, did I?"

"You might have helped some good people," Jack told her as he got back into his Land Rover.

Sister Gabriel took notice of the concern on Jack's face. "Fear not, for I am always with you," she said.

Jack wasn't religious, but he was happy to take all the help he could get.

CHAPTER 43

JENNIFER HADN'T EXPECTED TO see an armed guard when she arrived at Marshall's estate. He was a big man tucked under the overhang at the front gate, smoking a cigarette. She assumed he was there to protect Marshall, which made her optimistic that he hadn't left yet and the Aquariva was still be there. But she had to get past this sentry first.

Jennifer tossed a rock in the opposite direction to distract him. As he left his post to investigate, Jennifer lunged from behind, striking him just above the scapula and knocking him unconscious. In a few hours the man would wake up without his .38 pistol or his job.

Jennifer climbed over the wall and onto the property. The lights were on in an upstairs room. Marshall had to be in there. And if he hadn't left yet, his boat would be in the dock.

She trekked down a muddy path until she found the inlet. When she got to the embankment and found the boat slip, it was empty. No Aquariva Super.

And no Jack.

She waited there for fifteen minutes but he didn't show. Her mind ran away to the dark side. Had she misjudged him? Did he take her passcode, so he could escape with Eloise Concord's trust fund? Was she about to get ambushed on Marshall Shore's estate? Was this a setup…?

A voice boomed from above: "Stop right there!"

A flock of frightened flamingos around the pond flew off together, flapping noisily.

"Flamingos," the voice said. "They are very skittish. When disturbed, they fly away to safer havens."

Marshall was spouting his bird metaphors with glee from his veranda. And he was pointing a shotgun right at her. He had a clear shot.

She was trapped.

The .38 pistol she had ripped off the security guard at the gate was tucked in the back of her pants, but she needed the right moment to pull it out.

"You have a lot of gumption," Marshall continued. "I would have liked the chance to get to know you better."

She thought that maybe she could talk her way out of this one; after all, she had a lot of bottled up ammunition ready to spew. "You should have thought about that before you left when I was five," she retorted.

He didn't look surprised that she knew he was her father, but he did look more intrigued. "Come here," he said. "Come closer so I can have a better look at you."

She took a few steps forward. When she entered a pool of light glimmering off the rain-drenched mangrove, he shouted at her, "That's far enough."

She stopped.

His left eye squinted through his scope. "I can see the resemblance now." He chortled. "Good genes."

She wanted to puke. "Now we can compare all the wonderful traits we have in common."

"Flattery will get you everywhere, my dear."

"Why don't you put that gun down so we can finally have this talk? I'm sure you want to know why I'm here."

"I already know why," he said, not lowering his gun an inch.

—

THE RAIN HELPED DROWN the noise Jack made when he pounded out the hinges on a side door and entered Marshall's manse. He wore the stuffed Balenciaga bag like a backpack and gripped a black Beretta as he hiked up the stairs, hunting for the keys to the Aquariva Super, and the New Deals.

Marshall's raincoat was on the landing, waiting, proof of his intended defection. Jack searched the pockets. No keys. Only a note with an order number for a helicopter scribbled on it. Marshall was leaving by bird, not by boat. That gave Jack hope.

He continued into Marshall's master bedroom. Bags were packed and stacked, ready to go. Then he saw the two Burberry briefcases taken from his office.

Jack found a metal comb in the bathroom and used it to pry open the latches on the first Burberry. Inside were files, A through M, packed in tight. In the second briefcase were all the other current Flamingos, N through Z. The New Deals were all there, every detail about every Flamingo transformation, all their untraceable, buried secrets about who they were and who they became.

Jack heard voices outside. He looked out the windows facing the backyard and saw Marshall on the balcony below, pointing his shotgun, bidding Jennifer farewell.

He had to move fast.

—

MARSHALL FELT A BLUNT cold object push into his neck, and he heard a familiar voice. "Drop it."

"Surprised to see me alive, Marshall?" Jack asked, pointing the Beretta.

Marshall was actually, and his face went pale. Marshall set down his shotgun and saw his two Burberry cases in the doorway.

Jennifer looked up at Jack as if she were staring at the Messiah. "Thank God," she heard herself say out loud.

"You okay?" Jack asked.

She nodded. "I am now."

Jack turned to Marshall. "Give me your keys."

"My keys?"

"Your keys," Jack said as he raised his Beretta up to Marshall's head.

Marshall reached into his pocket and ceded a bulky keychain, along with a cheeky grin.

"Why are you smiling?" Jack asked.

Jennifer answered for Marshall. "Because his boat isn't down there."

Marshall laughed.

Jack looked pissed. "It's in the shed with your speedboat, isn't it? So you can have it shipped to you once you helicopter to another island…? Too bad your plan just got hijacked," Jack nudged Marshall forward. "Walk down to the water."

"Why?" Marshall spewed. "Like you just said, my boat's not down there."

"I'm going to tie you up on the dock."

"You haven't thought this through. Flamingo security won't let you leave the island alive unless I stop them. You need me—"

"Walk!" Jack ordered with a forceful shove.

Marshall headed down the steps that led to the lawn. His blood boiled. "Ungrateful son of a bitch," Marshall said to Jack. "I brought you up from nothing. I gave you a decent life. All I asked in return was that you were loyal."

"Actually, you asked a lot more than that," Jack said. "For a guy who's an expert in gaming the system, finding loopholes, and taking advantage of people, you sure had a lot of rules for everyone else to follow."

"We all make sacrifices, don't we?" Marshall snapped. "Success comes from the opportunities we take, not from the opportunities we turn down. The more you have, the more you want. It's just human nature. True for cops and robbers. True for me. True for you—"

"Some of us seem to know a lot about human nature," Jack snapped back, "and very little about being human."

"And some of us would rather be ruined by praise than saved by criticism." Marshall's voice dropped an octave. "What did you think you were doing at Flamingo, Jack, hiding angels? Your idealism was one of your most charming qualities. I played into it, sure, even indulged your naïveté sometimes, if that's what you want to blame it on, but you always knew the deal. There was a price to escape your miserable birthright. Let's not play the fool here. You betrayed me. You betrayed Flamingo. And you knew the consequences—"

Marshall stopped himself, realizing that Jack was no longer right behind him. When he turned around, he saw that Jack was several paces behind, his finger on the trigger; he was shaking, deciding.

"Don't! Please!" Marshall begged.

Jack's eyes were full of hate.

Marshall turned to Jennifer, desperate. "I'm your father, for the love of God. Stop him!"

"Don't shoot him, Jack, please," Jennifer said.

Marshall looked like he had a glimmer of hope.

Jennifer pulled the .38 from the back of her pants and said, "Let me do it."

Any glimmer of hope faded fast. Marshall pleaded, "Please, no, let me explain—"

"What's there to explain?" Jack said, his gun still on Marshall. "Why you ordered Dex to kill me?"

Jennifer took a step closer and said, "Or why you let me believe that you were dead all these years?"

"I was forced to leave you. I didn't have a choice. The CIA made me—"

"Bullshit!" Jennifer shouted. "I know everything. You set up offshore havens for your clients, saw that they could get away with it, and just got greedy."

"For Christ's sake, no," Marshall shouted. "My clients were just a cover. The offshore bank was for the CIA. They hired me to set it up. I used my clients and their money just to make it look legit. It was for them. It was all for the CIA."

He had her attention.

"I was one of the most knowledgeable specialists on offshore tax havens at the time," he continued. "The CIA needed to launder a lot of money. They needed a bank that could be discreet and flexible. So they came to me. I told them that the Bahamas were their best bet. They hadn't had any taxation since 1717 and their privacy laws were upheld. They asked me to help. I set them up at Nassau Bank & Trust, a bank I had a good relationship with, and I agreed to oversee and execute all their transactions. They couldn't pay me on the books, so they bought me a stake in the bank. I would have even more control that way, and so would they—"

"It was a win-win for all of you," Jennifer interrupted, "until it wasn't. The Briefcase Affair happened. The IRS accidentally exposed the CIA. You and your clients got off. The IRS didn't like how arrogant you were, so they sent an auditor to make your life hell. That auditor was Roberta Coscarello. For some reason, she fell for you. When she told you that she was pregnant with your child, you took the opportunity to run away from all your mistakes."

Marshall didn't see that one coming. And he didn't have a response.

"You faked your death and moved to the islands. Your relationship with offshore banks made you the go-to guy for hiding money, and so you built Flamingo—"

"No," Marshall objected. "I was too good at what I did, and the CIA needed banks all over the world—"

"More bullshit!" Jennifer shouted again. "You don't do any work for the CIA any more. You have them working for you. You pay off a few greedy ones and they provide surveillance, authority, and security for Flamingos. The tax payers pick up the tab. That's called bribery, treason, fraud."

Marshall didn't counter.

"Roberta Coscarello came here to save me," Jennifer told him. "Your henchmen chased us over a bridge and she was killed."

Marshall didn't flinch.

"And your son's name was Marcus, by the way. Did you even know that your other child was a boy? He was killed this morning. Your security apparently reaches all the way back to New York."

Marshall looked away. He was trapped. And he didn't have any words that would make a difference to his daughter.

"I always knew you were scum," she said, her voice shrill now, "but you're even worse than I had imagined. I spent my life wondering what happened to you, hoping that one day I'd learn that you were more than just a selfish prick, that you had one redeemable quality. Just one. I hoped that you really did have a boating accident, that you were dead. At least then you'd have a real excuse. For so long, I missed you, even wanted to be like you. Until I learned about the real you… Then I became the person I thought you would dread. I went after guys like you for pure pleasure. And you want to know something? I was good at it. I reveled in it, seeing the look in their eyes when they realized that they hadn't beaten the system like they thought they had, that they couldn't run, that they would pay."

Marshall tried to speak but nothing came out.

"But I was miserable, resentful, and angry," she continued, "and that's no way to live. It's finally clear to me…I was wasting my life trying to get back at you. But I'm done with that. I'm done with you." Jennifer raised her gun, pointing at his head. "Do you have any regrets? Any at all?"

Marshall was no longer listening to Jennifer's rant. His eyes fluttered. Reminiscences flooded his head, about Vera, Roberta, the dead son he never knew, the life he left behind—

"Answer me!" Jennifer shouted.

Marshall looked wary. "What was the question?"

"I asked if you have any regrets—"

"We all have regrets, young lady, and you're going to have a big one if you pull that trigger."

Jennifer's eyes showed no mercy. "You think I would regret pulling this trigger? Are you kidding me—?" Just then,

Jennifer noticed the keychain Jack had taken from Marshall and she reached for it, "Can I see that?"

Jack handed it to her. It was the rabbit foot keychain she had given her father on the day he walked out the door for the last time. She rubbed the soft white fur.

Marshall knew what she was thinking of the day he left:

"Daddy has to go away on a business trip."

"You have to take this with you for good luck."

Jennifer looked up at Marshall. "I gave this to you—"

"My lucky rabbit's foot. Yes, you did. I've carried it with me ever since..." He saw a tear fall down her cheek. "See, I'm not the monster you are making me out to be."

Jennifer lowered the gun. "I'm not going to pull the trigger. Not because I think you deserve a second chance, or because I forgive you. I don't..."

Jack lifted his gun back on Marshall.

Marshall's eyes shifted to the bushes over her shoulder. Dex was sneaking through and he had a gun in tow. Neither Jack nor Jennifer noticed.

Marshall had a surge of hope, proof that his system of checks and balances worked. He would have banked on Jack being his most loyal protégé in the end, but it was Dex who turned out to be his savior.

Marshall had told Jennifer on her tour of Flamingo Enterprises that human nature is profitable. He also said that people were as unpredictable as stocks, the reason he always delegated jobs to different Flamingos and never put all his eggs in one basket.

Now she was about to learn how he enforced the rules that protected his enterprise, and about rule number four, which was often referred to, but never spoken, until now:

"Any threat to Flamingo must be eliminated, without hesitation," Marshall seethed.

No one was aware of Dex yet. He moved slowly and aimed his gun at Jennifer.

Jennifer looked at her father's fraught expression, and her eyes swelled. "I've carried around the anger you left with me all these years," she told him. "I don't want to carry around anything of yours anymore. You've always been dead to me anyway—"

Jack shouted, "Get down!"

Dex fired his gun.

Jennifer hit the ground and heard the bullet whir over her head.

Jack squeezed his trigger.

The bullet hit Marshall square in the back of the head. He fell hard and died easy.

Jennifer took cover, diving behind nearby shrubs.

Dex charged her, howling, firing.

Jack trained his gun on Dex. It was difficult to stay with the moving target. Jack got two shots off. Both missed.

But the third was a charm.

CHAPTER 44

Dex and Marshall were both lying face up; bodies frozen; goggle-eyed gazes; gob smacked.

Jennifer couldn't take her eyes off her father. "You've always been dead to me," she mumbled. "This just makes it official." Then she allowed herself to fully cry; a bountiful release, long overdue. She wasn't sure if it came from finally knowing the truth, letting go of her past, pure exhaustion, her love for Jack, or all of the above—but the tears flowed.

Jack held her for a while and she welcomed his warmth. When she spoke again, she was stone-sober—*qui vive*—and ready. "We need to go back to the harbor," she said.

"It will still be blocked off," Jack reminded her. "Flamingo security has been ordered to stop us, and you were chased by CIA agents when you tried—"

She cut him off, "Are those the New Deals?" She was looking at the two large Burberry briefcases Jack had brought out to the veranda.

"A through Z," Jack confirmed.

She felt a chill and a thrill. They could finish the job. And she couldn't imagine a better partner.

Jack retrieved the briefcases, then they rushed across the lawn, through the front gate, and past the security guard, who was still unconscious.

When they got to the street, Jack said, "I still didn't understand what you're thinking. The harbor will be blocked—"

"We're going to use a diversionary tactic." She stopped and looked around.

Jack pointed to the right. "The harbor is this way. About a twenty-minute walk."

"Driving will be faster." She approached a Buick Regal parked on the street. The door was unlocked. Jennifer reached under the seat, crossed some wires, and the engine turned over. "Let's go."

Jack got in the passenger side and they drove off.

"What's the diversionary tactic?" Jack asked.

She touched the Balenciaga bag Jack was still wearing like a backpack. "I'll explain everything if you tell me what's inside this thing."

He looked out the window, contemplating.

"When I saw you the other day going into a church with that bag...I thought you were playing Robin Hood—"

"I wasn't playing Robin Hood," he said.

"Were you stashing away money?"

"No."

"Then what's inside?"

"All the New Deals that never made it to Marshall's cabinet, the ones that I stole."

"Why did you—?"

"I pulled all the files of people I believed in, who deserved a second chance," he explained, "Flamingos that didn't come here because they were running from the law or because they screwed over a bunch of people, but because they just wanted a fresh start."

She smiled at him. "The innocent ones?"

He smiled back. "The innocent ones."

"I thought you weren't supposed to judge."

"Sometimes a little judgment's a good thing."

"Is Jim Thompson's file in there?" she asked, remembering to the story he had told her at Club Flamingo about why he liked helping people that deserved a second chance. "Will it show that he had fallen under the love spell of an aboriginal Semang woman and is living off the grid, happily ever after?"

"I don't have Jim Thompson's file, no." Jack smiled. "But I have yours."

"You planned on protecting me?"

"I still do... Take a right at the first stop sign," Jack said as she approached an intersection. "It's the quickest way to the harbor."

She turned left instead. "We have to make a quick stop first."

—

JENNIFER STOOD BEHIND A large palm tree, hiding in the shadows, waiting for her resourceful bartender to arrive for his evening shift.

When he arrived at the hotel, she called out, "Alex!"

He turned and saw her waving. "Ms....Pelican?"

"I need to talk to you."

He approached cautiously. "Our staff was briefed last night to alert our manager know if anyone saw you... Are you okay?"

"I'm fine. But I need a big favor."

"I hope you're not getting hooked on that Devil's Breath shit—"

"No drugs," she assured him. She handed him a hundred-dollar bill. "Please don't tell your hotel manager you saw me." She handed him another hundred. "Or anyone."

He pocketed the money. "What's the favor?"

"I just need you to get something to one of your guests." She went behind the large palm and brought out the two heavy Burberry briefcases.

Alex looked nervous.

"I promise you, there is nothing illegal inside," she told him. "No drugs. No money. Just papers. Very important papers."

He nodded. "You just want me to leave these at the front desk?"

"I want you to get them to a guest. Sheldon Strom, he got married at the hotel—"

"I know who he is." Alex lifted the heavy briefcases. "Is this some sort of wedding gift?"

"Kind of." She handed Alex an envelope. "There's a note inside for Mr. Strom that explains everything."

"Don't worry about a thing," he assured her. "I'll make sure he gets it."

She gave Alex another C-note and kissed his cheek. "Thank you."

Thunder cracked, as if on cue. Alex looked satisfied and put on his hood. "I got you covered," he said as he started toward the hotel. "I just hope there's not a bomb in these things." He turned back to see if Jennifer thought that was funny, but she was already gone.

———

THE MARINA PARKING LOT was nearly empty when they arrived, so Jennifer immediately recognized the dark sedan near the entrance. CIA agents Shannon and Perretta were sitting in the front seat, waiting.

"Is there another way onto the pier?" Jennifer asked.

Jack pointed to the right. "Drive around the back. They won't see us enter from the other side."

The harbor administrator under full Flamingo-sanctioned rainwear was making his rounds to ensure all the boats were docked and secured. He stopped at *Lucky*, the fifty-five-foot power cruiser that was being trussed by Anthony Marino and Grant Hall.

Jack and Jennifer tucked behind the lighthouse where they had a view of the yacht. They couldn't hear what the administrator was telling the Flamingos, but Jennifer was sure he wasn't just warning them about the weather.

"Do you see Marshall's boat?" Jennifer asked.

Jack pointed to a private slip adjacent to the boathouse where two powerboats were under a corrugated shed. "Those are both his. The Aquariva Super is the one on the right. The other one is a vintage Chris-Craft Capri, a classic Italian speedboat, which he's had for years. Treated them both better than his people."

Jennifer recognized the Chris-Craft Capri immediately. The last time she had seen it, she was five years old. It still had its name stenciled in black on the stern: *The Great Escape*.

She shifted back to her earliest memories of her father taking her on joyrides: how the mahogany speedboat shimmered along the rippled surface like a skimming stone, and how the warm breeze felt flowing through her long, curly hair. This was the boat that her father wanted everyone to believe he had died in thirty years ago: his vessel of lies.

They never found his body or the boat. Now I know why.

"Are you sure about this?" Jack asked, startling her.

"About what? My plan?"

"About splitting up here."

Jennifer looked back at the CIA agents' dark sedan in the parking lot and nodded her head. "They'll never let us go," she said. "Even if we get away in this storm, they'll come after us. And I don't want to be running for the rest of our lives."

Jack nodded. "Promise you'll be careful."

"I promise." She kissed him deeply, uncertain if it would be their last.

And then she made her move.

CHAPTER 45

Anthony Marino went down to the cabin. He was carrying two plastic crates with Bank of the Caribbean logos. "We'd have to be crazy to leave in this weather. Maybe we should crash here until it clears. What do you think?"

Grant didn't respond.

"Did you hear what I said?" Anthony shouted.

There was no answer.

When Anthony came back up on deck, he saw why. Grant was gagged and tied to the dock. "What the hell—"

Jennifer grabbed Anthony from behind, her arm wrapped around his neck, and she squeezed hard. "I hope you socked away more money than what's inside those Gift Baskets because I'm taking those with me."

As Anthony eked out a venomous response, she reached into his pockets and found his keys. "Say goodbye to *Lucky*, too, because you're never going to see this baby again."

She eased up on the chokehold and Anthony spoke with a gurgle, "You won't get away with this. We know who you are—!"

"And I know who you are—or were," she said as she tightened a line around his wrists. "At Lehman Brothers they called you Tony-the-Tiger. Grant Hall was Daniel Mann. You're both wanted for nine counts of pandering and fraud, and when I make sure the banks know, you won't be able to sell your Flamingo home. All your assets will be frozen. You'll be just like the people you sold toxic loans to, the ones that lost everything—"

Anthony made eye contact with Grant who was grunting weakly.

"Guys like you will always be able to make a good living," she said. "I'm sure you'll do well dealing Devil's Breath, in prison—"

Anthony used all his force to spring backward. She was nearly half his weight and went airborne, slamming back into the fiberglass side. He got back up first and scrambled away.

In a pocket under a seat was a flare gun. Anthony fumbled with it in a panic. Just as he was about to fire, she leapt on top of him and twisted the wrist back she had tied a line to. He screamed, but his finger was able to squeeze the trigger. A flare shot toward the back of the boat and splayed red.

It was enough for CIA agents Shannon and Perretta to notice from the parking lot. They didn't say a word to each other. They had been waiting all day for Jennifer to try to escape the island.

Jennifer tied the line from Anthony's wrists to a cleat hitch beside his partner in crime, so they were both bound, hogtied on the dock.

Flamingo was unraveling, their financial fugitives and illicit businesses would all be exposed, including the support received by the CIA. Jennifer knew that when Perretta and Shannon's superiors learned about their extracurricular activities, especially piggy-backing on Operation Caracas to produce the world's supply of a deadly recreation drug called Devil's Breath, they too would end up in prison. She also knew that they would do everything in their power to prevent that from happening; they had to stop her, which meant they had to kill her, and they were now sprinting toward her through heavy rain and bleak darkness, desperate and determined.

Lucky's engines started with their heavy baritone hum, preparing to launch. Shannon got there first, just as *Lucky* was pushing off. He gripped the rail around the stern and pulled back with all his strength. Perretta leapt too and landed right beside

Shannon, also gripping the rail. Together they tried to pull the boat back to the dock.

Jennifer was up at the controls, joggling the throttle, just enough to keep them hanging on. She wanted them to come on board.

Anthony and Grant squirmed wildly on the dock, grunting through their gags to relay the severity of the situation.

The CIA agents didn't need to be reminded. They gripped the boat lines and hung on tight. When Jennifer finally pushed off, they flailed, bounced, and writhed like a Roman Priests at an exorcism.

Jennifer eased up on the throttle just enough for the agents to pull themselves on board. As they got on board they were each greeted with a wooden paddle across the head.

Whack! Whack!

They both went down. Lights out.

—

LUCKY'S ENGINES ROARED AS the yacht charged out to the angry sea. The cruising speed was just over ten knots, and the jerky swells made it feel twice as fast. Perretta and Shannon huddled together in the back, realizing that their guns were no longer in their waistbands. Had she tossed them overboard when they were unconscious? Lucky for them, they ankle-carried as well. They took out their wepons and moved around the quarterdeck, prepared to take her by surprise. When they arrived at the controls, she was nowhere to be found.

—

JENNIFER SLIPPED THROUGH A teak hatch and found her way into the engine room. As she rigged a detonator to the fuse box, her mind drifted back to the earliest memory of her dear old dad, when she was barely five years old and he had taken her for a joyride on his most prized possession—a vintage mahogany Chris-Craft Capri—befittingly christened *The Great Escape*. She remembered how the classic Italian speedboat shimmered from endless pampering as it cut through the rippled surface of the sea like a skimming stone with the warm summer breeze flowing through her long auburn curls, and how safe she had felt as her father preached life lessons: "When it comes to money, people will do unthinkable things…"

She was too young back then to know that *The Great Escape* was more of a decision than a desire, or to understand the scope of her father's betrayals. Three decades later, it was payback time. She would soon feel safe again, or so she hoped as she set the time delay.

She had two minutes. An eternity. She tucked behind two bolted-down ice chests, prayed for the first time in years, and asked to be forgiven for the sin she was about to commit. It was a big one, she silently confessed, but justifiable, and well deserved.

—

ON THE DECK ABOVE, the agents searched every corner; their pistols pointed and ready to fire the moment Marshall's prodigal daughter reappeared.

"I'll circle around," Shannon said with a swirling finger motion.

Perretta nodded, gripped his gun, and crouched down to cover.

Shannon lapped counterclockwise, and before he was halfway through he noticed a loose hatch door flapping. He waved back at his partner.

Perretta joined him and they approached. Just as they were about to fire into the porthole, *Lucky* crushed a crestless six-foot swell, lifting them off their feet. They both landed face down. The yacht shimmied through a series of whitecap rolls, sending them back to the quarterdeck.

—

JENNIFER CHECKED THE TIMER.

Twenty seconds left.

Her father's deep, throaty voice continued to echo in her head as she pulled herself back through the porthole: *"Whatever you desire—love, money revenge—doesn't matter…"*

Perretta noticed her and fired.

Jennifer dived behind the downriggers.

The yacht struck another enormous wave and knocked the shooter back down.

Jennifer climbed up to the ledge.

Ten seconds left.

The islet lights were barely visible now. The cruiser had drifted too far out for anyone to see them. Jennifer shut her eyes and her father's final words resounded: *"The more you have, the more you want. And the more you get, the harder it is to protect yourself. Unless, you take it all and disappear…"*

Everything that had been murky was now perfectly clear.

Jennifer leapt, jackknifed into the raging sea, and descended into the ink-black void.

"…And there is only one way to truly disappear."

—

Agents Shannon and Perretta heard the splash. They shared a moment of horrorstricken resolve; both knew there was only one reason Jennifer would go overboard this far out at sea, at night, in the middle of this gale storm.

Three, two, one…

The cruiser erupted into a massive ball of flames; bodies surged.

Jennifer looked up through the turbulent flow and saw the blaze and charred fragments evanescing into the apoplectic sea.

When she could no longer hold her breath, she ascended.

At the surface, through the smoke and smoldering rain, she saw a dreamlike apparition, a vision: Jack was coming for her on the classic mahogany Chris-Craft Capri, his smile beaming through the miasma.

She would be leaving with the man her father had groomed to be his legacy, in her father's most precious possession, *The Great Escape.*

Ironic, she thought. *My life can finally begin.*

In the end, her father had fallen hard, died easy, and set her free. She felt safe again.

EPILOGUE

SHELDON STROM RACED DOWN Madison Avenue amongst a herd of bundled New Yorkers trudging through slush and snow as darkness fell and Christmas Eve approached.

He stopped at a Barney's window display of a mannequin in a wedding dress, reminding him of his new wife, Monique, their destination wedding, and his serendipitous run-in with Jennifer Morton.

Sheldon recalled checking out of the Flamingo Hotel and receiving the two large Burberry briefcases, which he was now holding. If the contents inside the briefcases could bring down other financial fugitives—as the note promised they would—Jennifer Morton had come to the right guy.

At seven o'clock on the nose, CNN correspondent Kelly Keefer arrived, unrecognizable in her long coat, ski hat, and scarf. She stood close to Sheldon, pushed her scarf off her face so he could see that it was her.

Sheldon set down the two briefcases, nodded, and smiled.

Kelly Keefer lifted the heavy briefcases with some effort. "By the weight alone," she said, "I can tell that this is going to be a big story."

"I hope so," Sheldon said. "It deserves to be."

"I still need to know how the evidence was obtained, it will have to be verified—"

"I'm just the delivery boy," Sheldon told her.

The note Jennifer left for him was clear: *"Do not give Kelly Keefer your name. Or mine. Just make sure she gets both briefcases. She'll know what to do."*

Sheldon walked away and disappeared into the mass of humanity, feeling proud that he had done his part to help bring down the liars, scammers, schemers, and cheaters.

———

THERE WAS STANDING ROOM only for the financial district crowd at Delmonico's bar. It had been a grueling week. The Feds raised interest rates again. The markets took a dive. But everyone's eyes were on the TV waiting to see if the rumors were true of a story breaking about leaked financial documents that were promised to be more incriminating than the Panama Papers and Paradise Papers combined.

Kelly Keefer's face was beaming with plume. A graphic flashed, "The Flamingo Affair." She delivered what was sure to be the story of the year: "Hundreds of files were acquired recently by an anonymous source, exposing individuals that have hidden money in offshore accounts, using shell companies for illegal purposes, including fraud, money laundering, tax evasion. Some of these people had been on international sanction lists, known felons with affiliations ranging from drug and gun trafficking to crime syndicate ties... "

The crowd around Delmonico's collectively gasped. Kelly Keefer continued, "The IMF had formerly thought the total amount of American citizens' cash in foreign banking institutions to be in excess of seven trillion dollars. This proves that the number is closer to ten trillion, as some of us have suspected, and now something can be done..."

Mike, the lawyer that had pursued Jennifer and failed, turned to an attractive woman on the next stool told him and asked, "Did they say who leaked the story?"

She shrugged. "I bet it was WikiLeaks."

Frankie the bartender turned up the volume and Kelly Keefer said, "Our sources wish to remain anonymous as they are protected under reporter's privilege as well as international law, but one of the files explains in detail how this man, who was recently convicted of balking investors out of billions of dollars, got away…"

A mug shot of Max Culpepper came up.

Mike turned to the attractive woman and smiled. "I don't think it was WikiLeaks."

The head of the New York City Bureau of the Internal Revenue Service, Simon Brisco, was drinking at Delmonico's that night. In his gut, he knew that Jennifer Morton, his protégé, had gone after Max Culpepper on her own like she had wanted to. If she had done all this, she got results without being seen or heard. Finally. And he felt proud.

Kelly Keefer continued, "These documents explain how many more of the most wanted financial fugitives in the world have been sheltered through Flamingo Enterprises, a Cayman Island–based company. How they were able to keep personal financial information private through bank manipulations and identity change is revealed in detail. Sources at the IRS, SEC, and CIA have assured us that a full investigation will pursue these financial fugitives under the Freedom Act…"

An apple martini sipper at the bar announced, "The president just tweeted that it's fake news."

The crowd at Delmonico's laughed.

—

THE US DEPARTMENT OF the Treasury and their Financial Crimes Enforcement Network didn't think the Flamingo Papers were fake news. They praised the outstanding efforts of the media that helped create a financial trail they could use to track criminals, their activities, and their assets. FinCEN's motto was "Follow the money" and their 147 Financial Intelligence Units did just that; they coordinated all the efforts of the IRS, SEC, and CIA, and hunted down the hundreds of financial fugitives with unbound fury.

Flamingo Enterprise was shut down. All their real estate holdings were sold off, and the proceeds were distributed to victims of financial crimes.

It was an arduous process, but it helped many families get back on their feet.

The CIA worked with the Venezuelan State oil and natural gas company to shut down all production of Devil's Breath and help them fight incompetence within the company that has led to endemic corruption.

Special Agents Shannon and Perretta were confirmed missing in action. The CIA suspected they had fled with the money they made from their involvement with Flamingo businesses and they remained on their Most Wanted List. There was no evidence that would have connected them to the yacht that exploded out at sea. The carnage was too annihilated, and the storm had scattered most of the remains.

The investigation of the explosion, however, was able to identify the boat, *Lucky,* and its owners, Anthony Marino and Grant Hall, both of whom were wanted for nine counts of pandering and fraud (as their former selves, Tony Romano and Daniel Mann).

They were captured at Bermuda airport a week later.

Hundreds of other fleeing Flamingos were hunted, captured, tried, and punished as well.

—

MAX CULPEPPER WAS TAKEN by surprise in his stucco room behind the Carthusian monastery in the far-flung rainforests of Granada and dragged back to the States for a rapid sentencing for the crimes he fled from, as well as several new ones.

He was going away for life.

His lawyer, Barry Lynch, was unable to provide his defense because the entire firm of Lynch, Arnold, Heller, and Gold were pending their own trial for aiding and abetting fugitives, and collusion and conspiracy with criminals mentioned in the Flamingo Papers, as were several other law firms, tracking back four decades.

Federal prison turned Max Culpepper into a miserable recluse. Never in his wildest dreams had he imagined he would end up in such prison, hunkered down, alone, and shamed. Once a day he was allowed to watch TV in the mess hall, the only thing he had to look forward to. Unfortunately, his designated TV time was always at 7:00 p.m. during the Kelly Keefer show on CNN, where she would inevitably report the latest Flamingo captured. His singular attempt to change the channel did not go over well, resulting in one of the inmates throwing a shoe at his head. A guard blamed Culpepper for inciting violence.

He gave up living just then. That evening, he hanged himself.

—

Five Years Later

A HANDSOME MAN WAS building a treehouse in a Magnolia tree overlooking a stunning fjord. His cell phone rang and he answered with the name of the company he and his wife formed when they first arrived on this secluded islet, "Pelican Properties."

The caller told him that she had been referred by a friend.

He asked her who her friend was, and she named someone he trusted.

"My situation is complicated," she told him.

"I'm sure it is," he said as he climbed down from the tree. "Why don't you tell me what you're looking for."

"I need to know how you can guarantee privacy and protection—"

"We have a flawless record," he assured her as he headed down a pathway lined with stone statuaries and up to a beautiful hacienda. "If you deserve a second chance, we can give it to you."

As the caller explained her predicament and desire to drop off the grid, he went out to the Italian stone deck that wrapped around the home and looked out at the exquisite archipelago they called Pelican Cove. His lovely wife and son were returning from a joyride on their Chris-Craft Capri, glimmering amber in the setting sun. He waved with an ardent smile; there was living proof why he believed in new beginnings and second chances.

—

SHE WAVED BACK AS the speedboat careened the jutting canyon walls, half-hidden by dense dusk mist. She loved him dearly. And she loved their life together in this unspoiled paradise. It was the perfect place to raise their family.

She was six months pregnant with their second son. Her first-born was sitting on her lap, steering the boat, listening intently as she preached life lessons. "When it comes to money, people will do unthinkable things…"

The End.

Acknowledgements

I AM DEEPLY THANKFUL for the love and support of my incredible wife, Elisabeth, and our amazing children, Jasmine and Jake. I am also profoundly grateful for the encouragement of my mother, sister, extended family, and wonderful friends, all of who invariably inspire me.

Big thanks to Tyson Cornell, Julia Callahan, Hailie Johnson, Guy Intoci, Jessica Szuszka, and all the hard-working staff at Rare Bird Books.

Heartfelt thanks to Talcott Notch Literary and my awesome agent, Paula Munier.

As they say, we stand on the shoulders of giants, and I have been lucky to have had the guidance of many awe-inspiring mentors from the International Thriller Writers community.

They also say (and I often wonder who "they" are) that the truth is stranger than fiction. I sometimes find it more fascinating, too, and that's the reason I framed backstories in this book with historic IRS and CIA operations. I changed the names to protect the innocent—and guilty—but my intention was to show an authentic parallel to the plight of my protagonist. The results of those investigations were based on my own interpretations of federal court cases, which are public record, and off-the-record interviews, which shall remain confidential. I want to extend a special thanks to those who gave me insights about offshore banking, tax evasion, and how government watchdogs can push the limits of the law in the name of justice. If the truth is in fact stranger than fiction, then hopefully fiction mirroring reality will help my themes resonate more believably. Thanks to everyone that helped me do that.

This novel is dedicated to my father, in memoriam, because it carries a message about what we pass on from one generation to the next. Now that I am a father, I realize how much my dad taught me about being a parent, and how lucky I am that he was mine.

For more information about *Flamingo Coast*, *The Second Son*, and my other projects, please visit martinjayweiss.com and connect with me on Twitter (@martinjayweiss) and Facebook (@martinjayweiss).

About the Author

MARTIN JAY WEISS IS the author of the acclaimed novel *The Second Son*. He has written, directed, and produced numerous award-winning commercials and films and has worked throughout North and South America, Eastern and Western Europe, and Southeast Asia. Born and raised in Chicago, he now lives in Southern California with his wife and two children.